The Silent Treatment

The Silent Treatment

A Novel

Abbie Greaves

HARPER LARGE PRINT

An Imprint of HarperCollinsPublishers

A hardcover edition was published in 2020 by Penguin Random House UK.

HarperCollins books may be purchased for educational, business, or sales promotional use. For information, please e-mail the Special Markets Department at SPsales@harpercollins.com.

FIRST HARPER LARGE PRINT EDITION

ISBN: 978-0-06-297877-6

Library of Congress Cataloging-in-Publication Data is available upon request.

20 21 22 23 24   LSC   10 9 8 7 6 5 4 3 2 1

For my grandfather Robert Walls, who taught me to read.
Truly, the greatest gift of all.

The Silent Treatment

Prologue

From above, Maggie looks to have everything under control. She deposits the tablets onto the dinner plate with her usual fastidious care. If anything, she moves through the motions of breaking the coated capsules free from the foil with even greater precision than usual, tipping the blister slowly so as to enjoy the sharp clanging sound that announces each one hitting the ceramic. Anything to break the silence.

When she has eight in front of her, Maggie retrieves from the sideboard her glass of water, untouched since lunch, and checks the oven setting one last time. Chicken pie, ready-made, so it will be twenty-five minutes. Plenty of time to finish up here. She pulls out a chair and takes a seat at the kitchen table, her back to the door. There is a sheaf of bills in front of her, all settled but spilling over untidily. Maggie reaches into her handbag and fishes out her most treasured gift, a paperweight fashioned from a rock, decorated especially for her, and places it on top of them.

Mess contained, she clicks her pen. A rollerball, one of the few with ink in the desk drawer of no return, with a smooth glide that seems unlikely to reignite the claw-fisted cramp a week writing in Biro has induced. Her script is as neat and sharp as ever as she finishes her last sentence to Frank. If there is any fragment of doubt in her mind, there are few visible signs. Maybe a little wobble on the comma, if you look closely.

Maggie shuts the red leather planner, and without further ado, she gathers the pills in her hand, drops them on her tongue, and takes a small sip of the water, casting her head back in the extravagant swallowing gesture she developed in her teenage years and has never quite outgrown in the half century since.

At first, nothing occurs. Without moving from her seat, she goes back to trimming the beans, pushing the ends and their peculiar fibrous tails to the corner of the chopping board. The waves of relaxation arrive after a minute or so. Maggie's slicing begins to slow, her right hand trembling on the cutting knife.

Just seconds later, she slumps forward. Fortunately, it is far too swift to process, her head suddenly dropping in the way it always would during the French-film marathons Frank lined up for wet Sunday afternoons. It is a shame he is not there to cushion the fall this time.

And this time, there is no chance she will jolt back awake.

In his study, Frank fixates on the screen in front of him. The end is in sight: a knight, a bishop, and a pawn, all controlled by the computer, on a beginner's setting, no less, pen in his last bastion of hope—his queen. All those academic achievements, and still he has yet to progress past level two. It gives a whole new resonance to his most favorite of phrases: *Persistence is key.*

In the past, when Maggie called him for supper, he would be so engrossed in his strategy that he couldn't register the sound of her voice, let alone shut down his game. Once she had plated up, Maggie would come and retrieve him herself, resting her hands on his shoulders and stroking between the blades with her thumbs until the checkmate screen inevitably appeared. "Next time!" she would say, to buoy Frank back up. The algorithms might be stacked against him, but Maggie could never stand to see him disappointed.

Today, however, there is nothing quite so kind to

rouse him. When the fire alarm cuts through his consciousness, his surprise is more that it still works than that it has gone off. Maggie has never been a very attentive cook, though at least it means they don't have to go through the ceremony of testing the smoke-detector battery with a broom handle every three months. What's more, their early years together were marked by a string of now-infamous culinary defeats: the Lopsided Trifle of '78 (the fifth or sixth date); the Concrete Cranachan of '79 (a title that earned him a night in the spare room); Gastroenteritis-gate at a birthday party hosted in their wildly unkempt back garden (fortunately only attended by forgiving close friends). Once the aftereffects had subsided, each one, miraculously, made him fall a little deeper in love with her.

The alarm is shrill and insistent enough by now to cause him to exit his game and, after a minute wondering whether Maggie is already on to it, to go and tackle the bugger himself. He can smell the smoke before he sees it. Ahead, in the oven, something has burned, been forgotten perhaps while Maggie takes one of her increasingly frequent lie-downs. Turning off the dial with one hand, he reaches for the souvenir tea towel looped on the door handle to begin to disperse the smoke. It is thicker than he first thought, and even Cornwall's finest dishcloth isn't going to cut the mustard. Fresh air. That is what he needs. It is only when he moves to open the door that he sees Maggie.

It is not the empty pill packet at her side that gives it away. Nor the spilled water glass, nor the vegetable detritus sprayed around her wrists. It is the pain in his chest. It is the carpet being pulled from under him, the walls giving way, the ceiling caving in—every awful infrastructure analogy unfolding as he realizes what Maggie has done.

He touches her wrist in the hope of finding something there: a flutter, a twitch, anything. Maybe it isn't too late.

His hand hovers over the telephone cradle. He has never been good with calls, and there is a moment when it is touch-and-go whether he will back out altogether.

"Hello, emergency service operator. Ambulance, fire, police, or coastguard?"

Silence.

"Hello, emergency service operator. Ambulance, fire, police, or coastguard?"

Silence.

"May I remind you that making a call to the emergency services as part of a joke or prank is an offense and a risk to lives?"

"A-a-ambulance," Frank manages, just in time, the

vowels rattling in his throat before tumbling out in a barely audible torrent.

"Sir, you will need to speak up for the ambulance operator. I'll connect you now."

"Ambulance service. What's the address of the emergency?"

"Forty-three Digby Crescent, Oxford OX2 6TA." Frank's voice sounds hoarse, unfamiliar, so unlike how it has sounded to himself, these past few months.

"Can you tell me exactly what has happened?"

"It's my wife, Maggie. She's . . . she's taken too many of her pills, her sleeping pills."

"We're sending someone now. Is she conscious, sir? Can you feel if she has a pulse? Any sign of her breathing?"

"I . . . I don't know. I can't say for sure."

"Sir, do you have an idea of whether this was intentional?"

Silence.

"Any additional information you can provide at this stage may prove invaluable to our response. Has your wife recently mentioned any desire to harm herself? Any previous depressive episodes?"

"Well . . . the thing . . . the thing is, we haven't spoken for a while. I mean, *I* haven't spoken to her for a while . . . It's been . . . nearly six months."

Her Silence

Chapter 1

There is nothing as unsettling as the hospital waiting room. The banks of plastic chairs with their picked and pinched vinyl covers, the quiet hum of the vending machine, the collective intake of breath when the intensive-care consultant comes in with news, more often than not directed elsewhere—it's as if every aspect of it is designed to keep you on edge. And that's before you consider why you are there in the first place.

Maggie always said patience was *my* virtue, as if good qualities were something to be divvied out in a marriage, along with the weekly chores. I can see her now, waiting for a text or an email or a guest, one knee jiggling up and down on the sofa, the other stilled under my palm as I try to calm her down. So much energy compressed into such a small person. I often wondered how she didn't exhaust herself entirely, worrying about everyone and everything. I never wanted to change her; I just wanted to make sure that all that nervous energy didn't get her tied up in knots so tight that even I couldn't unpick them. I had forty years of success in that regard, and now here we are. It's never too late for things to change.

Above my head, the clock releases an extra-heavy tick as it announces the hour. Being kept waiting this long cannot be a good sign. Maggie would know. Four decades as a nurse and she would surely have a good handle on her own diagnosis. That and the sheer volume of hospital dramas she consumes. "Awful tachycardia," she would tell me with great confidence as we sat side by side on the settee on a Saturday evening in front of the latest episode, reaching across for the remote and amending the volume to compete with the sound of her own commentary. "Shame, though, such a young man to be found that ill . . . It does always seem to affect those city-slicker types, doesn't it? Awful stress they put up with every day . . ."

"Professor Hobbs?" A doctor is standing in front of me with his hand extended.

"Yes, yes, that's me," I say, beginning to rise from my seat. There is something sharply efficient about this doctor that radiates from the slick parting in his hair all the way down to the shine on his shoes. Even his name badge is pinned perfectly parallel to the seam at the bottom of his shirt pocket. I suddenly feel very aware of my own appearance and redundantly run a hand through my hair.

"I'm Dr. Singh, the consultant in charge of your wife's care. Could you come with me, please?"

I follow him back through the double doors, and for one hopeful moment, I imagine I am being taken to Maggie. Instead, I am ushered into a side room opposite the lobotomy bays and feel the final dregs of my wishful thinking sink away. The doctor takes a seat at the computer and gestures me toward the other chair as he starts the machine and shuffles through a wedge of papers on the corner of the desk. A freestanding fan behind him tickles at the edges of the loose documents.

"Sorry. Bit hot today, eh? No idea when this will break."

I feel the doctor's understatement in the sweat that is beginning to pool under my arms. I don't have the strength to make even a halfhearted remark about the weather and look down at my feet instead.

His computer burbles to life, covering up my awkwardness. After a minute or so, he exhales. "Professor Hobbs, I will cut straight to it. The prognosis is not good. When your wife arrived here last night, her central nervous system was shutting down. Fortunately, the paramedics managed to secure her airway, which was a feat, given how long she might have been unconscious by the time she was found. However, it is still too early to say what the effects of the oxygen deprivation will be. For now, she is in an induced coma. Once we have a clearer idea of the extent of the damage we can look at all our options, with your input, of course . . ."

This is my cue to speak. I have missed enough of those this past year, but I still know by rote the signs that come with it—the querying eyebrow, the tilted head, the impatient throat-clearing. The doctor settles for the latter.

"Ah, Professor Hobbs, I can appreciate how difficult this is for you, but please rest assured that we are doing all we possibly can for your wife. In the meantime, there are resources at your disposal. Our family-support team has—"

"I don't need family support," I cut in, my voice coming out hoarser than I remember, quieter too.

"Well, yes, Professor, I agree that it is not for everyone. I see from your records that you have had a referral before? To the support team here? Not followed up on . . ."

He looks up from his screen, and I reach for my

glasses. I take one of my loose shirttails and begin to rub at the smears across the lenses, although I am not sure that I am improving the situation. "An avoidance tactic," as Maggie always put it. She was right about that.

"Look, it is not for me to say what you should do. I can't force you to see them. Just, well, bear it in mind, Professor? They are here for you and available twenty-four/seven. We see situations like this more often than you would think, and they are specially trained . . . The important thing is that you know you are not alone here."

The irony. That is exactly it. I *am* alone. More alone than ever before. More alone even than before Maggie, because how can you truly know what it is like to be alone until you have felt complete?

"As I say, there is little we can do at this stage beyond observe Mrs. Hobbs's progress, so we would advise you to return home at some point for some sleep, some food. First, though, if you would like to see her, we can bring you to your wife now."

"Yes," I murmur. "Yes, yes, I need to see her."

"Professor, I'm sure I don't need to reiterate this, but we do so to all relatives: your wife is in a very delicate state. Please do not be alarmed at how she looks, and if you have any concerns at all, please don't hesitate to let myself or one of the nurses know. We have kept her in a private room for the time being, but there are a lot of staff around, should there be any problems."

The doctor begins to stand, and I follow suit, knowing all too well that it takes a little longer these days but not wanting to draw his attention to my sixty-seven years any more than is strictly necessary. Do they give up earlier if they feel you are too old? If you don't have enough grieving children at your side? For Maggie's sake, I hope not.

I accompany the doctor out, filing past the queues of walking wounded, down a corridor of discarded wheelchairs and hurrying, harried staff navigating the endless complexities of eye contact with relatives. I wonder which other families are greeting their worst nightmares today. Soon, the curtained bays peter out and the doctor swipes us through to intensive care. Beyond, there is a series of single doors, each one with a metal handle to depress.

Maggie is behind one of them. I can tell by the way the doctor slows, reaches up to check he has his pager, looks left and right. I want to say "No," pinning his arms to his sides and holding him stock-still. But what difference would that make in the long run? I cannot avoid facing up to what I have done forever. I try to tuck my shirt in as best I can and then shove my hands deep into my pockets to stop them from shaking.

There is a quiet click as he pushes the door open with both hands. He goes through, holding it ajar for me, only my shoulders are broader than he has calculated and there is an awkward moment when I have to shunt sideways to follow him, bending my head as I do so but still managing to knock it against the top of the door frame. I have never quite got the hang of being the tallest person in any given room.

At first, in the dim lighting of the room, it is difficult to make Maggie out. The bed is elevated and surrounded by an arsenal of machinery clunking away. It is hard to believe her life now relies on a machine not altogether dissimilar from the dehumidifier I would heave down from the attic on Maggie's instruction for its annual winter stint in the cellar. I move closer, and as my eyes adjust to the half-light, I feel a breath catch in my throat. It exhales as a low moan that clearly concerns the doctor.

"Professor, I'm so very sorry—"

"May I touch her?" I ask, brushing over his apology and inching closer to her side.

"Yes, that should be fine. One of the nurses will be in shortly to explain more about the routines they have in place. They will be well placed to discuss Mrs. Hobbs's day-to-day care. Here, let me give you some time alone together."

For a second, it is as if we are newlyweds again, the B and B owners beating a hasty retreat in case we are about to jump each other before the door has even swung shut. I would give anything to be back there now—Maggie wild and impulsive, me straitlaced, awkward, yet somehow always enough for her.

She seems smaller here, propped up against those awful hospital-issue pillows. Her hands rest on the sheet, as dainty as ever, the cannula sitting flush against the prominent veins and her papery skin. There is no chair by the bed. Clearly I am not expected to stay. How can I leave her here? She would be so frightened, were she awake. Frightened by the situation, certainly, but more by having no one to speak to, no one with whom to share her observations and every other waking thought. I know I have let Maggie down. I know she has needed so much more than a silent sounding board over the last few months.

When I touch her now, slowly, as if trying not to frighten a skittish neighborhood cat, her hand feels warm. It is so horribly unnatural. Even on the warmest summer evenings, I could always rely on Maggie to place her cool hands on my forehead after the cycle home. I have spent a lifetime being called upon to act as a human glove and draw some circulation back into her palms. Now this? We needed each other. But more than that, we chose each other, we wanted each other— you will never know just how great that feels until it is taken from you.

Behind me, there is a shuffling. I turn gently, without breaking contact with Maggie. A nurse has arrived, the blue plastic covers over her shoes rustling on the linoleum as she takes readings from the screens at the back of the room. I have no idea how long she has been there, but she notices when I look round, and I sense she may have been sent to keep an eye on me.

"I can bring you a chair, if you'd like?" she asks, her Yorkshire accent warm and reassuring. "It can't be good for you, all that standing." She is clearly young. She can't be more than, what, twenty-five? She has the sort of easy charm that Maggie always had, a way of lighting and lightening up a room all at once. It sends me right back to forty years ago, the drizzle and the streetlamps and a drunken rendition of "Good King Wenceslas" providing the soundtrack to our first encounter.

"Shall I?" she prompts, interrupting my trip down memory lane. "Really, it's no trouble, I promise."

"Thank you. I'd be very grateful."

For the best part of twenty-four hours, I have kept

it together, but it is at this very act of human kindness that I feel I am ripe to come undone. The nurse returns shortly and even goes to the trouble of folding the seat out for me. I suddenly feel like the guest of honor at the most unpalatable picnic of my life.

"What's your name?" I ask, not bothering to try to decipher her name tag in the dimness or run the risk of scrutinizing another woman's chest at my wife's bedside.

"Daisy," she says. "None too dainty like one, though, I'll admit."

I try to smile. The whole bottom half of my face feels as if it is cracking with the effort.

"I am sorry, really very sorry to see this," Daisy says, noticing as the corners of my mouth begin to drop. For a minute, maybe more, we both watch Maggie, her chest rising and falling with regimented efficiency, her lips slightly parted as if in a permanent state of surrender. Everything about this is not her. The discipline, the hush, the fuss of nurses providing the sort of kindness Maggie spent a lifetime expending and eventually being punished for.

"You can speak to her, you know," Daisy says. "It's so quiet here, often people feel scared to speak aloud. But you have to push through that. Let your wife hear your voice."

I gulp. I wonder what Daisy would say if she knew. She seems so much wiser than her years, and I'm sure she has seen more than her fair share of suffering in this line of work. Even so, could she understand?

I think back to the day my voice first failed me. I was so close to confessing what I had done. I'd seen the consequences laid out before me, and the guilt was so pure, so overwhelming, that I knew I had to tell Maggie. The words were on the tip of my tongue, or at least I thought they were. I had braced myself as I tiptoed up the stairs to our bedroom.

Then I rounded the corner and I saw her in the half-light, struggling to sit up to reach a glass of water on the bedside table, a shadow of who she used to be, and I knew I couldn't risk hurting her any more than she already had been. She was barely hanging on; I couldn't bring her more bad news. I couldn't tell her what I had to, not when it meant she would leave me. Every day when I couldn't speak, in the silence, I lived with that same guilt, the same burning shame. I was suffocating myself, but somehow anything was better than the thought of telling Maggie what I had done and losing her forever.

Daisy clears her throat lightly to bring me back in the room. "I'm no doctor, don't get me wrong, but I can say what I have seen, and sometimes it is a familiar voice that will do it, more than these tubes ever will. The patient hears you. It reminds them of all the good things they have to wake up for. Spurs on the recovery, you know?"

I don't know, but I nod regardless. I can see how much she cares about Maggie, even if she is just one of an extensive list of patients. Daisy has large fingers, long and thick, but they move so tenderly as she works to straighten the fabric at Maggie's neck where it has bunched up under the tubes. It's the sort of gesture I know Maggie would appreciate.

"You could tell her your news," Daisy prompts. "You've probably got plenty to say anyway, after the day you've had. Or maybe there's something that's been on your mind that you want to share?"

"Well, I've certainly got that." My attempt to sound lighthearted comes out as it really is—sheepish and forced.

"Pardon? I didn't catch that. You're muttering," Daisy says, taking one final reading from the monitor next to Maggie and flipping her pad shut.

"Sorry—yes, I do have something I need to tell her. Something important. I don't know why I didn't tell her before."

The understatement alone is enough to crush me. I press my fist hard against my lips and force myself to look at Maggie square on. How did I never realize just how small and fragile she has become? She has always been tiny—a good foot shorter than me. The first winter we lived together, I couldn't wrap my head around the sheer volume of jumpers she needed to wear on her minuscule frame just to function around the rental flat. The dubious central heating didn't help matters, Maggie hopping from one foot to the other like an aerobics instructor while I bashed at the buttons in the boiler cupboard to no avail. I learned early on that she brought her own warmth wherever she went.

"Now isn't the time to be hard on yourself. Ease Maggie in. Don't blurt it all out, mind—you don't want to scare her away. Definitely not at first. Try to keep it positive. Remind her she's loved. Tell her about all those times you showed her that."

My face must read wild-eyed panic, as Daisy lays a hand on my shoulder, a subtle pressure that flattens the crumples in the cotton of my shirt.

"Don't worry about it too much. Just talk to her. Don't let this time get away."

Chapter 2

I don't stay long that first day. The moment Daisy is gone, I feel my reserve creep back, despite my best intentions. It has only ever been Maggie who has had some way of cracking through it: my studious awkwardness, the well-meaning remark delivered always that bit too late, my inability to "just gel" with new people. In all our years together, Maggie has never felt as much of a stranger to me as she does here, a little, lined face among the network of taut tubing, reduced to a series of regular beeps and timetabled measurements.

There is so much I have to say that I have no idea where to begin. I can't start with the reason why I stopped speaking. Not when Daisy has told me to go easy, to coax Maggie back to me. Talking has never been my strong point. "Not a man of many words," my sixth-form tutor wrote on my university application by way of a character reference. My own mother used to describe me as a "quiet sort" to friends and relatives; even the traveling podiatrist got a version of that when she came to visit, every fourth Saturday, foot file in hand. It dawns on me now that I am about as much use here as an umbrella in a hurricane. I'm not sure I can do this after all.

I wait for the little bus that comes direct to the hospital. Pity on wheels. No one on board makes eye contact; it would tip us over the edge—the sufferers and the ones watching the suffering unfold in all its grotesque, undignified detail. What about those who inflicted the suffering in the first place? I doubt I would be welcome. I find a window seat and place my bag next to me.

At the traffic lights, a couple idling on the pavement nearly miss the green man as they cradle each other's waist, their eyes intently focused on each other as they delve deeper into their conversation; behind me, a family with two children and a boisterous Labrador pack out a battered station wagon; a group of students ride their bicycles three abreast, unconcerned by the queue of angry, honking cars behind. I have never felt so alone. Wasn't that what marriage, our marriage, was meant to keep at bay?

It has been swelteringly hot today, not that I felt it in Maggie's artificially cooled room. When I get off the bus and stumble the short distance home, I feel as if I am being blasted by a hundred hairdryers, dry and intense, and wonder if anything will ever feel comfortable again. I get the key in the door after a few false starts with my faltering fingers. The last of this late August evening's sunlight illuminates the hallway, a ribbon of dust dancing and swirling toward the scene of the crime. *Hers or mine?* I ask myself as I head up the stairs.

I can't bring myself to go back to the kitchen, not yet. Without turning on the light, I head straight to our bedroom. *Our.* I hardly remember a time before I spoke in the plural. What I would give to have her back, here, on her side. In reality she had all the sides. I never knew how much space such a small person could demand, wriggling like an octopus throughout the night until I was squashed up at the precipice of the mattress edge, just a corner of duvet to my name. God, I never knew I could miss it.

I trail my fingers along the stack of books that has accumulated on her bedside table—some from charity shops, a slim gift book titled *The Wife* that I bought as a stocking filler a few years back, one in its plastic library jacket (firmly overdue). After she retired three years ago, she decided she would go and volunteer there, at the library in Summertown that was earmarked for closure. "In solidarity!" she'd said when she told me. I wasn't sure if she meant with the books or with the overworked professionals who had enough on their plates without the threat of government cuts teetering over their heads. Either way, it was something to distract her until I retired a year later as well. She loved it there—the people, the sanctuary. She gave it up, though, when everything happened. I suppose you can't help others until you are able to help yourself.

In recent years, she hasn't been sleeping so well. She still tries to read but when I lean over, to plant a kiss behind her ear or to stroke the inside of her arm in the way she likes, I can see she's still on the same page, her eyes fuzzy in the mid-distance. I make the call on when to turn out the lights, knowing full well neither of us will drift off easily. Instead, I draw patterns on the soft skin at the base of her spine, which is exposed by her pajama top. It takes me right back to our first dates together, when I was too scared to tell her I loved her but traced the letters out on her back instead, a coward's compromise delivered with a trembling hand.

I kick off my shoes and lie down on top of the duvet. I am so desperate to touch her again, to spell out all the ways I love her. When I drift off, all I see is Maggie cocooned within it, one hand poking out to pull me in.

At the hospital the next morning, I am welcomed by my first name at the nursing station by a woman I don't recognize in the slightest. I hope this is not a sign of how long they expect me to be visiting. At first, I don't see Daisy and feel a rush of panic. She was so calm, so nonjudgmental. I can't afford to lose her too. I scan the reception space with its bewildering array of staff, assessing their backs, their hair. Eventually I catch sight of her, busy at one of the computer booths in the corner, her back to me and her hips straining at the seams of her scrubs. My heart rate slows just a tad, and I clear my throat, loudly enough to feel like a nuisance. Loudly enough that a pregnant woman waiting five feet away covers her mouth with her scarf.

"Ah, Professor, good morning," Daisy says, beaming as she wheels her chair round to face me and levering herself up, palms on thighs. She is even taller than I remembered from yesterday, only three inches or so shorter than me. She has the sort of build Maggie would have affectionately described as "sturdy," as if she were assessing the stability of a tree in the back garden.

"Is that what you want to be called, eh? Professor?" she asks as she weaves herself out from behind the counter and leads me down the corridor. Her dark brown hair is pulled back in a ponytail that swings sleekly in time with her step.

"Well . . . er . . . ," I begin.

"Cat got your tongue, eh? Don't know your own name now?" Daisy smiles with the sort of easy complicity I always wished I could generate with my own family, let alone strangers.

"Frank," I say decisively. "Please call me Frank, Daisy."

Daisy turns to smile at me, and for a second I feel as if maybe, just for once, I have done some infinitesimally small thing right. Then we reach Maggie's door, still closed, and I feel the weight of my own frustrated hopefulness crash down around me again. The blinds in her room have been opened, and I am able to take in the space fully. It is sparse, and I suddenly feel conscious of arriving empty-handed.

"We need to keep it all very clean here," Daisy says, somehow sensing my embarrassment. "But I kept your chair, Frank, so you two can talk."

Daisy moves behind me to adjust the blinds, lowering them slightly so I don't have to squint.

"How did it go yesterday?" Daisy asks.

"Not well," I admit.

"It's hard, Frank. I get that. But our Maggie is going to want to know that you are here."

"I'm scared." The words slip out before I have the chance to think better of them.

"I know, but trust me, you'll be more scared if you don't talk. If you don't, then you'll have regrets. And regret is something to be far more scared of."

I sense Daisy is about to leave, and I am overwhelmed by my desire to keep her here. She is safe—a reliable conduit to Maggie.

"Daisy," I call, as she heads for the door. "What shall I say?"

Daisy's face remains unchanged, bar a slight smile that breaks at the corners of her lips. Evidently, I am not the first visitor to need schooling on their bedside manner.

"That's up to you, Frank. If you're struggling, why don't you tell her your story? You and her, huh? There's a reason people tell you to start at the beginning. It's easiest that way. Only this time, you can do it right. Tell her all the things you should have said before."

I nod.

"Not all at once now, remember."

With that, Daisy is gone.

I pull my chair a little closer to Maggie's side, careful not to knock the cables. I am struck by how much there is to say, how much I should have said, and yet how very little feels appropriate. And how do you start to talk again, when you stopped so long ago?

"Morning, Maggie." My voice comes out as a croak. "The things I should have said before, eh? Well, you better get comfortable."

In the silence, I remember her laugh, light as a feather and quick to humor me—my bad jokes, the dad jokes.

I see the cannula strain where I have grasped at her hand, and I quickly place it back down before one of the contraptions signals my disruption and I am unceremoniously hauled out by the staff.

"I . . . I . . . Can you hear me? Did you hear that, what I just said? No? Oh. Well . . . Oh God, Maggie, I'm terrible at this, aren't I?"

For a minute I think of leaving, of making a repeat performance of yesterday's nonstarter. Then I think of the house, each room achingly empty, a memory of Maggie imprinted on every chair and wall and light switch. What sort of husband would it make me to leave her here? Not a very loving one, that's for sure. I have had plenty of failings over the years, but not loving Maggie enough has never been one.

I sit up taller, imagining each vertebra slotting back into its proper formation, and rise out of my half slump.

"Look, Mags, you are going to have to put up with me being terrible at this because I am here to stay. I will stay as long as it takes for you to wake up. See, I even have a chair."

Nothing.

"You need to know what happened, Mags, why I switched off."

I half expect her eyes to open wide at this. Finally, an answer. The answers that she spent six months looking for. The answers that nearly took Maggie from me forever.

"I can't let you go without telling you that."

It sounds so morbid, out in the open, and I kick myself. This wasn't what Daisy meant about keeping it positive, quite the opposite.

"I can't let you go full stop, Maggie. I can't be without you. Really, Maggie, I can't," I whisper, reaching for her hand. "I'm so sorry. I'm sorrier than you can ever know.

"Do you remember that was the first thing I ever said to you, Mags? Do you? 'I'm sorry.' And do you know, I have spent the last forty-odd years thinking what better lines I could have tried out on you instead?"

The first time I saw you, all I could make out were your eyes and the very tip of your nose, ruby red like a beacon in the cold. You had a thick woolly scarf pulled up over your lips, your hair bunched up under it so that only a few wisps could escape. When you arrived, it was as it ever would be, like a cyclone descending, all flailing limbs and air kisses, a flurry of hugs and exclamations and the sort of warmth everyone in the vicinity could feel, even at three degrees below.

I hadn't seen you around before, that much I knew for sure. I'd been in Oxford for five years by that point and I was knee-deep into my PhD; the lab was hardly swarming with women and it wasn't as if I was dripping in them in my spare time either. No, I definitely would have remembered if I had seen a girl like you before.

With its cheap lager and large outdoor seating area, the Rose & Crown was a stomping ground for the developmental biology department, if such a thing could be claimed by a group of scientists who didn't see much daylight, let alone the social evening hours. It was far enough from the Dreaming Spires to dodge the Canon-wielding tourists but close enough to stumble back to halls if anyone did manage to land it lucky at the end of the night. I know it is a cliché to say that I noticed you straightaway, but it would still be true, even if your elbow hadn't half caught Piotr's glass as you barreled past and into the arms of your equally excitable friends.

That close to Christmas, there were plenty of new faces in our local, some of them home in time to spend the week with family. Our group of academic exiles was either too far from home to enjoy the festive season in the comfort of our own front rooms or, as in my case, would rather prolong the inevitable awkwardness of returning to our parents at the age of twenty-six and without a bride in tow. So much for the social upheaval of the seventies: the liberal ideals of the decade had scarcely reached the Home Counties, let alone brushed the doorstep of my parents' three-bed terrace in Guild-ford.

It was a relief to be free, really, as much as my family meant well. I loved them, and I knew they loved me; it was just that everything at home felt so very small. We didn't really discuss things. Not the important stuff, the big questions that kept me awake at night. No, it was polite, and it was comfortable. There was an unspoken assumption that I would follow in Dad's footsteps, take over the garage and shore up the business. As they saw it, science was all very well, but it was best left at the school gates in favor of a mortgage-able career. My choices took some getting used to, but I knew they were proud, in their own way at least.

As for Oxford, well, I felt at home in a way I never had before. I made great friends, many as socially inept as I was, and no one at the back of the lecture hall shouted you down for sitting in the front row or taking too many notes. I did worry that I hadn't made quite enough of it, though. In my mind, my time there should have been spent smoking cigars on the roof-tops or attending parties with women called Camilla or Cordelia or something else that sounded suitably exotic to me until the sun shot through the curtains and took us all by surprise. In reality, the only place I pulled all-nighters was at my desk. That was my version of a good time. Until I met you.

I was looking forward to that evening, a Christmas party of sorts, only the budget didn't stretch far enough for any sort of planning to have been required. Instead, the two supervisors had come and put a fistful of notes in a glass for us to buy rounds. I wonder what would have happened without the departmental Dutch cour-age? If I could have focused on the merriment on hand instead of mooning at your table, reading into your mad hand gestures and facial expressions as if I were at a mime performance, not in a pub garden?

You are, naturally, the center of attention, a habit, I will come to realize, holding court and magnetizing all eyes to you. To your left, a man with sandy hair and a tweed jacket hangs on your every word, laughing a little too loudly and a beat or so before the rest do. There is some distance between you, though, and I write him off as another acolyte, in thrall to your charms.

It doesn't take long for the boys to cotton on that my mind and attentions are elsewhere, Piotr nudging me in the ribs and delivering the sort of crude remarks that make me thankful the last four years of his doctorate haven't entirely thinned out his Polish accent. It is Jack, our lab technician, a man who dedicates forty hours a week to breeding newts, who makes the only sensible remark of the night.

"What have you got to lose, eh, Frank?" he says. "Another night in a cold single bed?"

When I see you stand up to get your round in, I know it is my chance, and the boys aren't going to let me lose it. The moment you are up, squeezing yourself off the bench and holding the empty glasses precariously between your fingers, I am sent in with what is left in the kitty.

The pub is warm inside, and my glasses steam up quickly. I curse my eyesight and almost wish I had taken the risk of leaving my frames at home. I'd tried that once before, on the sole date I'd managed in the last two years, with a research assistant over from

Glasgow. Let's just say Fiona wasn't too pleased when I came back from the bathroom and sat down at another woman's table.

I blot the lenses on my jumper. It is one of Mum's finest creations, a Christmas-tree scene, and the little glittery threads from the knitted baubles keep catching on the screws. Finally, I manage to clear away the condensation, but my resolve seems to have dissipated with it. I suddenly feel ridiculous—what was I thinking, hoping a girl like you would cast your eye on me, let alone agree to a date? I am about to concede defeat and send Jack for our next round when Piotr enters, en route to the loo, and he is as unsubtle as ever when he slaps me on the back, enough to turn me back around and, in the tight squeeze of bodies by the bar, knock me straight into you. For a second, there is terror that your stack of empties will fall, and I stick my hands out blindly, catching one, then steadying myself just in time to save some face.

"I'm so sorry—" My face flushes as red as my hair, my words pouring over one another. Blessedly, you cut me off.

"Thank you!" you shout over me. "I am always biting off more than I can chew! Here, can I get you a drink—token of my appreciation and all?"

"No. Thank you, though. I mean I'd love to, but"—I

jangle the coins in the pint glass as a weak explanation—
"I've got to stand my round!"

"I admire a man with principles." You smile. I
cannot tell if it is my imagination or if you are taking a
step toward me.

Before I can analyze you any more, you turn around
and make your order, winning over the barman, who
laughs at something you say while you peruse the
ciders on tap. As your drinks line up, it is on the tip of
my tongue to ask if, actually, we could postpone that
drink—another night, after Christmas, just us?

Instead, I burn up, my cheeks on fire, my palms
sweating. In a bid to calm my flaming face, I think of
the evolution and gene-mutation paper folded in half
and rammed in my back pocket. "DNA Mutations in
Xenopus Toads," I seem to remember. But no data set
or scatter graph on adaptive change is sufficient distraction from my crippling embarrassment. Not for the
first time, it strikes me that if I carry on at this rate, it
will be a biological marvel if I survive my twenties and
have any chance of reproducing.

All too soon you have your drinks, and a tray this
time too. You look up at me, pushing your curls behind
your ear. "Well, thanks again . . ."

"Frank," I offer. "'It's Frank."

"I'm Maggie," you say. "Margot, really, no thanks to my mother. It seems so old-fashioned, and besides, I'm not French, no delusion of being either."

"I'll remember that."

"What? The not being French or the not being deluded?"

"Both, I'd say."

You smile at that. "And how will I remember you?"

I am not imagining it this time. You take a step toward me, so close now that the lip of the tray brushes my chest.

"Frank, the man of principle. Despite what this jumper might say to the contrary."

The garish metallic baubles flicker under the harsh light overhead. You laugh, head thrown back, and for a second there is nothing. The roar of the pub dulls to silence. My peripheral vision goes blurry. You become my foreground, background, and everything besides. This is my chance to ask, but it feels almost sacrilegious to break this moment.

It's Piotr who breaks it. "Frank! Frank, get the drinks, eh?"

"You're being called!" you shout over the din of some drunken carolers who have just arrived and slam their palms down on the bar. "Better get the round or they'll worry where you've been." And then, more quietly, as if it is a secret, just for us two, "Merry Christmas, Frank."

And just like that, you were off, back to the garden. I'd missed my spot at the bar and I'd missed my chance.

What should I have said, Mags? Well, asked you on a date, that's for sure. But that wasn't enough. You would have had other men chasing you, I knew that as good as certain. I wanted you to know that how I felt was different. How, when my glasses steamed up, I knew exactly how far in front of me you were because there was something about you that felt programmed into me. I knew then that you were it, that you were my Forever Girl. I wouldn't have said that then, though. I didn't want to scare you away. But I knew then what I have always known. You were my Forever Girl, Mags.

Chapter 3

After our first meeting in the pub, there weren't five minutes that went by when I wasn't thinking about you. That magnetic smile, your easy charm. And to think there was just a tray between us. A day later, still kicking myself for losing my opportunity, I went back to Guildford alone, much to my parents' disappointment, although Chessie had brought her fiancé, and that diverted the spotlight somewhat, even if she is two years younger than me.

Regular as clockwork, all the relatives asked in turn, "Is there someone special? A lady you are going steady with?" and I brushed off their inquisition brusquely, pretending to be reading for my next paper or doing battle with the crossword. My perpetual singleness had always been a great source of amusement at home.

I'd yet to bring a girl home, and in between bouts of concern, there was plenty of fodder for their entertainment as they mimicked me trying to analyze patterns in flirting on a scatter plot and applying them to my own chaotic attempts with limited success.

How on earth was I meant to explain that I had met the girl of my dreams and had let her slip away into a smoky pub garden without so much as asking for a date? I imagined you there, with my parents, on our Boxing Day walk, staying over in my childhood bed and sharing the single duvet, generating our own heat when that didn't suffice. I tortured myself over the turkey with images of you with another man on New Year's Eve, ringing in the New Year with a sparkle of your infectious laugh and a sparkler on your ring finger too.

Try as I might, I couldn't get you out of my mind. Back in Oxford, the boys from the lab didn't help matters, refusing to let me live down my failure to launch. That January was grueling by anyone's standards; I barely slept, barely ate (although a researcher's stipend made that practically a prerequisite), and was barely surprised when I developed a hacking cough.

Eventually the father of the family I lodged with packed me off to the doctor, more from his own frustration than from kindness, I imagine. And so it was that I found myself in a walk-in clinic in Jericho—wheezing my way through the appointment with enough vigor to warrant a prescription for antibiotics and a firm warning to take good care before it developed into something worse.

I was ushered out of the consulting room and into the reception area, which had packed out in the past ten minutes. I could hardly see where I'd entered for all the sick: mothers jiggling their fussy babies, a couple with matching plaster casts on their wrists, teenagers with glazed eyes and restless feet slumped against the wall when there wasn't room for them on the waiting-room seats. As I was squeezing my way past, muttering my apologies, the attention shifted to the front of the room. From the community-nursing office, a voice emerged, a voice I would remember anywhere.

"All right, all!" you say. "We'll be seeing you all individually, so please do make yourselves comfortable until then. I'm a newbie too, so be kind. You have been warned!"

In an instant, I am back at the Rose & Crown: the same studied irreverence and the same ability to disarm and win over any audience with that self-deprecating charm that had sent my head into a tailspin.

I know it is now or never. I'll never know how I summoned up the courage, but the word is out of my mouth before I can overthink it.

"Maggie . . . Maggie!"

You stop in your tracks, rising onto your tiptoes to survey the room and find the source of the voice. By this time, I have reached you. "Nurse Marbury, rather," I manage, quickly assessing the name badge on the breast pocket of your pinafore and ensuring my eyes don't linger too long.

For one cruel second, I suspect you can't place me. Then you exhale, beaming. "Frank! My man of principle. What brings you here?"

With impeccable timing, the rattle in my chest rises up and I find myself coughing a chunk of phlegm straight into my hankie, crumpled from overuse and a few days spent stuffed at the bottom of my pocket. I don't think I have ever been so grateful for a cough before or since. I tell myself it is fate, that this is meant to be.

"Ah, well, I might be able to guess that one." You smile, placing your hand on the top of my arm. The spot where your hand rests tingles, and in that one gesture I realize just how hungry I am for touch, your touch.

I imagine we are being watched, and you are careful not to cause a scene. "Take good care of that cough, Frank, lots of hot chest compresses, tea every hour . . ."

"Look, Maggie, I wanted to ask you something. And not about the cough." I haven't much of a voice left after weeks of coughing, but what little there is comes out with uncharacteristic decisiveness. "Maggie, would you go out with me sometime? Just the two of us?"

Our interaction seems to have attracted an audience. I can sense the row of patients behind me leaning just an inch forward. In the far corner, the receptionist peers suspiciously in my direction, one minute away from tapping her watch at me, if she gives it even that long.

"Yes. Yes, I'd like that."

I haven't given much thought to being taken up on my offer. I feel very much out of my depth but manage to relax my face into a smile that I hope says how delighted I am, without putting you off. It works. You offer up your availability as if you have spent a lifetime arranging dates.

"I'm off a week tomorrow, which should give you enough time to clear that cough. You can pick me up outside the surgery at two thirty. I'll leave the rest up to you."

And with that, you call your next patient.

I stumble out into the fresh air, relieved to be away from the smell of stale human bodies and its unconvincing antiseptic mask. On the cycle ride home, I am elated; I have found you again and convinced you to go on a date. What were the chances? Surely that was fate in action? And it was on my side for once too! It isn't until I get into bed, the duvet pulled right up to my neck, that I realize we haven't even hit the hard part yet.

Our first date rolls round quickly enough. I arrive horrendously early and do laps of the nearby streets, hoping there aren't any residents hovering at their net curtains, primed to call me out on my suspicious lingering. You are true to your word, perfectly on time. From a hundred yards away, I catch a flash of your bright red skirt. Hardly your usual uniform and more likely to cause a cardiac arrest than cure it, I find myself thinking, feeling my own pulse surge with each step you take toward me.

"Hi, Frank," you say, your face flushed. From cold or nerves? I wonder. "Where are we off to, then?"

"I thought we could go to the Ashmolean? There's meant to be a good exhibition there at the moment, Japanese screen paintings . . ." I trail off, suddenly not so sure of my romantic sensibilities or my ability to plan anything remotely "fun." I sound thirty years older than I really am and cringe, scouring my brain for last-minute alternatives.

"How cosmopolitan, Frank. That sounds wonderful!"

For a cruel second, I think you are mocking me. Then, from nowhere, you link your arm through mine, and suddenly I don't care. I know I have got something right, and the warmth of your enthusiasm floods through me.

At the museum, you are keen to pick my brain on the exhibition, which is, mercifully, empty. I'd had visions of schoolchildren watching me floundering from their crocodile formation; worse yet, the students I supervised making use of their university discount on a weekday afternoon. There is something about the way your face lights up when I impart a titbit of information, your head cocked to one side, looking up at me from under the curtain of your fringe, that makes me want to impress you.

I overreach myself. Before I realize it, I am an expert on the Edo period. I provide all manner of observations on the shogun's favorite ceramic vase, the screens saved from the battle of Osaka. I pray you don't know enough to see straight through my invented tales, which grow ever more extravagant in my bid to light you up, to sustain the glow and glee on your face. For the first time in my life, I feel confident. Calm, at ease, not aching with the overwhelming desire to be someone, anyone, else. You are here, freely, with me. For some unfathomable reason, you seem to be very happy about that too.

At the final case, there is an array of fans, painted silk with bamboo handles, each one decorated exquisitely. On the table beneath, there are some less antique equivalents for school visitors to practice their own fanning, or to hit each other with, whatever might buy their teachers more time. Picking one up, I extend its cheap gauze across the lower half of my mouth and look down at you with a gaze that I hope looks coquettish.

"And how did the empress like the exhibit?" I ask.

You laugh, your head thrown back, your neck bare and beautiful. It has been a risk worth taking. When you gather yourself, you take a step closer to me.

"Oh, you are an odd one, Frank," you say. "Oddly brilliant too." You fleetingly cast your eyes left and right before pushing the fan aside and placing a kiss on my lips.

I knew then that I loved you, Mags. I have loved you since that moment on and in every minute since. I should have told you then. I worried that it was too early. We had all the time in the world to grapple with our emotions, for me to admit just how deep you ran in my veins. Only now, when we have used up that time, can I see my mistake. I see them all. These past six months, I haven't been your clown, and I certainly haven't been your samurai. Forgive me, Mags, please?

Chapter 4

I can't help but think how much Maggie would hate all this fuss. She could fuss with the best of them when it came to others, but herself? That was out of the question. When I arrived this morning, I started counting the staff who come in to assess the monitors, her vitals, and whatever else might go awry while she lies there, as still as she has ever been, still utterly unresponsive. I counted six nurses then stopped. I figured my attention was better spent elsewhere.

At least I have, to some extent, begun to open up. I am speaking. Slowly—yes. Sticking to the good bits—yes. But speaking nonetheless. There is nowhere to hide when there is a bedside I need to be at. There is nowhere else I could be either. I cannot retreat to my study, bury myself in some papers or lock eyes with the cryptic crossword to avoid engaging with the gulf between us. How has it come to this? I never thought I would be saying the things I should have said for the past few months—hell, for a lifetime—to a face that has not moved an inch in forty-eight hours.

"You're staying, then?" Daisy asks as she takes over the rearrangement of Maggie's breathing tubes from an assistant who seems to be shadowing her.

"Pardon?"

"Here. You're staying, then?"

"I can't leave. I can't, Daisy."

"Hey, now, I didn't say you had to, did I? Some doctors will say visitors ought to keep to their hours, but luckily for you, you're dealing with Daisy. What Daisy says, goes. And Daisy says that if you want to stay, then that can be sorted. I can get you some bedding before I head home, if you'd like?"

She rubs her eyes with the edge of her wrist where her rubber glove ends. When she opens them again, they seem larger, discs of dusty blue awaiting my answer.

"Will you, please?"

"Sure, Frank. But mind, there's no glamour here, I warn you. Think camping, then think less comfortable. Saves you going home, though. Saves you time. Unless you need to get back for something?"

Time. Yes. The eternal enemy. How long do I have left? Before they try to pull the cord on Maggie? For "compassion." For budgets. For everyone's sanity. The thought sends fresh waves of nausea crashing through me, and I try to suppress the image of a doctor's hand wavering at the plug socket behind the bed.

Daisy has finished her adjustments, and for a second we hold each other's gaze. I am the first to look away. There is something confessional about her presence, and this is a confession I am not yet ready to make, however big my first step has been. Not yet. Eventually. I'll get there eventually. I hope I have enough time.

When Daisy excuses herself to locate a camp bed, I move a little closer to Maggie. In doing so, my stomach drops a fraction, its age-old response to nerves. I have spent a lifetime trying to get closer to her. Now I am too scared.

"Do you still recognize this voice?" I ask, running my finger down the soft skin of Maggie's cheek. When it reaches her jaw, I can see my finger tremble. "Do you still want to hear it anyway? Please, Mags, just wake up and tell me it isn't too late."

In an unbelievable stroke of good fortune, you agreed to a second date. My nerves skyrocketed. There was so much more at stake. I wonder if you noticed my palms sweating, Mags, when I stood up to greet you. That awful moment when you went in for a double-cheek kiss—so sophisticated, so natural—and I stuck my hand out instead, like I was being interviewed for a job, not trying to start a relationship.

We met down a narrow alleyway. Do you remember it? The one near to where Edie moved a couple of years later. Anyway, it hardly screamed safe, let alone romantic. Earlier in the week, I had put instructions on a notelet and left it with reception at the surgery, half fretting whether my missive would make it to you, half terrified you wouldn't turn up after you read it. As I would come to learn, you lived for that thrill of the unexpected. You would bring it out in me too. I always did say you were a miracle worker.

"So?" you ask.

"So, what?"

"So, what are we doing today?" You look so excited.

"I thought we might do a little boating." I try out the voice I have been practicing in the shower this week. Confident. Assertive. One that suits the new Frank. If I'm honest, it is the sort of Frank I didn't even know could exist.

"Ooh, I'd love that!"

Just as I am about to mentally toast my own victory—
Two for two! Can I make it three?—there is an ominous
rumble in the clouds above. We both look up at the gray
overhead, only one or two white curls visible in a sea
of slate. I look down before you and see that there is a
smile hovering on your lips.

"They did say on the radio that it was going to be
mild. The beginning of spring . . . ," I begin. It is late
February. We are both bundled up in coats and scarves.
I wish I hadn't been so trusting of the peppy weather
presenter. "But now I'm wondering if perhaps this isn't
quite the weather for it . . ."

"Or maybe it's the best weather for it after all?"
You fix me with a look that is blatant in its mischief.
"You've got me this far—there's no way we're not
getting in a boat now."

My heart thumps so loudly in relief that I wonder if
you can hear it.

"Right, well, shall we?"

Logistically, things go from bad to worse. The boat
I have rented, from a "close friend" of Piotr's (not a
phrase I would ever trust again), has a crack running
horizontally under one seat and a set of the shortest
oars I have ever seen. In a fit of gallantry, I take the
seat above the crack and offer to do the rowing. You
push us off, taking a run-up that sends me shooting off

from the bank far faster than either of us expected. To get on board, you end up half splashing into the river and have to hoick yourself up with a violent push that sends the whole boat rocking from side to side. By the time you are in, we are both in hysterics.

You barely pause for breath before you are pulling off your loafers and emptying out the greenish-brown water that is sloshing around the soles. You stand up and immediately begin pulling down your tights. The first patch of skin that emerges, mid-thigh, is peppered with goose pimples. I feel indecent for looking and end up manically checking over my shoulders instead, as if on the lookout for the bank. Too late. We hit it with a judder that sends you flying forward. Just in time, I manage to catch you. My hands grab your shoulders inches before you crash into my face. I avoid a bruise, but the intimacy shakes me.

"My hero." There is something playful in your tone that makes me stir. I imagine what would have happened if I had let you fall just that tiny bit farther, until our bodies touched . . . Then, in desperation, I think of my grandmother, down in Dorset, and the way she would pick the food out of her teeth with her nails after supper, collecting the larger bits on the side of her plate. I think of the black mold on the shower door, the blocked sink in the little side kitchen at work . . . anything to distract me from the tightness in my trousers.

Before I know it, you have sat back down again, opposite me. The moment has passed, and my breath returns to some semblance of normality. In all the excitement, the boat has continued on its own path downstream, and when I finally take up the oars, I realize the hard work may have been done for me. We are in a small inlet, the surface almost emerald with a series of large, overlapping lily pads. The boat has a hard time cutting through them, but for once, now that I am in your presence, I feel no need to be chopping and changing lanes to get on in life just that bit faster.

On the far bank, two mallards, a male and a female, make their haphazard procession out of the water.

"Would you like a family, Frank?"

Do you know, I had never thought about that until you asked? I felt it was out of my reach to find someone to share a night with, let alone enough days for that to be a question on the cards.

You were the first woman I'd ever felt this way about. My first love, a decade later than everyone else seemed to experience theirs. I'd spent the last few years seeing all my friends coupling off while I languished on the starting blocks. I'd had enough trouble finding the right person, without the issue of the right time coming into play too.

I often found myself wondering why I hadn't met anyone before. Since Fiona, I'd had trouble getting up the confidence to ask anyone out, but even on the rare occasions when I did, I never seemed to have any success. At the pub, I could laugh it off, but once I was home, curled up in the single bed in my room (a good two inches too small for me, but beggars can't be choosers), I ran through what had gone wrong. I wondered if my potential love interests had noticed the tremor in my voice when I asked? That off-putting quiver that suggested I wasn't a leader or a man's man or whatever else they might have wanted. Did I not lay enough groundwork? After a few failed attempts, I drew my conclusion: I was kind, reliable Frank. The friend. I didn't have the self-confidence, the *pizzazz*, to be the great love of anyone's life. Until you, Maggie. You magicked something new out of me, all right.

Your question hangs in the air.

"I'm not sure. Perhaps. Yes, I suppose. I'm sorry, that's not a very good answer, is it? Anyway, what about you?"

"Yes, yes. Very much so." You answer without so much as a pause for breath.

"Are you close to your own family?" I ask, running my right hand through the water. I watch as it cuts the surface like a blade and then glance up at you.

"Not really. My dad died, two years back . . ."

"I'm sorr—"

You cut me off, almost as if you didn't notice the apology at all. "It's fine. Now it is, at least. We weren't very close, but well, it's still sad, isn't it?"

For the first time since we met, I see a new side to you. Gone is the gregarious, good-time girl, the joker, and the raconteur. You are contemplative and wistful. You are struggling to meet my eyes, and I sense there is something darker afoot too. You fiddle with the sleeve of your cardigan, twisting the loose fabric against your wrist before hooking it over your thumb like a tiny cotton cap.

"What about brothers and sisters?"

"Two brothers, both older. One's in New York. The other's . . . I'm not sure, actually. He's an artist. Last I heard he was in Scotland for an exhibition."

"And your mum, is she . . . ?"

"Alive? Yes. Just not very present. She left when I was thirteen. Remarried." There is something in your tone that is more than matter-of-fact. What is it? Resignation? Despair?

"Do you see her much?"

"Every now and again. She lives abroad, moves around a lot with her new husband. It's all . . ." You make a gesture with your hands, circling them and then opening the palms up to the sky as if to say it is out of your control.

"Complicated?" I suggest.

"And difficult. But that's family, huh?"

Just as that familiar worry is settling at the base of my stomach—*What will I say next?*—I feel a cool rush on my forearm. A frog has temporarily mistaken me for a lily pad. Slowly, so as not to startle it, I bring my left hand over and, in one deft motion, close my hand over its body. There is a second of panic when its eyes bulge, but then, safe in my cupped hands, it settles.

"What on earth?" Your attention snaps back to the boat.

"Oh, this guy? Just a friend."

"You are very good with him, Frank."

"Cheers. A compliment at last." Teasing you comes easily, but I am still keen to tread carefully. "I work with frogs."

"Really?" Your incredulity is almost as wide-eyed as the amphibian chirruping in my hands.

"They're great. Honest. To look at how far we have evolved. At the moment, we're looking at something called 'genetic drift'; that's the part of evolution that produces random changes over time. So, not selection, not what Darwin says. But at least it gives a chance to those of us who wouldn't make the cut in the survival of the fittest."

"Helpful for me too, then." There is a little color in your cheeks, a pinprick of red that is spreading out wider and wider. I didn't know you had the same bashfulness as me. What else had I read wrong?

"We all have silent genes—well, that's the current theory. Little bits of us that we can't see, not obviously, at least, which can cause mutations—good and bad."

"I like that." Your voice is barely above a whisper. "The little things that no one sees that could make the biggest change of all."

I reach over to you and begin to trace my finger in a circle over the goose pimples on your knee as if they were Braille. What silent secrets will I find there?

Just as my confidence is increasing, the tremor in my hand quietening, there is a rumble in the skies above.

"Shit," I say as I fumble for the oars. "Better get back."

Luckily, we haven't gone far. It is only as I am heaving our dinghy out and draining it under the boathouse awning that the rain starts. You don't rush for cover, not like me. No, you don't move an inch. You throw your coat at me and continue to stand in the full spray of the downpour, your arms above your head as you let the drops, fat and heavy, course down you.

"Maggie, you are a madwoman—you must be freezing!" I shout.

"Yes, just a bit." It is as if the thought of the cold has only just occurred to you. You head toward me, and I rush over with the coat outstretched.

"We need to get you home, before you get a chill." There is a fumble as you struggle to wriggle your arms into your coat sleeves, which I have straightened.

"Whose home?"

I have a distinct sense of being tested. I know what I want to do, but I am wary of pressuring you. I'm scared I will lose you altogether. Besides, I am a lodger, and the sort of hospitality I would like to share is hardly appropriate for a family home with two children under ten.

"What about mine?" you offer.

Silence.

"Jules and Edie will be in, but they'll keep themselves to themselves, I'm sure, and I've some food that needs eating." You are remarkably perky for a woman whose teeth are chattering.

"Yes." You appear not to have heard as you begin a

full inventory of your cupboards and our supper options. "Yes, I'd like that," I say, a little louder than I
had hoped this time, and rather too loud for the empty
river path we are on.

"Oh, well, great then—grab your bike!"

I learn then that you are a demon on two wheels,
powering down the cobbled lanes and main roads that
lead back to your shared house with the sort of vigor I
had previously assumed you reserved for conversation.
So much for a romantic cycle, side by side: I play a ten-
minute round of quite literally chasing your coattails
before you squelch off the saddle and brandish your
keys.

"Home sweet home!"

It takes me a good minute to catch my breath.

The house is much as I have imagined, small and
made smaller by an assortment of clutter strewn on
every surface: the teapot acts as an unofficial paperweight, holding down a stack of bills, more than one
of which bears a red OVERDUE stamp; a shelf of LPs
has overbalanced, leaving a puddle of discs and covers
surrounding the record player below; half the crockery appears to be either lodged on the sofa's edge or
wedged behind it. Everything is a little too much, no-
tably disorderly.

There was no doubt you lived there, Mags, although

it was amusing to hear you'd only moved in three months ago. It never did take long for you to make an impression.

In a change to the billed proceedings, Jules and Edie do little to make themselves scarce. I learn a lot then. About the nursing course the three of you met on in London, the digs you shared near Tooting Common, and just how close you had come to being suspended after an incident involving a skeleton, three meters of bandages, and a particularly debauched Halloween party in Balham. I don't need to worry about impressing with my conversation over dinner: there is no way I can get a word in edgeways in the hours that follow.

"Race you for the bathroom?" Jules turns to Edie, whose fourth hot toddy of the evening has left her yawning uncontrollably.

"Outta my way!" Edie hollers, pushing her chair back with such force as she lurches off the starting block that it careers backward, landing with a thump on the floor.

"Not fair, no way!" Jules is up, after her, the two shrieking and cursing all the way up the stairs.

"Is it any wonder we aren't our landlord's favorites?"

It is just us, finally.

I have spent the past few hours navigating the space between us in a state of constant anxiety. Now we are the closest we have ever been, our chairs adjacent at the square dining-room table, our knees brushing. I know now is my opportunity to kiss you, properly. I can feel myself shaking.

I inch my face forward and am relieved to see you do likewise. In anticipation, I reposition my hand on the table to steady myself but unwittingly place it on a slick of spilled gravy. My upper body hurtles far too fast toward you, and my forehead bashes into yours. You laugh, kindly. I wipe my hand on my trousers and set it back next to my glass. You reach over, and your skin on mine feels reassuringly cool as I start burning up with shame. I wait a beat or two, for my cheeks to go down, for my stomach to dislodge from my throat.

"Will you stay tonight, Frank?"

There is nothing I want more and nothing I am more scared of.

"I'd like that," I manage. "Shall I . . . ?" I gesture at the mess you and Jules managed to make in the preparation of the sausages and mash.

"Oh, all this? No, no, leave it for me, tomorrow."

We both know you are being optimistic there. As if in protest, the tower of pots, pans, and miscellaneous crockery gives a tinny groan. You rush to the sink and create some makeshift scaffolding with your arms. I manage to move some of the dishes into the sink, both of us doubled over with laughter. Just as I am going to turn on the taps, you place your hand on mine and draw it away, intertwining our fingers.

In the doorway, you turn off the kitchen light and lead me up the stairs. You don't turn on the light in your room either. I find the bed and sit on the edge of it. For a second you let go of my hand—have I done something wrong already? But then you are back, slippers off, and so much better than I could have hoped for, your knees straddling my lap, your upper body curved to reach my lips.

Looking back, I am grateful you didn't give me the time to begin down the inevitable path to overthinking: Would you assume there had been others? Would my inexperience be noticeable? Would it put you off?

No, none of that. Just you, me, and our bodies, giving ourselves up to each other with the overwhelming sense that whatever detours the day might have taken, we had ended up in the right place, with the right person, after all.

I remember our first time like it was yesterday, Mags. I couldn't believe how soft your skin felt, how perfectly we seemed to fit together. I hadn't dared to hope things could get even better, that there was more to come. You always did prove me wrong.

When we finish, a little abruptly on my part, you

will have none of my whispered apology, placing your index finger across my lips in a stylized shush. With your head nestling in the hollow below my left shoulder and arm, I wish I had told you that you made me the happiest man alive.

"Thank you," I whisper.

Chapter 5

I doubt it happened that first time, although I may be wrong. There were a few times in short succession, blissful nights at yours and the hurried mornings after as you set an alarm ambitiously close to the surgery's opening hour. You had to drag me out of bed by the ankles, still half asleep and with my hands slammed against my ears to drown out the noise. I looked like a scarecrow as you flapped me out of the house—no time for a shower, let alone breakfast, and my hair sticking up every which way. You, by contrast, managed to look as impeccable as ever.

I think it's fair to say that we didn't get *much* sleep in those first few months, not that I begrudged it for long once the fug of the wake-up call wore off. We would stay up into the early hours talking, both of us folded on our sides and propped up on our elbows until the feeling went right out of them. When I think about it now, it's hard to single out particular subjects we talked about. Some nights you would just riff on small snatches of nonsense—imitating a particularly amusing patient or the latest visit from the landlord. Other times, you wanted to deal in the heavy stuff—did I believe in God? How did I vote? Oh no, you didn't mean to ask that, but mind, it would be helpful to know if I was a Tory or not.

Despite your inquisition, we touched on the subject of protection only once, that first night, just before. You told me you were covered, that it was a perk of the job and not to worry. I did what I was told on that front and I never thought to bring it up again. What was the need? Besides, it always amazed me how quickly you would begin to doze off the moment I tried to turn the high beam of conversation back onto you. As your eyes began to give the succession of tiny flutters that announced you were drifting off, I settled on tracing a series of hearts on the almost transparent skin at the nape of your neck, my body tucked like a parachute against your back.

There was never a dull moment with you, not even close, and I knew that was what I wanted for the rest of my life. I liked who I was with you, Mags. I could be spontaneous! Funny too. I remember the day I borrowed a car from Sam in the physiology lab upstairs and took us on a last-minute trip into the Cotswolds. It was the perfect introduction to spring proper—warm enough for a T-shirt, and that satisfying sense of the sun licking at the back of your neck. We went on a walk that the map advertised as circular. Funniest-shaped circle I'd ever seen. Six hours and several wrong turns later, we were back at the pub where I'd parked the car, parched. We were still topping up our hydration when last orders were called.

In the car, you drifted off almost immediately, the side of your face squashed against the glass as if your skin had melted in place there. For a problem sleeper, you put in a good performance then, so much so that it was almost tempting to hide the issues that I could feel starting under the bonnet, barely ten miles out of the village. I could feel the steering wheel vibrating under my hands, little tremors that kept intensifying until they were big enough to run right up my arm. I pulled in at the nearest service station.

"What's up, Frank?" you say, dropping your right arm to my knee and rubbing at your eyes with the other.

"The tire needs changing."

"Ah. Are you going to call someone?"

It's dark, but the forecourt is lit brightly enough that I can make out the phone box on the other side of it, taped up and with a hastily scrawled sign jammed in the door: DON'T USE.

"No," I say, surprising myself with my own resolve. "I've got this. You head in." I nod in the direction of the petrol station.

Of course, that doesn't work. You never have been a great one for following instructions, and instead you insist on standing out there with me. You must have been freezing in just your polka-dot summer dress, but no one would know it from the way you patiently hand the wheel wrench back and forth, steadying the spare, placing the jack back where it came from.

"Ta-da!" I tighten the final nut and stand up. In the process, our foreheads smash together. I hadn't noticed your approach.

"Ah! Sorry, Mags, sorry!"

One hand scoops under your nose to plug the bleed, and you flap away my apology with the other. "No." You flap again, this time toward my nose. A double nosebleed.

That was it, wasn't it, Mags? The moment we both lost it. We were gone, the pair of us seized by the sort of hysterics I hadn't had since I was a child.

I manage to usher you back into the vehicle, and

it is then that the full absurdity of the situation takes hold. We are both laughing so hard that the car starts shaking all over again.

"I didn't have you pinned as the practical sort, Frank," you say, when you have recovered enough to talk. You are still pinching the bridge of your nose, and your voice is distorted like a cartoon villain's.

"My dad's a mechanic—this sort of thing is in the blood." I look at the mess all over our hands. "Fitting, eh?"

You have found a tissue down the side of the glove compartment and are shredding it into four tiny plugs. I try not to think about how long it may have been down there.

"A mechanic," you say, as if you are mulling over the veracity of my statement. Gently, you bung my nostrils with the twisted paper before fitting your own. Satisfied with your handiwork, you reach over the gearstick and tap the side of my head. "Are you hiding any other talents in there?"

"Plenty. You'll just have to wait and see."

"I have no doubt you're sitting on a wealth of secrets."

"I love you, Maggie."

The words are out of my mouth before I have the chance to think better of them. It is the secret I have been nursing for weeks now. I have never felt it as fully as I do then, with you smiling in the passenger seat, wedges of paper stuffed up your nose.

"I love you too," you say. It is so matter-of-fact you could have been reading out directions. There is none of the ceremony you see in films. No red roses or choirs or anything else besides. It just is.

"Shall we?" You tap the wheel and crank up the radio. You certainly aren't sleepy anymore.

All the way home, I was treated to your personal rendition of the chart hits, minus the top notes that you were nowhere near hitting. When you were like this, high and alive and so fully in the moment it seemed as if you could barely breathe from it all, you were like the beacon on a lighthouse. The glare was square onto me, and it was all I could do not to go blind from your brightness and the way it lit up everything you touched. It was a miracle I didn't miss our turning off the motorway.

It would be fair to say I was enthralled. In fact, I was so wrapped up in you that it took a month or two for me to notice something was awry. We saw each other as much as we could, and for the most part you were your usual effervescent self. But that was never the full picture. I'd seen hints of something darker on our day on the river, in snatches of conversation since. There was nothing straightforward to you—there never has been, Mags—and I was mesmerized by the subtle waves of contradiction in you that bled into one another to form an overwhelming whole that I couldn't shake. You were like a watercolor painting: from afar, perfect; up close, blurry, messy, a combination of a million hues I never knew existed. I loved you fiercely, Mags, but more than that, I wanted to understand you.

So, you can see why I would take to studying you, in those moments when you would withdraw, burying your arm in mine as Jules and Edie babbled away in the kitchen and hiding yourself behind a heavy drape of silence. As you lay beside me in bed, I tried to read into the subtle flexing and uncurling of your muscles. Was this just you? Or was there something more?

Once, I awoke in the middle of the night and you weren't there. En route to the bathroom, I heard voices from the living room downstairs—Edie and another, whispered. I didn't mean to eavesdrop, Mags, but I was concerned—scared, really—for you. I tiptoed just far enough down the stairs to see you pressed against Edie's chest, shaking.

I wanted you to want to confide in me, Mags, but as you know all too well, you can't force someone to talk against their will. When you came back to bed that night, I made sure to envelop you in my arms.

Usually, at this point, you would curl into me, your head landing on its special spot beneath my collarbone. That night, you rolled away, your back to me and your hands tucked under your head. It was as if you barely registered I was there. Even now, I can still feel the iciness of your feet when they accidentally brushed against my calves.

Later that week, I tried to open you up on our walk home from the surgery. Our bikes bumped uncomfortably between us, but I had made a scene of needing a tire change and you were too distracted to interrogate the story. Not for the first time, I realized how much you always led our conversations, nineteen words to the dozen until you came up for air, gulping it down greedily before embarking on a new observation or anecdote.

"Good day, Maggie?"

"Yes, fine, the usual, but Aoife was off sick—more work for us all."

For you, this is positively monosyllabic. I want to drop the bikes and take your face in my hands, kiss it better until I hear my usual torrent of Maggie tales again, delivered with their inimitable panache.

"Mags, look, I hope I'm not intruding, but I feel like something is up. Is there something wrong?"

Silence.

"You've been so quiet, so withdrawn. It's not me, is it?" I whisper.

Silence.

"If it's me then I'll understand. Just say what I need to do to make you happy again." I am babbling, but I know that's the fear kicking in. I won't be fine if it's me, if I stand to lose the best thing that has ever happened to me . . .

"It's not you, Frank." You look up from the pavement and fix your gaze on me. There are tears glazing over your irises. The green-gray pools I am drowning in, now fully submerged before a thunderstorm. I am too afraid to move to blot your eyes in case it stalls you. "I don't want you to hate me."

"Mags, you know that couldn't ever be the case. Whatever it is, we can work through it." I take one hand off my handlebar and press it against your hand in a gesture that I hope is calming. My mind is in overdrive—have you been unfaithful? Are you calling us off?

"I'm . . . I'm pregnant, Frank. With our baby."

Whatever I was expecting, it certainly wasn't a child.

"I can't get rid of it, Frank, I just can't." With that, you drop your bike on the pavement with such force that it takes mine down too. For a minute we stand and face each other across the tangled heap of metal. Your face shines with the track marks of fresh tears. You have never looked so beautiful, or so afraid. Slowly, as if you are a wild horse that will buck away at any minute, I make my way round to you and take you in my arms. I press my stomach hard against yours.

"It'll be fine, Mags. We'll be fine." I have no idea if this is true, but I do know that it is what you need to hear, and I will say whatever I need to in order to take away just a fraction of your fear. I don't know how long we stand like that before I guide you back to the house.

That night, as you are putting on your pajamas, I get down on one knee.

"We better make this official, Mags. Marry me?"

You are visibly taken aback, as much as is possible when stuck half in your blouse, but you nod before the tears start again. I rummage in my pockets. There is no ring, not at this short notice, but I find an old receipt, roll it lengthways, and tie the ends in a most ungainly knot. It does the trick—you laugh. Just a little at first, a tinkle, as if you are testing it out again, then louder, longer. My paper monstrosity dwarfs your tiny ring finger and it has a nasty habit of leaving cuts on my chest where you rest your hand throughout the night, but it has solved something, temporarily at least.

For the first time in a long time, you fall asleep before me. I don't sleep at all. Instead, I am afforded eight hours to think about how our lives will change. In the middle of my panic, I feel happiness unlike anything I have ever known. A lifetime with you, Mags? A family? It was beyond my furthest hopes and dreams. I had never imagined myself as a father. I have no idea how to parent. But then I think of my own—their quiet, contained existence, their reserve, their uncanny ability to dodge discussion of any remotely awkward issues, and I know I want to do better than that, for the baby and for you. I would lay down my life for any tiny ball of cells that bore your magnetic imprint. We would be just fine. Far better than fine, in fact.

Chapter 6

I don't see Daisy until she enters the room to carry out her observations the next morning. At first, she is blurry. My gaze has been fixed on the middle distance, my eyes are swollen, and my glasses are smudged from several days without a polish and from the debris that comes with keeping your fists balled into your eye sockets. Wordlessly, Daisy places a box of tissues on the stand next to the bed and begins her rounds by straightening the cover over Maggie.

"Do you know that Maggie knows when you are here?"

"I doubt it," I say, immediately hating my own cynicism.

"Really, Frank, she does."

"I hope so," I say, trying to summon a smile this

time, but the corners of my mouth remain resolutely tight.

"I see it in the readings that are taken at night, once you've dropped off to sleep. Everything is a little lower—her heart rate, oxygen flow. She wants to be back with you. Whatever you have to say, she clearly wants to hear it."

"It's hard." I try to swallow as it strikes me that I have yet to get anywhere close to the difficult bit. With Mags, it has always been so easy to be blinded by the positives.

"I know. No one ever said otherwise."

"How do you do this?"

"What? The job?"

I nod.

"Yeah. I'd say it's hard too." I catch Daisy's eye before her gaze moves to the window. She looks exhausted: some of her hair has escaped from its elastic band and frizzes at her hairline; her previously impeccably pressed scrubs have a network of creases daggered down their back. "You see some terrible things. Course you do. But there are some brilliant weeks too. The recoveries. You have to remember them when it's tough, or you wouldn't last long around here."

I am too scared to ask whether I will be one of the lucky ones, the sort that gets the patient home and pretends this was all a bad, bad dream.

"Thank you." My voice comes out quietly, but it is enough to stall Daisy as she heads for the door. "For everything, Daisy. And you were right, about the talking. I mean, I don't know if she hears, but I hope she can. There's so much I should have said already."

"We all feel that way, Frank, but you're lucky you have still got time. You've got the time to say what you need."

How much time, though? Enough for me to get there, to explain myself in full? To let Maggie know that my silence had nothing to do with her? No, it never could have done. It was about me, my failings. How I let her down. The fact that she could never forgive me for that.

"You all right there?" Daisy goes to separate one of the cardboard sick bowls from the stack on her trolley. "Frank? Here." Daisy passes one over and lays a hand between my shoulder blades. "You're going to be OK, Frank. You and Maggie both. Don't stop now."

The cardboard feels rough and grainy in my hands, its woody smell doing nothing to settle my stomach.

"I can't," I mumble.

"You can, Frank. If anyone can, you can. You will get her back, and you will get her home, and you will take good care of our Maggie. I know it."

That was always the plan.

———

You were three months along when you told me. You had eaten something bad and spent a night vomiting, rendering your pill ineffectual. For some reason, you hadn't thought the incident bad enough to warrant some additional protection. I remember being pretty unsure of what they had been teaching you at nursing college, but I bit my tongue regardless.

We decided to tell our families of the engagement but held off on news of the pregnancy while we found a place of our own and worked out how quickly we could get a registry office to take us. You ended up falling for the first flat we saw, something about the light and the way it fell in the living room. The minute the estate agent stepped outside, on the pretense of checking the parking meter, you spun around, arms spread wide, and declared it our home. I nearly balked when I saw the size of the deposit on the rental agreement, but then I caught a glimpse of you, running your fingertip along the windowsill in that very same light, and all my doubts dissipated. I signed on the dotted line. We would move in a month later.

In all honesty, I was mainly happy to be out of my poky single room and catapulting into a life with you, Maggie. I'll never forget how, in advance of our moving day, you led us on a quick-fire tour of the charity shops of Oxford, on the hunt for the cheapest and cheeriest furniture we could find. We took that sofa missing a back cushion on the proviso you would make a replacement yourself, and a kitchen table so old that it might have seen the Industrial Revolution. They never did get the renovations you promised, did they? Dare I say it, I grew quite fond of them as they were.

Our first night in the flat was perfect. Two beanbags, a large pizza, and a six-pack of that disgusting orangeade you had been craving for the past few weeks. In the corner, the one item we had unpacked so far: a cactus with tiny pink flowers that I had bought you on one of our earliest dates at the Botanic Gardens. "Short and spiky. Like me," you'd said. We had been so busy moving in the boxes that you fell asleep mid-slice, one hand sprawled out in the direction of the spines. I tucked your abandoned crusts back in the box, cleared some space, and shifted my beanbag so we could fall asleep under the uncovered duvet together. I could replay that night on a loop forever, Mags, I really could.

The next morning you were up and at the unpacking before I had so much as rubbed the grit from my eyes. You were in your element as you set about making the flat a home, and I thought it best to leave you to it. Do you know, Mags, that to this day that is my greatest regret? Leaving you to it? God knows you were—are— the vision of competence, but at that stage? I should have known better.

After tightening the odd handle and oiling some hinges, I could sense my aimless standing about was getting in your way and on your nerves. With my stomach growling, I set off for some interim supplies. I can't have been gone long. Long enough, though. When I think back now, I wonder when exactly it was that I realized something was wrong. When you didn't get the doorbell? When I couldn't see you in the sitting room? Whatever it was, it was the quiet that confirmed it.

"Mags! Mags! I'm back. I've got stuff for tea and toast—shall we have it now? Mags, where are you?" I go from room to room, popping my head round the door frames. Upstairs, the bathroom door is locked. I knock, quietly.

Silence.

"Mags, are you in there? Is everything OK?"

Silence.

I've never been a door-barging type of man, and I'm not going to start now, however terrified I might be. After a few seconds, I hear the bar of the lock being drawn back. Slowly, cautiously, I inch the door forward.

You are sitting on the toilet seat, tights bunched around your knees, your head in your hands. You don't look at me. I follow your gaze. Crimson against the crisp white of the floor tiles: a pool of blood.

You don't say a word. Not then. Not for three days. Your silence is louder than any scream could ever be.

I run the bath. You offer no resistance as I strip off your clothes, leaving them in a pile to soak up the soiled reminder of what we have lost. Your naked body is as limp as a rag doll as I scoop you up, one hand around your torso, one under your thighs, and carry you, childlike, into the tub. In the cruelest twist of fate, you have become my baby. I run only a small amount of water, fearful that you cannot, or will not, hold your head up and will drown if I so much as blink. There is still a small orange blotch on your sternum where some of the tomato sauce from last night's dinner fell short of your mouth. I have to rub hard with my thumb to remove it, but you don't register it at all.

I am out of my depth. Should I call a doctor? Can I do that without your permission? My only reassurance is that this is, or was, your area of expertise. You must have seen women like this before, you must know what needs to be done.

Kneeling at the side of the tub, I use my hands to scoop the warm water over your body, watching as the first clear palmfuls turn increasingly rosy. You have yet to unpack any towels, so, when the water begins to feel tepid, I lift you from the bath and wrap you in the sheet from the single bedroom. Cloaked in the bobbly white cotton, you could be a child playing dress-up as a bride, your dainty features dwarfed by an event that feels too adult for us to bear.

I get you to bed and close the curtains. In the darkness, I can see you curled in the fetal position, your back to me. When I am certain you will not move, I tiptoe into the hallway in search of your handbag. I have thought no further than that I must find Edie. Her number is in your address book, tucked, as I had hoped it would be, in the inside pouch. We have yet to meet our downstairs neighbors, but I need a phone and my awkwardness pales in comparison to my need.

Thankfully, they are in. My distress must be obvious, because the surly-looking kid who answers waves me right through to the hallway. Edie does not pick up on the first few rings. I can feel a knot of anxiety tightening in my bowels. There is no plan B.

At last . . . "Hello?"

"Edie, it's me, it's Frank. Can you get here as soon as possible?"

"What is it, Frank, what's wrong?"

"It's the baby, Maggie, she . . ."

I don't know how I will say it, but Edie knows.

"I'm leaving now, Frank, go sit with her. Leave the front door open."

When Edie arrives, I am on the edge of the mattress,

tentatively stroking your hair. Some of the strands have dried crisp and dark. Edie gets into bed, next to your shrouded body. There is something about the intimacy of the moment that leaves me feeling as if I am trespassing, and I go back to the bathroom, on the pretense of cleaning. Should that have been me, Mags? Did I let you down? I'm sorry, so sorry if I did.

Edie finds me perched on the side of the bathtub, halfheartedly scrubbing at the rusty marks along the waterline.

"We're going to take Maggie to the maternity unit. I've got a friend on duty who should be able to take her quickly. She's getting dressed now, then I'll drive us all down."

I do not know if she is including me to be nice, out of pity, perhaps. Then again, it is my loss too.

There is fresh hell in you being taken to the ward you shouldn't have been admitted to for another few months, in seeing all the new mothers being wheeled to their cars, their eyes sunken with exhaustion but somehow still beaming with delight. You keep your eyes on your shoes, but I still see you wince with each newborn's cry.

For the procedure, you go in alone. Edie and I sit, outside, an empty chair where you waited between us.

"You will still be there for her, won't you, Frank?"

"Of course."

"The wedding . . ."

"I still want to marry her."

"I know—it's just . . . the timing. Ten days?"

I nod. "I'll wait as long as it takes, though."

"You're a good man, Frank. She knows that."

I hope desperately that what Edie says is true. I can't stand to lose you too.

When you emerge, you look as if you have shrunk. Your coat hangs off one shoulder; the hollows of your cheeks are more sunken than before. The doctor gestures to Edie but, oddly, I don't feel affronted. All I want to do is to be with you. I wrap an arm around your shoulders, shepherding you back to the car.

I only notice that you are crying when we reach the main entrance. Your body slips from under my arm, bent double and shaking. It is just us two.

I didn't say anything then. Not that night, not in the days just after. This wasn't about me. I was terrified of making things worse. I always have been. It's paralyzing, Mags, it really is. If I had my time again? Yes, I would do it differently. There was so much I wanted to say, so much that I should have said. "It's not your fault" would have been a very good place to start.

Chapter 7

Our marriage could not have gotten off to a worse start. Indeed, it almost didn't get off at all. For two whole days after we returned to the flat, you barely moved from the bed, didn't say a word. I brought cups of tea and poured them away an hour later, still full and cold. You didn't even try to make the toast appear nibbled. Torn between wanting to be near you and wanting to give you some privacy, I tried to make myself useful, unpacking the remaining items and stocking the cupboards. Anything to make the place feel less empty.

On the third day, I was at the kitchen table, marking a stack of undergraduate scripts, when you came down wrapped in a toweling dressing gown. Your hair was sticking up at all angles, and there were pillow crinkles crisscrossed on your cheeks. Do you know, Mags, that you never looked more beautiful to me than in that moment? My girl, my darling girl, come back to me. Or so I hoped.

"Hey." You take a seat adjacent to me and stretch your left hand into the gap between us. The paper ring I fashioned has long since disappeared.

"Hello, darling—how are you feeling?"

You nod. I have no idea what that indicates, but I carry on anyway.

"Mags, look, I still want to marry you. I'll understand, though, if . . . if . . . you don't feel—"

"Well, that's a relief," you cut in. "Because I cannot lose you too." There are tears brimming in your eyes, threatening to send you back to bed, far from my reach. I lean over, clumsily using my thumb to blot your tear ducts and making you smile in the process.

"You'll need a ring in that case—about time, eh? Shall we go this afternoon?"

"Shouldn't you be at work?" you ask, biting your lip with a look of concentration that tells me you have lost track of the days.

"It doesn't matter. I needed some time off . . ." I am gabbling in my anxiety. I take a deep breath and try again. "You're the only thing that matters to me, Mags."

I have never meant anything more.

I offer to cancel the wedding guests, to do it just us, but you are insistent that we go back to normal, put on a "good show," whatever that means. The last-minute preparations seem to take your mind off things, as far as I can tell at least. By the time the day of the wedding rolls around a week later, there is nothing to indicate the shaky start we have overcome to get there.

And we had a beautiful day for it, didn't we, Mags? Cool to start off with but bright, the sun radiating off the city spires and leaving us with a series of group shots where every member of the party is either squinting or shielding their eyes. Our decision not to announce the pregnancy works in our favor. To our families, my colleagues, and the girls from home, you are every inch the blushing bride, not a care in the world.

All our friends love your resolve to walk yourself down the aisle—a modern woman! I was sure it would be a bit unorthodox for my own parents, but they have the good sense not to mention it; you don't say that you wish you could have had your father there to do the honors, not in so many words, and I decide not to probe either. Not with everything else going on. I already know that you two never had a straightforward relationship, but I do wonder how much you miss him now—a memory rather than a steadying hand on the way to the altar.

Instead, I turn my attention to trying to bond with your mother. It's only the second time I've met her, what with her being abroad, but she keeps herself to herself, on the arm of your brother the artist; the other is stuck in the middle of a big deal, or so he told us. I'm not sure that I make much progress with her, and after a half hour of increasingly tenuous questions (me) and curt answers (her), I make my way over to the rest of the guests. Our friends haven't had the chance to mix much before, and the social experiment is well and truly under way. At least the novelty allows you a little bit of space, the opportunity to divert back to the proceedings any questions that fall just that inch too close to the bone. Only Edie keeps close to your elbow the whole way through the reception.

A honeymoon feels extravagant, and we have both taken a week off work already, pleading a nasty bout of stomach flu. We make up for it with a long weekend by the sea as soon as the wedding has wrapped. The change of scene does us both good. My parents had bought us a Polaroid, and the photo I keep of you in my wallet has Brighton Pier in the background. Your jeans rolled up, you carry your loafers in one hand, the other thrown back in delight. The belt of your trench coat just touches the water. When I look at it now it reminds me of what I fell in love with, the wild abandon, the warmth and joy. It also reminds me of just how quickly that can be taken from me.

At the B and B that night, you allow me to touch you again. As ever, I am tentative, wary of trespassing where I am not wanted yet, but I am surprised by how you warm into me, urging me faster, harder, until the two single beds we have pushed together begin to split apart and your body caves into the crevasse between. You laugh, breathlessly, and, in the motion of hauling yourself back up, bring me prematurely to climax. There is an angry knocking on the wall by our headboard. And do you know what, Mags? I couldn't have cared less. They could have evicted us naked and still I wouldn't have cared. All I wanted was right there in front of me, smiling once again.

Soon we were back in Oxford, our lives taking on much the same form as third had before. For the first few months, there was no mention of what had happened or of trying again. Now, I don't know why I didn't do more to sound you out, to delve beneath the guise of good cheer that you wore from dusk to dawn. I suppose I was just too happy. God, what an excuse to make. It holds, though. I loved our newly married life, I really did.

All it takes is the smell of wet paint and I snap right back to those days, just after the wedding. You had decorating fever, and I was your willing assistant, in a pair of overalls a good four inches too short, tickling at my shins. The landlord was lax, to say the least, which gave you the opportunity to really go to town on the place. We had great fun painting every room (some twice if they didn't feel "quite right"), tore up two carpets, and hung hundreds of framed pictures. Any minute of any spare time was funneled into your renovations, and I could sense, even when you sat down, that you were itching to be up and back at it again.

For weeks, we'd go to bed every night with flecks of paint all over us, however hard we'd scrubbed in the shower. Some nights I'd try to kiss them all, but the tiny white drops had landed everywhere and I'd have to kiss faster and faster until I was dizzy with the action and had to crash out onto the safety of your lips. I'm sure that inspired you to make more mess with the paint than was strictly necessary when the next day we picked up where we had left off.

We'd work through the weekends, not a break in sight. Lunch was a standing-up affair, a hunk of bread and a slice of cheese propped on top while the teapot cooled. When we ran out of mugs, you would instruct me to just top up the pot with the milk and we drank straight out of the spout. You had taken down the curtains by that stage, so God knows what the neighbors must have thought. And me? Well, I stopped caring pretty quickly. All my self-consciousness had escaped through the open window with the paint fumes. You always had that uncanny knack of making me forget the rest of the world, Mags.

When you finished a room, I'd pin one of the dust sheets up against the door frame as a makeshift curtain so you could do the grand unveiling to your adoring audience of one. I'd play the estate agent, in my anorak, interrogating you on all manner of minor details. How many coats of paint? Was this design inspired by any artist in particular? Before we collapsed with the absurdity of it all, I made sure to give your efforts my "scores on the doors." It was never less than ten out of ten.

I suppose what I'm trying to say, Mags, is that we moved on from that loss. Not that we forgot it, you never do, but we were building a new bliss that wasn't contingent on anything or anyone but the two of us. I had never known happiness like it. I hoped you felt that way too.

Then, a few months into our marriage, I came home to find you in tears at the kitchen table.

"Everything OK, Mags?" I ask. Your back is turned to me, elbows propped on the table as you drag your fingers through your hair. You don't get up to greet me and barely seem to have registered my presence. I know something is wrong, but I have no idea what.

"Work OK? They aren't making you switch districts? Imagine the cycle!" My hand is on your shoulder. You haven't recoiled, but nonetheless the joke has fallen decidedly flat.

"Hey, Mags, come on." I walk round and catch your profile, tear-stained and blotchy. "You know you can tell me anything, *anything*, I promise. What's wrong?"

"I'm not pregnant," you whisper quickly, quietly. "I'm not pregnant again. I'm sorry."

"Sorry? What for? Mags, this isn't your fault. Say, it's only been a month or two."

"Ten."

"Ten, then." I feel the crushing hand of alarm clutching at my chest. I had barely noticed any time passing. "No time at all. Your body has to work itself back out. It's early days, Mags, we're young, we'll try again. Plenty of times. And, well, if it's not meant to be, it's not meant to be, eh?"

I wish I had never said that. The hollowest of all throwaway phrases. And what does it really mean? Who decided that you would suffer so much? No benevolent deity, that's for sure. You, the best of people, having to endure the worst of your own nightmares. The sort of mother who would love *too* much, if such a thing was possible. So, who was drawing straws for our lot and constantly pulling you up short?

I know I have said the wrong thing as I see your body drop, your shoulders round down an inch farther. I want to kick myself for rolling out a pointless platitude. I know how much the uncertainty kills you, how much you have always craved the stability you never had as a child. I want to tell you our son or daughter couldn't provide that, but I could, I did, I always would, Maggie. Somehow I have always found that easier to show you than to say.

"I want it to be, though," you say, pushing the kitchen chair back and slowly getting to your feet. "I want it so much." You are in danger of breaking down completely. I am almost too scared to touch you again in case it is the gesture that sets you off, that takes you beyond my reach. "I'm off to bed, Frank. There's some bits for supper in the fridge."

I watched as you walked away, down the hallway, and past the one room that had been left untouched by plastic covers and slippery-lipped paint cans—the one earmarked as the nursery. Fortunately, we had only bought one item, a mobile made of tiny, fragile paper birds that I'd had the forethought to remove and hide. Even without the reminder, the room was too much for you, and I never saw you go in. You skirted the door, moving a good few inches away, as if there were a force field humming around it.

Once I had heard you make your way upstairs, I realized what I should have said. For years the phrase rolled around my palate before I swallowed it up for another day: What would be so wrong with just us, Maggie? Isn't that what we signed up for? Isn't that what marriage is?

I'm sorry, Maggie, but when it comes to you, I am selfish. I want you, all of you. When I proposed, there were three in the picture, but when we said our vows, there were just two. That has always been enough for me. It always would have been too.

Chapter 8

"Ah, Professor Hobbs, I'm glad I caught you." The doctor is back. I have evaded him long enough, dodging his consulting room, keeping my head down along the corridors in the rare moments I venture away from Maggie. Maybe he saw me kick the water fountain in the canteen when the drum gurgled empty for the second time in a day? Most people did.

He hovers in the doorway. "Professor Hobbs—may I?" He tilts his head toward the spare chair.

I can hardly say no.

"So, how are you doing?"

"Er . . . not well."

"It's understandable." There is a pause when I know the doctor is considering mentioning that support line again, and I am desperate to stop him. I have hundreds of more pertinent questions for him, but somehow the words are all too jumbled to form themselves into anything resembling an intelligible order.

"So . . . your wife."

"How is she?"

"Well, Professor, as I'm sure you are aware, we are nearing the seventy-two-hour phase. By now we were hoping we would be able to begin to rouse your wife. However, her signs are not as consistent as we would like, and we feel it would be a risk to do so before we can see a pattern in her vitals emerging. I came to explain that we have decided to keep her sedated for the next twenty-four hours at least."

"So, this is bad news?"

"It isn't the best. Of course, we would all like Mrs. Hobbs to be brought out of the coma sooner. The longer she is under, the greater the potential damage. We have also yet to establish the cause of the fluctuations on her charts. That said, certain organs are showing some signs of activity. There seems to be the will to come through, if you will. She is in no worse condition than when she arrived, and we are doing all we can for her . . ."

A space has opened up for me to speak. To say I'm relieved. To say I feel reassured. All I want to do is scream.

"Thank you," I manage. "For what is being done. I know Maggie would be very grateful."

"Do you have any questions, Professor? I appreciate this is a lot of information to take in. You needn't ask me now either, but you know where I am should any crop up later in the day."

Can she hear me? When do you give up on her? What will I do if I lose her? What will I do if I don't?

"What happens after the twenty-four hours?"

He pauses. I have hit on the crux of the matter.

"Then there will be some important factors to consider in terms of the next phase of care."

I ask the doctor to repeat himself, but still nothing he says means anything solid. I know what he's inching toward, though. Time is running out. I need to get on. Cut to the chase.

"If there's nothing else at this stage, I'll be off."

"No. No, thank you. You have been very informative."

"See you soon, Professor."

When the door clicks shut, I turn back to Maggie. The bedside is surprisingly free from the sort of tat that usually accumulates with a long hospital stay: grapes, magazines, a family pack of sweets. I suppose it would be stranger if it had—there is no one I have told.

I fish my mobile out of my jacket pocket. I imagined

it would have run out of juice, now that Maggie isn't there to plug it in next to hers at night, but, remarkably, there is still some battery. It is a perk, I presume, of having avoided upgrades. Instead, I aimlessly scan the email notifications on the home screen. Among them there is a single text, from Edie. She hasn't been able to get through to Maggie—is everything OK? I hover over a response—Maggie sick. In hospital. Will text when better—and click send before I think better of it or allow the guilt to really take root.

After everything that happened, we cut ourselves off. A lot of people dropped away, understandably. But Edie has been persistent over the last few months. Constant in her kindness, in the sheer will to get through. And still we couldn't reach out. How much does she know? I wonder. Did my silence push her away too? I switch off my phone before I write anything else or find myself reading into the isolation of the unanswered gray bubble.

"Come along, Frank," I tell myself out loud. "Yes, Maggie, I need to get the hell on with this. All of it. The difficult stuff too. Because we really don't have long now."

I was never foolish enough to think you were OK about it, the fact that we couldn't have a child. But you have always been so very hard to sound out. Some months when you bled you treated it with the same brisk efficiency as paying the gas bill or taking the bins out. Other times, you were inconsolable, locking yourself away in our room. Those were the worst days, when you didn't leave the bed and I spent hours attuned to your every move. With every shift of weight on the floorboards above, my heart pounded with the hope that it was over now, that you were getting your dressing gown on and coming down to my outstretched arms. When I heard the flush of the toilet and the bedroom door shutting again, my whole body ached.

But as months became years and the years rolled on, those days became fewer and further apart. We were good together, the two of us, and, as I saw it, growing better with each passing day. Marriage suited us, didn't it, Mags? As we marked five, ten, fifteen years together with a candlelit meal out, two cards, and something other than the second-cheapest bottle of wine on the list, we could revel in the good life that we had built. We eased into each other, like shoes that require a little patience to wear in but that come to fit so perfectly you cannot so much as fathom the existence of another pair.

I could curl my index finger and thumb and know exactly how much spaghetti would do us both. Not a strand more, not a strand less. We reveled in long suppers together and long weekends away, the freedom to lie in on a Sunday. I can still see you now, sorting the supplements into two piles: technology and sports for me, the magazine and arts review for you. You always read faster and, in a bid to distract me the moment your attention was up, you would begin to fashion the main broadsheet into a paper roof of sorts, propping the edges behind the headboard. I'd give it two minutes (maximum) of you kissing down my neck until I abandoned the sports section entirely. Do you remember how crinkled the paper would be afterward? It must have made an ungodly racket.

I lived to make you happy, and I feel no less of a man to admit that. I brought things home that I knew would make you smile: Mateus rosé on the first sunny day of the year, which you would chill and then crack open on the patio. When the sun began to go down, I would head in to bring you your shawl, knowing that you liked to eke out every last drop of warmth on your face. I would even put your slippers on for you like a cheap and cheerful knockoff of Prince Charming. Then I would look at you, my polar bear in twenty-degree heat, and it would be so silly that the two of us would fall about laughing until it was dark. As I watched you carry in the glasses, I knew you made me the luckiest man in the world.

I remember exactly where I was standing when you

told me that this was all about to change. I was in the study, pacing by the window, the final clue in the *Times* cryptic on the tip of my tongue, tapping a battered blue Biro against my front teeth in an attempt to conjure it.

"Oh, Frank, will you stop pacing, it makes me nervous." You appear at the door, never shut in those days, in a gingham apron dusty with flour.

"How could it possibly make you nervous from the kitchen?" I feign exasperation but take a seat, to humor you.

"Frank, please."

"All right, all right. If it's the guests making you this stressed, you should have said. We could have canceled."

"It's not that, Frank. That's fine. It's under control."

"Then what?"

"Do you have five minutes for a chat?"

What a peculiar thing to ask your husband. I had signed up for a lifetime of five-minute chats. In your case, they usually came out at more like five hours anyway, what with the tangents and the inevitable embellishments.

"I know we have Jack and Sarah for supper, but I'd rather just say this now . . ."

It is then that I realize you are nervous, gathering the skirt of your apron in both hands and twisting it back and forth in a thick spiral.

"Go on then, Mags. What is it? What's wrong?"

I drop the paper on the desk and come over to you, releasing the fabric, now crumpled into a thousand tiny creases, and taking your trembling hands in mine.

"Whatever it is, Maggie, we'll be fine. You know that."

"Well, it's not bad news. Just . . . unexpected. Yes, certainly unexpected." You are off now, and I know better than to interrupt. "The thing is, Frank, I'm . . . well . . . I'm pregnant."

Silence.

I realize now that you only ever get one chance at a first response and that mine have always been lacking. Somewhere in the shock and sudden flash of terror, I notice you looking up at me expectantly. I am still holding your hands and give them a tight squeeze.

"Look, Frank, I know this is unexpected—"

"Yes, quite the word I was after," I mutter. It has been fifteen years since we met, fifteen years since the miscarriage. We would have had a teenager by now. "Unexpected" is an understatement.

You laugh gently. "But don't you see, Frank, we've wanted this for so long, and maybe it was just when we stopped thinking about it that it happened. Nature took its course—a bloody long one, but . . . well . . . it's a miracle, really."

I take a step into the gap between us and let my lips linger on the place on your forehead where a little flour has landed and diffused. It takes me back to one of our early dates, a picnic on a rug in Port Meadow on one of the first days of spring, our eating intermittently interrupted by you blowing the fuzz from dandelion clocks onto the surrounding grass.

"Oh, Frank, you'll be a brilliant father—just you wait and see."

In the kitchen, a timer begins its aggressive beeping, calling your attention away.

"God, is that the time? Right, Frank, they'll be here soon. Don't mention this, though? We'll speak more after. There's a fresh shirt for you on the door upstairs . . ." You are already off, your voice calling down the hallway.

I wish I could have said something, the *right* thing, then, instead of giving you just an openmouthed gawp. I knew how delighted you must have been, Mags, and there is nothing worse than someone throwing a dampener on one's happiness, even if it is entirely unintentional. I'm sorry. If I could go back and replay that all again, I would do so much better. I would manage some proper enthusiasm with my wide-eyed surprise. I know I would.

In any other circumstances, supper would have been

an easy affair. But that night? My mind was all over the place, and anywhere but on the beef bourguignon. *How had this happened?* At some point in the years following the miscarriage, you saw a doctor. Several, in fact. You had test after test. I had a few too. Weeks went by and then, eventually, a meeting for us both. They said it was unlikely, given the circumstances of the first pregnancy. *Unlikely* but not impossible, I reminded you as we walked home from the bus stop. You didn't look convinced. And as the years went by? Well, the needle slipped from unlikely ever more toward impossible.

I am brought back to the room with a thump. Sarah's fist lands on the table, steadying her as she laughs uncontrollably at something you have said. I catch a glimpse of you, mid-anecdote, your torso thrust over the green beans and your fork dangerously close to Jack's upper arm. I can't remember the last time I have seen you so uninhibited. One hundred percent light, not one speck of darkness to be found. When our eyes meet, I give you the smile that tells you I am over the shock, that I have processed it. I hope it also tells you how much this means to me too.

When we did discuss it the next day, properly, that was when the excitement kicked in. You were twelve weeks at that stage. We talked about the room we would do up and the cot we would buy, the leave we could take.

Finally, when we ate out, we could look at the families at the circular tables set aside for them and know that it would soon be us. I insisted on carrying your handbag, collected anything that fell on the floor. At night, I knew the exact spot on your lower back that I needed to massage to help you get some sleep.

In fact, I became so accustomed to our new normal that I almost forgot the pregnancy had an end point.

"Frank! Frank! We need to go." Your voice ricochets down the stairs.

I am slow to unearth myself from whatever review I am immersed in.

"Frank!"

When I get out to the hallway, I can see you have only made it down one stair and that you are gripping the bannister with both hands. Behind you on the landing, a dark pool on the carpet where your waters have broken. I don't move. I never have had a head for logistics, have I, Mags?

"Phone. Now."

It takes me such a while to find the phone, buried as always under the papers or one of those pointless sofa cushions you love so much, that by the time I am back you have made it down the stairs by yourself. You are folded as far forward over the bannister as your bump allows, fists pressed into the wall. I try to rub my hand over the base of your spine, but you wriggle it off.

"How long?" Each syllable comes out like a huff. I try to tell myself it isn't me, not altogether convincingly.

"Ten minutes max. Can I get you anything? Tea? Water?"

I have no idea what I'm saying. I half expect you to bite my head off but instead you just don't reply. Every few seconds you exhale with such force that I wonder if it would be worth sourcing the sick bucket.

"Bag. Shoes!" you shout. I know where the bag is; it hasn't moved for weeks. I have nearly tripped over it on at least three occasions, the canvas straps tangling with my laces. Your shoes are quite another matter. I find something slip-on in our bedroom, comfy, I think, until we have to deal with navigating them onto your swollen feet.

"How much longer, Frank?" You have started kicking your shoe against the wall in time with your breaths.

"Er . . ." I check my watch. It's been fifteen. I figure it is better not to tell you that. "Soon, soon, darling. Here." I weave my fingers under yours, and they are slammed hard against the wall, the bones crunching together as you press down.

It is then that the paramedics arrive with the right

equipment and, fortunately for one of us, the right words. When we arrive at the hospital, I cannot tell if I am welcome in the room with you. There are scores of people offering their medical advice and intervention. I feel inadequate, just offering my hand, and even that manages to get in the way. On the pretense of heading to the vending machines, I take the opportunity to grab some fresh air outside the labor ward. By the time I get back, there is a bundle in your arms.

I missed it.

"Eleanor," you whisper, transfixed on her tiny head, bluish purple and mottled. "Will you hold her?"

I nod.

You pass her over, and suddenly she is crying and I am crying and there is no feeling on earth like it. I press Eleanor up against my nose so I can smell her and examine the folds on her tiny hooded eyelids. I don't want to squeeze her in case I hurt her. And the relief. She is safe and you are safe and I know then that whatever I have done before or since is nothing. Nothing if I can't keep her safe.

Chapter 9

"I hear our Maggie isn't quite ready to wake up yet." In Daisy's hand, there is a basin with a sponge.

"Yes," I mumble. I feel ashamed, as if this is somehow my fault. It *is* my fault. Perhaps not medically, but she wouldn't be here if we had talked, if I hadn't shut down. I only did it to protect Maggie, and look where that has left us.

"Don't be too hard on yourself," Daisy says, shutting the door lightly behind her. "And don't give up what you are doing either, Frank. I walk past and I see you talking to her. You obviously have a good story to tell her."

"I'm not sure about that. It's just . . . us, I suppose. Our story."

"Well, whatever it is, it is doing her good, even if we

can't see it yet. Less thinking, more talking. You can think again when she is back with us."

Back with us. I can't begin to imagine what that would look like. Hoists? Round-the-clock help? It is terrifying, but no more so than the alternative.

It appears I am not the only one on borrowed time. When I don't respond, Daisy shakes the basin to startle me out of my reverie. "Right, then, Frank, I was going to give Maggie a bath. But I can get someone else to come back later—what would you prefer?"

"I don't want to get in the way." Gently I remove my hand from beneath Maggie's and begin to stand up.

"Do you want to help?" Daisy offers. "With the bath? We can do it together. Then I'll leave you two in peace."

I am unsure how to respond. In my mind I reel through all the times I have washed Maggie. Always when she was at her lowest ebb, too weak to move. Even so, it feels almost too intimate, as if this is something I shouldn't be intruding on.

Daisy senses my hesitation, even with her back to me, as she fills the bowl with warm water from the sink.

"Look, Frank, it's easy, I promise you. I can talk you through it."

She comes around to stand beside me and places the basin on the chair where I have been sitting.

"First we need to get this loosened." Daisy reaches behind Maggie's head, gently propping it up on her forearm while she undoes the ties of her gown. Her motions are smooth and slow, trained not to disturb the fragile network of machinery keeping Maggie alive.

Daisy wriggles the fabric down, exposing Maggie's neck, shoulders, and chest, pulling the gown as far as it will go without taking her arms out. I am struck by how thin Maggie has become, her collarbones jutting out like sharp shelves, her ribs visible in the cavity between her breasts. When we touched in the past months, it was in the darkness, our hunger so great that the details of our bodies evaporated and the comfort of touch stretched like a blanket between us. I see now how pain has hollowed Maggie out. How it has scooped out her soul and left just its bony surrounds.

"We just want to moisten Maggie, to keep her fresh. Just a little water under her arms, around her neck." Daisy has wrung out the sponge and passes it to me with one hand while supporting Maggie's torso with the other. "That's right, lovely, easy does it."

I run the sponge over Maggie's chest and watch how the gauzy skin glistens temporarily with the moisture before absorbing it back to quench its thirst. I move the sponge up to her neck, carefully weaving it between the few strands of hair that fall down below her chin. I watch as a single drop of excess water, plump and heavy, trickles down from below her earlobe, skirts the bright blue veins of her throat, and then traces its path down her chest, coming to rest on the bunched fabric of her gown. There is such tenderness to its progress, slow and halting; I remember how my fingers felt running there for the first time, the last time too. I wish the times in between felt less indistinct.

"Right, good job there, Frank. That's fine." Daisy extends her hand to collect the sponge, and my stomach sinks with the realization that the moment is over. I wonder if Maggie recognized my hands.

"So, what is she like, then?" Daisy asks as she empties the basin. "Our Maggie?"

God, what a question. I have no idea where to start. How do you go about explaining someone who is everything to you, so much a part of you that you haven't needed the words to describe them for four decades?

"What did she do?" Daisy prompts gently, upturning the bowl on the trolley to drain.

"She was a nurse . . . like you. Well, not quite like you. She worked in a GP's surgery. Minor illnesses, vaccinations, that sort of thing. She loved it. She really did. She was so good with people, not like me . . ."

I look up and see a glimmer of a smile dancing at the corner of Daisy's lips.

"She was fun, wild, even. Again, not like me. Chalk and cheese, huh?"

"They often are—the best couples."

Is that how Daisy sees us? It was never a competition for me. With Maggie, I knew I had already won. My eyes zone out, flashing through stills of our life together like slides under a microscope, blurry and then getting brighter and sharper until the image drops altogether.

"How long have you been together then?"

"Forty years."

"Wow." Daisy's eyes widen, and I notice the tendrils of red at each corner. I have an overwhelming desire to tell her to get to bed. She and Eleanor might even be the same age. "And you spent all of that together?"

I nod. "There was the odd conference, a month here or there when I was away, but otherwise . . ."

"Well then, I better let you get on." Daisy smiles. I catch a flash of her top teeth, one incisor slightly overlapping the other. "Keep it up, Frank."

There is a rattle as Daisy begins to nudge her trolley toward the door.

"I didn't realize there was that much bathing to be done."

"You know what I mean, Frank. I don't know if you were much of a talker before, but now is the time. You have to use it. I'm sure you have plenty things Maggie wants to hear about from all those years together."

The door clicks shut, and we are alone again with that same sense of fear and relief that makes my bowels turn.

"So where were we then, Mags?" I reach for her hand, using my thumb to wipe away a drop of water that has come to rest in the crevasse between her index and middle fingers. "Eleanor arrived. She changed everything, in ways I didn't even know were possible . . ."

It wasn't until I had her in my arms that I really understood it—why I had been so scared. I couldn't admit it before then, not even to myself. I had spent your pregnancy with everything—the excitement, the joy, the anticipation—undercut by a fear that met me the minute I woke up and occupied me until the second I went to bed. I loved you so fiercely that I didn't know if there was space left in my heart for someone else. I was a house rammed to the rafters and straining under the weight of everything I felt for you, terrified that there was no room at the inn for another. Until Eleanor. A whole new annex, without her saying or doing a thing.

Once we had Eleanor home, I really came into my own in the midnight shifts, the rest of the world cloaked in darkness, aside from the glow of the owl-shaped nightlight in the corner of Eleanor's room. I would scoop her up and out of her cot and into my study at the back of the flat where we could do a little beginners stargazing. We covered Orion's Belt, the Big Dipper—Eleanor liked that one; it always generated a chuckle or a second or two of awed silence.

As she grew bigger, together we would take her outside in the evenings in that mad papoose my sister sent over, Eleanor's body strapped to yours and her head bobbing against your chest as we made our way to Port Meadow. We must have spent twenty, thirty minutes pointing out the ponies, the bike lights flashing as they laced through the bridge railings. Nothing but the odd whine at the injustice of the fresh air. Then, with great ceremony, she would jab her chubby digits up at the first sight of the stars. It made my heart swell with pride. She was smart, yes, but more than that she was so curious, so perceptive. There was so much of you in her, Mags, and I wouldn't have had it any other way.

Eventually, we'd reach the kissing gate at the edge

of the field. By this stage, with Eleanor asleep, it was almost like the old days, me stopping to kiss you and your wellies squeaking with the effort as you got up onto your tiptoes. Only now there was an additional happiness dangling between us. Before we shut the gate, we would take it in turns to kiss the top of Eleanor's head, at the spot where the fragile, fiery tufts of red hair peeped out from beneath her hat. With Eleanor there, happy and healthy, we had our own third dimension. Everything felt rounded, whole. I could breathe out fully again.

Well, nearly fully. I could see how it took its toll on you, motherhood. In the early days at least. I had worried about this during the pregnancy, in the exhilaration just after. It wasn't a reflection on you as a mother, not at all, it was just that I knew you, Mags. I'd seen the soaring highs, but for you they meant nothing without the unshakable sense that we were perpetually teetering on the brink of a fall. There were times when she wouldn't stop crying and I could feel the panic radiating off you. *What are we doing wrong? Is it something serious?* All the heartache and there we were, threatened with falling at the final logistical hurdle of how you actually went about raising a child. You wouldn't dare move until she was calm again, even if that took six, seven, eight hours.

I managed to bring Edie in, and with her assistance, the darkness did lift. With something approaching your usual aplomb, you announced your decision to put your nursing on hold until Eleanor started school. It was nine months or so after she was born, not long after I'd taken that new job at the university. Although the pay was better, this would mean things were still tight. I was totaling everything up in my head, all the beads whirring on my mental abacus, while you talked nineteen to the dozen about how you didn't want to "miss any time with her." I did wonder if this was you compensating for the months when you had been struggling? Either way, I decided it was best not to ask. There was such excitement in your voice that I ended up emphatically agreeing before I had any idea if the sums worked out.

Luckily, we made it add up. I still loved my work: that thrill of the unknown, the potential breakthrough, the odd glimmer of recognition. But it was the evenings and the weekends that I lived for. In those first few years, Eleanor was changing day by day. It was like a flip-book, all the individual images so familiar, but run them together and suddenly the passage of time floored me. I wanted to catch hold of as much as I could.

There was nothing better than coming home to you both. Eleanor would be propped on your hip, or once she was too big for that, on the kitchen counter, pajamas on and her head leaning against your chest. You would be giddy with the show you had lined up for me—some rock Eleanor had painted and repurposed as a paperweight or a collage still gummy with glue. Sometimes I would barely have the chance to get my coat off before I was chased up the stairs and onto Eleanor's bed, where she would be sitting, still warm from the bath, awaiting a bedtime story.

Your voices just didn't cut it, I'm afraid, Mags, so you were relegated to the rocking chair, with whichever members of the furry menagerie had been evicted from the bed to make room for me on your lap. I was never very good at saying no, which meant we did some stories two or three times before Ellie began to doze off at my side. If I'd really delivered a lackluster performance, you would drift off as well and I would be met with the sight of two sleeping beauties when I returned the book to its shelf. I could never work out how I had got so lucky.

There was a real structure to those evenings. We could have been the example in a parenting-book exercise, our routine polished to perfection. It wasn't so much us driving that, though, as Eleanor. She was so sensitive to change. Even the slightest difference would set her tiny internal barometer plummeting. If I was so much as ten minutes late, she'd be peering at the window, her face blotchy and contorted with the distress. We had to keep to the same stories, to my side of the bed. At the time, I assumed that was all children. I didn't have much experience to go on.

Looking back now, I wonder if that was the first sign that maybe she wasn't as resilient as she should have been. But then it was such a small issue in the grand, happy scale of our family that we could brush it off, at least until she started school. She was going to be the youngest in her class, a given for an August baby. Still, when I saw Eleanor coming down the stairs in her uniform, just four years old, her socks pulled right up, the skin above the elastic still chubby and dimpled, she looked so small that I couldn't believe she was ready for it. I snapped a few photos with the camera, all the while wishing that the shutter button pressed pause and that we could keep her like that forever. Most days, I still do.

I don't think either of us would call that first morning a success. She was sandwiched between us, a hand each, and she wouldn't let go. Such a viselike grip for such a tiny hand! Trying to leave was a trauma—for Eleanor, for us both. I'm sure you haven't forgotten the sound of her crying, Mags, those great big, snotty sobs that broke us in two. "Don't leave me," she said, over and over, her voice hoarse from the tears. The teacher managed to prize her away, but that was all I heard for the rest of the day, a loop of her pain at the forefront of my mind as I ran through my lecture notes.

When did she settle at school? Now, of course, there is the temptation to say never. Hindsight has a horrible habit of distorting everything through the lens of the present. I suppose once she made a few friends. That took a while. The teachers were forever telling us that she was behind, socially, as if that was a kind way of saying that she was the child left reading in the playground while the rest roamed in tribes. *Does she have these problems at home? Who does she socialize with there?* Well, us. We would try to explain that our friends' children were older, that she was happy and chatty at home. Every time, the same tilted head, the same skeptical smile.

Eleanor got there eventually. Katie arrived, what, two terms into that first year? Our savior—all three feet of her. Her family had come over from America, which might go some way toward explaining why she gravitated to another quiet outsider. Within the space of a day, they were thick as thieves. It got the school off our back, given there was little else they could find to query. Eleanor was the brightest in her class. So what if she struggled to open up to the other kids at school?

At home she was kind, thoughtful. Highly sensitive, yes, but we told ourselves that if it wasn't a phase, then she would grow to reframe it as a strength. She hadn't even turned five. She had all the time in the world to toughen up or branch out or whatever else the school had suggested.

With Eleanor at school and you back at work, it was time for the three of us that became rationed. Holidays took on a new meaning. I remember the fervor of planning that accompanied our first trip abroad as a family. If I close my eyes now, I can still see you poring over the travel brochures every evening after work, one hand cradling the bowl of your wineglass, the other circling apartments and flights and pointing them out to me with an enthusiasm so infectious that I would have agreed to a trip to the moon in a heartbeat. In the end we settled on Portugal, in February, perhaps not the most obvious choice, but we had just bought this house and we needed somewhere cheap. Or at least as cheap as it ever is when constrained by school terms.

We knew it wasn't going to be scorching, but our packing was still far more optimistic than the reality, scenes that felt far closer to a wet winter in Wales than the year-round sunshine the Algarve tourist board would have you believe. The day we arrived, the rain lashed down outside the apartment and you were in a tailspin about Ellie's clothes. She was seven and still far too small to borrow anything from you. *Where can we buy tights? A proper anorak, not one of those flimsy bin-bag things?* I wasn't so bothered with excursions; all I wanted was time with you both, numbing our brains with cartoons and playing Uno until I ended up brandishing a Draw 4 card in my sleep. And after a little persuasion and some cajoling on my part, that was exactly what we did. With both of you bundled up on the sofa against me, I couldn't have been any happier, Mags. Honestly, I couldn't.

On our last night, we had supper out, in that restaurant where they had all fallen under Eleanor's spell. It was fortunate for us, as we ended up with the best table in the joint—just by the door, so we could see the sun setting on the ocean but without the full wind chill. By the end of the meal, you were giggly, the best part of a bottle of rosé down, your feet tapping on the floor tiles in time to the music floating up from the beach below.

You reach for my hand. "Come on, Frank . . . dance with me!" Eleanor is so engrossed in her book that she doesn't even look up. "You want to, really . . ."

"Fine! Just one," I say. "Eleanor?" She glances up, her finger running along the line of text she is on. "We're going for a dance—do you want to come?"

She shakes her head.

"We'll just be down there, darling." You are pointing, but she already has her nose back in the book.

The makeshift dance floor isn't far away at all, but it is more crowded than it looked from the restaurant. Still, with the beat and the sand and the wine, I ease into it, my arms wrapped around your waist. We call it a day after three songs; it's late, and the flight is early the next morning. I give you a piggyback up the last few meters of beach, the two of us in stitches as I try to avoid blinding myself with the heels of your cast-off shoes swinging in my eyeline.

We get back to the table, and you slide down with a thud.

Eleanor's book is there. But she isn't.

"Where is she?" you ask, dropping your shoes.

"I don't know. The toilet, maybe?"

Around us, other diners look up from their meals.

"You go check the bathroom, ask the staff. I'll stay here, see if anyone saw where she went."

I try the table next to us, the one behind. They're both German, and my O-level efforts don't get me very far. Fear has a way of cutting across the language barrier, though, either that or my desperation, and they do their best to try to calm me down until you burst your way back from the bathroom.

"She's not there. They said they thought she went with us."

My tongue feels dry, a huge fat slab stuck to the roof of my mouth.

"Fuck. Fuck. Frank, what the fuck are we going to do?" I have never seen you so afraid. I want to fold you in my arms and hold you and rock you and tell you that this will be OK. Only neither of us knew that, did we?

"She can't have got far. Let's keep calm. Divide and conquer. You head to the shops, ask everyone there. I'll take the beach."

It hits me then. The water. That Ellie could be somewhere in it. Somewhere under.

"You have your watch, right?"

You nod.

"Right—so fifteen minutes searching, ask everyone. Then we meet back here at nine. If we haven't got her back by then, well . . . then . . . we phone the police."

The gravity of what I have just said makes my stomach turn. I have never phoned the police in my life. Nearly five decades as a law-abiding citizen and now this. An image of Eleanor's face as the opening shot on one of those gratuitous, late-night crime programs comes to mind, and a bolt of heat spreads up the back of my neck.

I scour the beach with that action you see on the

news when there is a missing child—the relentless push forward, combing the ground for clues. But in the footage, there is always a thick line of volunteers, not a solitary father zigzagging the shallows in a daze and a group of bewildered customers trying to keep up. I keep thinking I see a knot of red curls. But in the end it is just my mind playing the age-old trick of wanting something to the point of hallucination.

The end of the seafront is marked by a cluster of rocks and huge boulders, most of them bigger than me. There's no way Eleanor could be beyond there, not if she was by herself. The alternative doesn't bear thinking about. A giant wave breaks to my left, crashing like a cymbal, so loud that for a second, one blessed second, it nearly drowns out the shrieks of my own panic.

"Frank! Frank!"

I turn, and there you are.

"Daddy!" Eleanor releases your hand and runs toward me. I've never known relief like it, the noose loosened just as the drop comes into sight.

Even in the dark, I can tell she's been crying because when I fall to my knees and we hug, her whole body slammed flush against mine, I can taste the salt from her tears as I press my lips against her forehead. Soon, Eleanor starts to squirm. It's cold, and we're near enough to the sea for the spray to catch us. Only I can't let go, not when I've stared into the depths of everything we stood to lose.

You garble something over our heads about Eleanor trying to join us and losing her way. How you found her round the back of the music tent, someone was looking after her . . .

"It's OK. It's OK," I whisper.

I'm not sure which of us it was designed to comfort.

Chapter 10

Over the last few months I have come back to that moment time and time again. The wind whipping the sand up into my eyes and the dampness everywhere—the seawater soaking through my trousers, Eleanor's tears, my own. I had been up to my neck in the riptide of every parent's worst nightmare, and it was enough to drown me. It scared Eleanor, our response, you could see that. As her parents, it was our job to keep it together, to be fine and strong and constant even when our world was about to fall apart at the seams. Only it wasn't possible, was it? For the first time Eleanor was forced to see us as we really were: human. We felt fear just like her.

In the immediate aftermath, we wanted to make it right again. To get us all back to normal. We caught our flight, we made it home. It was spaghetti Bolognese for supper. When Eleanor went back to school a day later, we were braced for reports of some upset. You even considered warning the school, mentioning that there had been an incident. In the end, I talked you down; we didn't need another eyebrow arched in the direction of our parenting. Weeks went by and—surprisingly—nothing.

While, on the surface, we had narrowly avoided disaster, there was still a subtle shift in the delicate tectonic plates of family life that to this day I feel was so much more insidious. In the supermarket, Eleanor no longer wanted to go off and source items by herself. She had started an after-school art club, and if I was so much as five minutes late to pick her up, you could see she had been chewing the ragged nail at the side of her thumb until little pinpricks of red bubbled up from under the skin. When we went out, I felt her closer to my leg, her hand gripping mine just that bit tighter. Some days, I wondered if I was imagining it. You had talked to her about it on the way to school that first day, in the weeks after. Eleanor insisted there was nothing wrong.

No harm done, as my own mother used to be so fond of saying. Only it was never as simple as that with

Eleanor. She was always so conscious of upsetting us, wasn't she? Holding in her own pain so there was no risk of her inflicting even a drop of it on us. We had seen glimpses of it before: a grazed knee she neglected to mention, an upset at school that was raised, casually, by another parent. And after Portugal? When she had seen on the beach that she was our world? Anything that hurt her was bound to tip us both off our axes. That is some burden for any child to carry, let alone one as hypersensitive as Eleanor.

For once, it was nice to feel a holiday drifting into the distant moorings of memory. With every day that passed after Portugal, we moved ever closer toward solid ground. And things were still so good—it's impossible to deny that. I loved seeing Eleanor grow. Physically, she shot up around her eighth birthday until she wasn't that much shorter than you. I didn't want her growing up to mean growing away. You two had always been so close. It was me I was worried about. It sounds tragic to say it, but I didn't want to be shrugged off now that she was older, cast off as an embarrassment like any of the toys that had gone out of favor and were now clogging up the space at the back of her wardrobe. I resolved to do everything I could to keep that bond we had, father and daughter.

When she was nine, her class did a project on but-terflies. Eleanor was captivated. Drawing them, read-ing up on them. She even had a pajama set with a print of tessellated wings. The school had planned a trip to a dedicated exhibition in the Botanic Garden, but when I suggested we go together first, the two of us, she took me up on my offer without so much as a moment's pause.

"Ells, come look at this one." It is as silent as a li-brary inside, the windows papered with laminated QUIET signs. There is something almost comical about the exaggerated tiptoeing Eleanor performs on her approach.

"What is it?"

"It's a swallowtail." I've seen one just once before, on a family holiday in the Norfolk Broads, back when I was Eleanor's age. They were rare then, even more so now.

"It's amazing." Eleanor is so close that I can feel her breath warm against my arm.

"Here." I pass her my camera. "Take a picture."

There is such fixity in Eleanor's gaze, her tongue creeping out of the corner of her mouth in concentra-tion as she steadies the shot. In front of us the pale yellow wings twitch, their inky veins throbbing. I have made sure the flash is off, the shutter snap too.

Eleanor manages to take her photos without a disturbance. It is only when she passes the camera back that she startles the butterfly by letting out an almighty sneeze. Half the greenhouse recoil in shock.

Eleanor looks up at me, eyes wide at the mere thought of a reprimand. Instead, I feel myself beginning to crack up. I take her hand and drag her through the fire doors to where we can laugh, freely, until our lungs are empty and our stomachs are sore.

I loved Eleanor's focus, her drive. A project would finish and she would throw herself into the next thing at school, often to the point of obsession. She still had such levity with it, though. I could see it as we creased up on the bench outside the butterfly exhibition, other families wondering just what was so funny as they walked past. It was in a hundred perceptive asides at dinnertime or in the commentary she gave in front of the TV. It was in the way she could mimic the exact tone of your voice when you harangued me for leaving my wet towel on the bed again.

It's a shame those skills don't count for much at school, not formally anyway. When she moved to secondary school, we were on tenterhooks. It wasn't as if we were expecting the same full-blown meltdown we had seen over reception, but there was the same sense of unease that we'd always had when it came to Eleanor going anywhere new, anywhere beyond our immediate reach. Saying it aloud makes it sound like we coddled her, which I'm not sure is entirely fair. We never wrapped her up in cotton wool, though I suppose we never went out of our way to expose her to the elements either. Does any parent? Maybe we just hoped she would develop a thicker skin with time.

As it was, she managed to make the transition well enough. Katie and the few other friends she had were all still in the same class, though I didn't get the sense they had expanded their tribe much. Her first report made mention of the fact that she was quiet in class, shy in group projects, particularly with people she didn't know. The final line was something about Eleanor needing to give herself a break every now and again, a little smiley face in the margin next to it. I remember you passing the sheet over to me with a wry smile. They were spot on about that.

Eleanor would stay up to all hours on her homework when there was something she couldn't do. You could see her chewing down on the edge of her pen until the plastic snapped and her lips were tinged blue. There was no "Just ten minutes more," no "I'll just finish this page." There was never any compromise with Eleanor. She was eleven, twelve. Saying that now, it seems mad we didn't put our foot down. But then it was learning, and that was important, right? In all honesty, it was probably just because we were never very good at saying no to her.

I admired her tenacity, really I did, but where had that pressure come from, Mags? It certainly didn't come from us, no matter what you might have thought these past few years. Perhaps it is just the nature of being an only child? All that focus honed in like a laser on her and her alone. That would be the easy explanation, though, and if there is one thing we both know about Eleanor, it's that she always managed to eschew those. More often than not, I wonder if it was just a part of her, that drive, hooked up somewhere to a complete inability to deal with even the slightest failure. It was up to us to try to keep it in check.

It always struck me as amusing that, while other parents in Eleanor's class were desperately coercing their children into doing homework, we spent our time desperately trying to coerce Eleanor outside. That bicycle we got her for her thirteenth birthday was a brilliant investment. Every weekend that summer, the three of us would go out together, up to the meadow, cycling side by side until one of the pretentious Lycra-clad types whizzed by from the opposite direction and we had to merge into single file.

At the pub, I'd get in a round of drinks. I can still

see her, Mags, mid-story, jabbing her straw between the melting fragments of ice while she regaled us with some new tale from school, every bit as engaging and animated as you. She couldn't have been further from the shy girl of her school report, that's for sure. I often wondered if we had raised two separate Eleanors, one for home and one for the world outside.

Sometimes I'd watch you watching her and my mind would wind back to that day when you told me you were pregnant. I hadn't wanted it to change us. I'd told myself it wouldn't. And do you know what, Maggie? I've never been happier to find myself in the wrong. Under the table, you would run your foot up and down my calf in time to the ebb and flow of her story. Having Eleanor had brought us closer, made us more compassionate with each other. There was no one and nothing that I would rather we had in common.

In the evenings, once you had gone to bed and I was marking scripts or drifting off under the patio heater, Eleanor would pad out to meet me in her slippers. Little fluffy things, moccasins you had selected for Christmas that collected dust like the particles were going out of fashion.

One night in particular is locked in my memory.

"Evening, Eleanor. Oh, thank you. That's very kind." She places a cup of tea on the battered garden table next to me. I nudge out the second lounger, its middle all loose and flabby, and take off my jacket so that it covers the loose spring. "Here, darling."

It is dark enough that the first stars are visible. It's on the tip of my tongue to start pointing them out, but something stops me. I take a sip of my tea—she always did make a good cup—and wait for her to speak.

"Do you ever wonder why we are how we are?"

I look over at her: she is fourteen, five foot ten, all arms and legs. She looks so young in a pair of pajamas that hasn't caught up with yet another growth spurt, at that fragile age when you are so blatantly still a child but so utterly convinced that you are an adult. I am seized by a desire to grab her, to cuddle her up in my arms and let her fall asleep in my lap like she did when she was a toddler.

Instead I clear my throat. "It's a good question. Maybe the best one of all. Although I would say that, I suppose."

"How much is nature, how much is nurture, you know? How much is just luck?"

Eleanor is impatient for an answer. She always has been, ever since she was a toddler, but in that moment it is so obvious; she leans forward in her recliner, her torso twisting toward me. There are two purple crescents under her eyes, the skin there a wafer-thin sheet of tiny raised pores. The result of hormones or the relentless fizzing in her mind—I can't tell which.

"It's both," I say, careful not to rush into an answer. "We inherit certain genes, though there will be those that are harder to trace. You can teach certain behaviors as well. And then, well, there's luck. I'd never underestimate that, even if it's not what I'm meant to say at work. I like to believe that there's always an element of fate, or destiny, or whatever you want to call it."

"Hm." Eleanor nods and turns back in her chair, lifting the levers on the arms so she is tilting to look up at the sky. Something I said has obviously given her pause for thought. We sit in silence for what feels like an hour but which can't in reality be more than ten minutes. "So, there is always a chance to change your own story?"

"Yeah, I'd say so."

I am desperate to ask where all this has come from, but before I have the opportunity Eleanor stands up and bends down by my chair so I can kiss her on the forehead, the way I have always done before she goes to bed ever since she was a baby. They are always your baby, aren't they, Mags? However much they catch up in height or intelligence or anything else besides.

I never worked out what Eleanor was getting at there—was it teen angst or something more? Now, after everything that has happened, I come back time and time again to that conversation, scanning every word and pause and gesture for a clue to what was to come. Hundreds of hours replaying that night and still I'm none the wiser. Even if I was, what difference would it make? If there is one conclusion I've come to in recent months, though, it's that try as we might, there would always be some part of Eleanor that resided in the wilds outside our reach. I only wish we'd had a firmer grasp of this and equipped her with better tools to survive out there.

Things began to feel strained after her fifteenth birthday. She was going into a big year at school, what with exams, decisions about sixth-form colleges and subject choices, and the sort of big statements about "the future" from teachers that are bound to get anyone's back up. On top of that, there was that falling-out with Katie and one of her other friends I heard about secondhand, from you, of course, most probably long after it had been patched up and laid to bed. By the time we reached the summer term, I was checking every phrase and sentence in my mind before I so much as opened my mouth around Eleanor. It didn't take much to earn a look like thunder and that gut-wrenching sense of being locked out of her confidence.

We blamed the work—after all, she'd been at her

desk six, seven hours a day for God knows how long. It was enough to make anyone snappy and irritable. We just needed to get through the exams and then we could crack the lid, let out some of that pressure. We could talk about better coping strategies for stress and anxiety, all of the subjects that were currently going down like a fleet of lead balloons. "Once you finish your exams, it'll be the longest summer of your life," you told her over supper, as she dissected her potato into ever smaller cubes. Little did we know it would end up being the longest of ours too.

We didn't see much of Eleanor after that final exam. All those years encouraging her to kick back, and suddenly she was doing it of her own accord, albeit with little heed for anyone else. Careful what you wish for, as you always liked to say, eh, Mags? She told us she was out and at least that much was true. It was like squeezing blood from a stone, trying to prize any more information out of Eleanor—who she was with, where they were heading. She had always been so open with us about that sort of stuff, and suddenly we were scrambling around for whatever scraps of information she deigned to throw in our direction.

To start with, it was a few missed dinners, nothing terrible in the grand scheme of things, but within a week or two she was turning up well past midnight. It was a scorching-hot summer that year, and I remember the agitation the hosepipe ban brought to everyone— horticulturist or not. No one could sleep, least of all us, tangled atop a cotton sheet, attuned to every sound, our ears filtering every creak of the house for that subtle click that announced Eleanor's keys in the lock and the end of our nightly ordeal. Our text exchanges were almost entirely one-sided.

> When will you be home?
> Call me when you get this.
> Your mother is sick with worry.

In the morning, we were too exhausted to offer any sort of coherent punishment. We'd felt it then, being that bit older. When Eleanor was little, the fact that our friends were ten, fifteen years ahead in the parenting game meant it had been hard to find playdates, that Eleanor grew up in a home full of adults or near enough. Fast-forward to her teens and it was the sympathy we craved, the immediate solidarity of our support network struggling with the same surliness. It would have been nice to hear from just one of them dealing with the same inability to enforce a curfew.

We were too addled from fatigue to get even our own party line straight. When I went to tell her it was unacceptable, you counseled patience—it was the summer holidays; she was doing what all teens do. When you were out of your mind with anxiety, surrounding Eleanor with it like a cage—*You have to tell us where you are. You have no idea what we go through*—I told you to calm down and back off. We didn't want to risk her pushing us away for good. Instead, every night as we tossed and turned, we passed our new mantra between us like an inhaler: "It's just a phase." In hindsight, I wonder if we should have spent more time figuring out at what point a phase ends and the real problem starts.

I couldn't work out what the hell was going on— where was my Eleanor, the kind, sensitive girl we had raised? I found it impossible to wrap my head around the fact that this was the same girl who used to devote a whole day to the manufacture of my Father's Day card, a masterpiece in macaroni shapes, now looking at me like an intruder in her life. If it was teen rebellion, it was so at odds with the girl we knew that, at first, I almost felt at a remove. *This isn't my life.* That's what I thought, Mags, when she stomped out the door without so much as a backward glance. *This isn't the daughter I have.* She was never around to come and sit with me on the patio. I couldn't find it in me to put my feet up on the spare lounger.

Amid it all, life carried on as normal. When one of my papers was published in *Nature* that August, just before Eleanor's sixteenth birthday, you hosted a dinner party in my honor, bringing chairs down from the attic so we could accommodate a cohort of collaborators and peer reviewers for the night. When the subject of children came up, we had our two-hander down to a T.

"So where is young Eleanor tonight?" Jeremy, the head of my department, nudges you as he leans across to help himself to more rice.

"Out. With friends. You know how it is." The lights are low, but I can still see you flush as you look down at your empty plate, willing this discussion over.

"Ours were like that too, never a bloody clue where they were from one minute to the next." Jeremy chuckles, long and low. "Isn't that right, Anne? Almost a relief when they fled the nest!"

"I wouldn't worry too much." Anne extends her hand diagonally across the table, weaving between the tumblers and strewn serving spoons. "God, if I'd had a pound for every time I felt like giving up on the whole sodding parenting malarkey when the boys were in their teens, trust me, I wouldn't still be working!"

The rest of the table have abandoned their separate conversations, presumably sensing something juicier afoot. The silence surrounding your response is deafening.

"Well, I wouldn't say it is quite like that." You retract your hand delicately, wiping it on your napkin. Your eyes flash up at me, screaming for help.

I begin refilling the glasses. "What is adolescence if not a state of biochemical lability and aggression, huh?"

My joke elicits a flurry of laughter from the table. The mention of aggression seems to have taken it a bit too far for you, though, and I notice that you are staring at the tablecloth to avoid meeting anyone's eye.

"Might as well enjoy it while it lasts, I say." Jeremy is off again, the Merlot clearly swimming in his veins. "You get to my age and realize that you are as unable and unaggressive as it gets. It's one foot in your slipper, one in the grave."

Jeremy's reverie is cut short by a heavy thud against the front door.

"Last-minute guest, eh?" My postdoc laughs. "I always admire someone with their metabolism trained on the dessert course."

"Eleanor," you whisper, willing me toward the door before she bursts through it.

I am out into the hallway like a shot, just as Eleanor finally figures out which key works the lock. Her hair has fallen over her face, and when she shakes it back, her pupils are wildly dilated, her eyeliner smeared under them, from the time of day or from tears, I can't for the life of me tell. Her arms appear to be twitching, her breathing slow and shallow.

"Evening, Eleanor." The door may be closed, but I'm scared of what they might be able to pick out. Through the walls I can hear you talking at top volume. I am not the only one concerned with keeping up appearances.

"Got guests?" Eleanor's speech is slow and slurred. I grab Eleanor's biceps, half pulling, half dragging her up the stairs and into her room before we are found.

"Don't want your friends seeing me?" Eleanor reclines on her single bed and begins undressing herself.

I am uncomfortable, all too aware this is your remit, Mags, and yet I can't bear for you to see Eleanor in this state.

"What have you taken?" I hiss. My stomach drops. I wonder if Eleanor can hear my heart thundering in my chest. There is no parenting manual on earth that prepares you for the shock of seeing your own child strung out. I catch a glimpse of her Jeffrey, the bear I bought for her when she was just days old, teetering on the shelf just above her head, and feel sixteen years of my life collapsing into this one moment.

"This is important, Eleanor—tell me what you have taken."

"Bit of this, bit of that."

Eleanor is down to her underwear by now, and I pray she won't take off anything else. Her clothes reek of smoke. I find her jeans, rummaging through the pockets in case they yield some more coherent answers. Nothing. A disintegrating tissue and some small change. Good to see my taxi fare has been spent on illicit supplies instead.

"I don't want your mother seeing you like this. Get into bed." Eleanor is fumbling with the duvet cover, and I end up stepping in, tucking the quilt around her in a way I haven't done for nearly a decade.

I go to turn off the light.

"Why don't you say it?"

"Say what?"

"You're ashamed of me, Dad."

Downstairs, I can hear the front door open, the air kisses and gratitude and exclamations that "we must do this again—soon!" Eleanor always has been so perceptive.

"We'll talk about this tomorrow."

We wash up in silence that night. I can tell that you are torn between wanting to know and knowing you aren't able to bear that knowledge, not yet. That night, you cry yourself to sleep. I can feel the cold dampness when I remove my hand from under your head the moment I can feel your breathing slow into sleep.

Carefully, I extract myself from you and make my way down the hallway to open Eleanor's door. All these years later, and the fluorescent stars we stuck to the ceiling in one of my mock astrology lessons have yet to come off. *By her choice or by the strength of their design?* I wonder as I lean down to check that she is still on her side, still breathing.

I settle on the floor and prop my head against one of the display cushions that has fallen off the bed. I reach for Eleanor's hand, which dangles off the side of the mattress. A fetus with a single unruly limb. It is cold, clammy. I look up at the stars, all the time holding the one that fell to earth for us.

"I'm not ashamed of you. I never have been. I never will be," I whisper.

I wish I'd said it to her face.

Chapter 11

When the doctor arrives, it is early evening and I am on my feet, shaking some feeling back into their numbness and assessing how much change I have in my pockets to spare for the vending machine. After days of going without, my stomach has started rumbling with such ferocity that I wonder, hopefully, if it might wake Maggie.

"I'm glad to find you here, Professor. Although you are most diligent with your visits to your wife." He glances at the camp bed with its rumpled blanket but decides not to mention it.

"Forty years of marriage requires more than diligence," I mutter, somewhat more darkly than I intended.

"Of course. I couldn't presume to know."

If ever there was a time to allude to his inexperience in this regard, at the bedside of my critically ill wife is not it. He senses my hackles going up.

"Apologies if that was taken the wrong way, Professor. What I meant to say is that your dedication to your wife has been remarkable. You have barely left her side."

I am too spent to give a smile, or anything else for that matter. I have no intention of being cruel, really I don't, I never do. The sad reality is that often our behavior will do it for us, unwilled and unwillingly. My silence is the very best example.

"Look, I know we spoke this morning about how Mrs. Hobbs was somehow behind where we were hoping she would be at this stage in her treatment. As you'll remember, with your consent we agreed to keep her sedated for another twenty-four hours."

"And?"

"Well, before I leave for the day, I'd like to set up a time to discuss some treatment options, some other decisions."

"What options? What decisions?"

"As I say, if we could fix a time tomorrow . . ."

"Now is good," I say, heat flushing up the back of my neck.

"Er . . . well . . . if you would prefer now." He checks his watch; another person on a deadline. "Take a seat, please, Professor."

"I'm fine." Instinctively, I cross my arms. I am defensive, but of what I can't quite work out. I know that if I sit down, there is a strong chance I will never get up again.

"As I'm sure you are already aware, the longer your wife is under sedation, the higher the risk of damage to her brain should she recover."

Should? I double over. The doctor nudges the spare chair out from behind him and spins it round for me. I press my hands into its back until I feel the plastic edge cutting into my palms.

"Professor, do you . . . ?" He gestures at the chair.

"No . . . no . . . Please carry on."

"It means that we are wary of keeping her under for much longer. When we stop the medicines that are inducing her current comatose state, it may take a number of days, perhaps weeks, for her to regain full consciousness. However, I have to stress that there are no guarantees. We recommend that you speak to one of our trained support staff here who can talk you through your choices, should Mrs. Hobbs not wake."

"Whether I turn off the life support, you mean?"

"That is one option, indeed. I don't know whether

you and your wife ever discussed what you would wish to happen in this situation?"

Does anyone? Hardly the most romantic pillow talk in the early days, is it? DNRs and donor cards. Then the comforting complacency and routine of the middle years. *I would know what my partner wants, wouldn't I?* I can't bring myself to reflect on the last six months, the absence of all discussion, even of the most pressing issues.

"Professor?"

I have been quiet too long. He is clock-watching; unlike me, he has other places to be. Selfish as it may sound, I don't care about wasting his time. It is mine I am worried about. I glance at my watch. Six P.M. Fourteen, maybe fifteen hours before he is back. Surely I can be finished by then? The magnitude of what I have left to say is enough to floor me, but I cannot waste what little time I still have peeling myself off the foot of Maggie's bed.

"I won't turn her off." My voice is quiet but determined.

"I can appreciate that. In some instances, it is, however, the best option for the patient."

"I will not give up on my wife. I will not." My voice is rising, in volume and in pitch. I have not felt this sort of anger, raw and clawing at the back of my throat, for years. I know that it emanates from something more than this situation, but I cannot rein it in.

"I have paid my taxes, lived within my means. Maggie worked for forty years for the NHS. I will not turn her off to save money or meet targets. I will not give up on her!" I am nearly shouting and wonder how long it will be before reinforcements arrive, a male nurse, perhaps, or a security guard if they can spare him. "I will not give up on her!"

The doctor begins to beat a retreat toward the door. There is no panic button that I can see. I am safe this time.

"Think about it, Professor." He threads his index and middle fingers into the pocket of his shirt, still as neatly pressed as the first day I met him. He produces a small card and places it on the spare seat by the door. "It isn't in your wife's best interests to delay. I'll be back tomorrow morning with your wife's support team, and we will need to make some formal decisions then. You know where I am should you need me in the meantime."

When I am convinced that he has disappeared far enough down the corridor, I pick up the card. *Emily Morris—Senior Family Liaison Officer.* I throw it back down and make my way round to Maggie. Time is running out. Everything else can wait.

"I meant that, Maggie. I'm not giving up. I never have. Not with Eleanor, not these last few months either. I'm sorry if you ever felt that was the case. I do not give up on my family, and I am not about to start now.

"I just hope you won't give up on me, Mags, when you hear . . . why I stopped speaking, what happened, why I just shut down. Please, Maggie, please, hear me out."

We talk about the winds of change, but that night was a gale-force storm. I think we would both agree that things had been far from easy in the year running up to the exams, in the sleepless weeks after, but from the dinner party onward we were dealing with something else entirely. We were clinging on to the Eleanor as we knew her like a plastic bag in a hundred-mile-an-hour gust, our knuckles white with the exertion of keeping hold of just a piece of her fragile form in our lives.

The next day, she didn't emerge until well into the evening. I went in to check on her around midday, a glass of water and a piece of toast in hand. Eleanor was curled up, facing the wall. I so desperately wanted to ask if she was OK, obviously, but also what the hell had happened last night? Did she remember any of it?

What she had said? I sat on the edge of the bed, lowering myself as slowly as my thighs could manage so the mattress didn't sink. Most of her hair was thrown forward over her face, but a single auburn curl trailed down from the nape of her neck and over the duvet. I went to run my finger over it, the way I had a million times before. As a toddler to get her to sleep, as a child when she needed comfort. The second my finger made contact, she flinched.

I headed back to my study but I couldn't focus at all. Was she sick? Had there been some falling-out? Maybe she was ashamed that I had seen her in that state? I had a horde of possible answers but none that felt likely to have caused this extreme a response. You had gone out—to see Edie, I imagine—so I was left alone in my confusion.

As I sent a fleet of pawns to the slaughter and the computer dealt me out checkmate after checkmate, I tried out a hundred openers in my mind for a second attempt at a conversation, sifting through them for one that wouldn't push Ellie further away. Every time I heard the floorboards creak, my heart raced. She was coming down, finally. Then the loo flush, and the door bang, and that horrible sense of déjà vu that brought me back to the early days of our relationship and made me wonder if I was messing up as a father as badly as I had done as a husband.

Eleanor emerged eventually, after you had gone to bed. I was fixing my late-night cheese and pickle, and she appeared like a specter, her outline momentarily illuminated by the fridge light. I knew this might be my only opportunity.

"Hey, Eleanor, how are you?"

For a second, I wonder if she hasn't heard. She sets the tap to a low flow and fills her beaker to the top, greedily lapping up the excess.

"Ells?" I am cautious about coming too close. "Are you OK?"

The moonlight streaks across the metal sink, casting a triangle of light on the floor tiles but keeping Ellie in the dark.

"Ells?"

"Do you mind?"

"Mind what?"

"Just—please?"

It was only after she left the kitchen that I realized she hadn't so much as looked in my direction.

All night that exchange ran through my dreams on a loop so intense that when I woke up, four, five, six times, restless and bashing at the alarm clock to check how far away morning was, I couldn't understand how next to no time had passed at all. When I drifted off, my mind zeroed in on that moment just before she stopped speaking. What was that quiver in her voice? Was it a thimble of upset? A shred of regret? I would have preferred anger. Whatever it was unsettled me far more.

I hoped you would have more luck. I gave you the bare bones of that night—the drinking, the slurring, the heady daze that I worried might be something else. At one point later that week, I was rooting in the cupboard under the stairs when I heard the word "therapist" and the mention of "something we could do as a family" drifting down the corridor from her bedroom above. I could feel the blood rush to my face. I've never been a talker, have I, Mags? And really, I couldn't think of anything worse. But for Eleanor? There were no lengths we wouldn't stretch to, no depths we couldn't plumb to make things OK for her again.

There was still a month to go until she started college. It should have been a relief when she stopped going out until all hours. But with the sea change in behavior that followed the night of the dinner party, even that would have been preferable to Eleanor holing up in her room, sleeping or pretending to, or staring out into space. Something had shifted that night, and we were both coming up blank in terms of hard explanations for what on earth it could be. We tried all manner of things, didn't we, Mags, to coax her out? Talking, imploring, bribing. Everything we tried was met with, well, nothing. It went beyond inertia. That would suggest she was at least resisting something, when in fact the worst of it was that there was no pushback at all. She was being smothered by an unknown darkness, suffocated so that all the curiosity and the focus that made Eleanor *Eleanor* had been snuffed right out. I've never felt so helpless, Mags.

She made it to the sixth form. But it was just a holding pen for her. Obviously they noticed things were bad, because a session with the counselor was mentioned at the college. You put us on separate waiting lists outside of that, definitely two that I knew of. But somehow nothing came to fruition. That was the most animated Ellie ever was back then—begging us not to make her go. Why did we give in to that, Maggie? Why did we back off? I have always been a softie, a "pushover," whatever you want to call it. You were the firm one, not me. I often wondered if it became a matter of principle to you. You wanted to fix whatever was going on with Eleanor yourself, that much was clear. But at some point, surely, we had to admit that it wasn't possible? I just wish we had come to that realization sooner.

Often I'd get home and her rucksack would be in the

hallway, but there was no sign of her; no coat, no shoes, no mess on the kitchen table to suggest she'd fixed herself a snack. All that time she'd been holed up in her room we had prayed for her to get out, and now she had and we had no idea where the hell she'd gone in the evenings. Once she started to miss supper, I went out to search. You were frantic, I was frantic, but it wasn't doing any good, the two of us staring out of the living-room window as if our desperation alone would be enough to conjure her up.

I had to be doing something, so I made my way round the neighborhood. I didn't ask anyone—that seemed too . . . final, I suppose. Admitting she was lost at a point when we were still telling ourselves that she would find her own way back to normality. No, I just sought out the signs, Mags. I loved the very bones of her. I told myself that meant I would catch her by a whiff of her shampoo, an artfully discarded tissue. A hunch would do. In reality, it seemed too much *Poirot* had addled my mind.

With no tip-offs to go on, I would try the meadow first, the benches we used to sit and picnic on. I tried down by the shops, in them too. I went into the abandoned cricket pavilion, once interrupting a session round a homemade hookah pipe. I trailed round the circumference of the adjoining sports field, even though the floodlights had broken and I had to resort to the torch on my phone. I went up and down every aisle in Tesco, as if she might jump out at me from between the cereals and the soft drinks.

By the time I got back, I would be exhausted. Sometimes, if I was out for a few hours, she would have made it home of her own accord. Others, I'd return and there would still be no sign of her, not until the early hours. As I waited, my head would pound and my ankles would be puffed up, like two sausages about to burst their casing. *How much longer can I keep this up?* Once, as I eased my shoes off in front of the monitor in the study, my elbow caught the mouse and my screensaver flashed to life. It was the three of us at her birthday supper the year before last, a selfie that was ninety percent Eleanor, ten percent us, only half of each of our faces in the shot, grinning away at what we could already guarantee would be a terrible composition. With just one glimpse, I knew I would carry on my search as long as it took. I would never give up on Eleanor.

After a few weeks of false starts, I found her hangout: down by the canal, near Jericho. Her back was to me, but I would have known it anywhere. I'd been faced with it enough times over the past few months. I was cautious of causing a scene and made sure I was hidden by the undergrowth, moving slowly in the late-autumn gloom. She was alone. I couldn't tell if I should be relieved or not. She had a handful of pebbles and was absentmindedly skimming them into the gap between two moored barges. None of them bounced, not like they should, not like how I taught her. It took everything in me not to come up behind her and curl her hand in mine to help her find just the right angle. I watched for a minute or two longer while her efforts sank, and then headed home.

I wanted to make a scene. I wanted to be that man—the authoritarian, the disciplinarian, the stand-up-and-come-home-immediately father who gets the job done. I have tried and tried and tried, but we both know that it is not the man I am, Mags. It doesn't mean I wasn't desperately reaching out to her, throwing every last item in my personal arsenal her way. For months, ever since the dinner party, I'd asked every possible question, I'd hinted and suggested and supported and nudged and needled. I had read into pauses and the smattering of words we exchanged, I'd interpreted her gestures and movements, the shape of a shrug and the speed of an exit. I gave everything, we both did, and still we were no closer to finding out what had happened that night that so obviously changed Eleanor. It is always hard to accept that sometimes your best isn't enough. When it comes to your children, it's impossible.

"Did you find her?" I am barely in the door before you ask.

"No. She must be at a friend's house. I'm sorry, Mags."

"She hasn't texted." You are practically wringing your phone in your hands.

"She's fine."

"How do you know?" There's an accusation in your eyes.

"I don't, Mags. But look, we have to trust her."

"How? How, Frank? She's a child. *Our* child. And we're losing her!"

The truth hits me like a smack, square in the face. I start to respond, but I have nothing. You drop your palms onto the windowsill and slump.

"Hey, Mags, hey, hey now."

I manage to turn you back around and steer you to the sofa.

"She knows we are here, that we are always here when she needs us." I wonder if you doubt my words as much as I do. "She knows we love her."

"Does she?"

I wasn't sure what I knew anymore. I suppose that was why I was so surprised one day a year later when

Eleanor came home, at the start of her second year of sixth form, with talk of university. I think it's fair to say that we were both concerned what her future would hold, but we were too scared to push. She never gave us much in terms of courses, university cities, what would come after. No, it was far more perfunctory than that. But it was progress, right? That was how it felt to me.

When Eleanor's offers came in—two that we heard of, at least—we wanted to mark the occasion. We settled for something low-key, a bottle of cava on ice the day she texted to say she had taken up an offer from Manchester. By the time we got home she was already in her room, curtains pulled and the light off. The bottle returned to its previous home in the dust at the back of the drinks cupboard.

Was there some part of you, Mags, that felt relief? Relief that she would be out of our hair, even if she was already out of our hands? I could never bring myself to phrase it quite like that, but you must have known what I was getting at when I joked about having the house to ourselves again. It wasn't me giving up as a parent, Mags. The very idea is a contradiction in terms. How can you admit defeat when that would mean turning your back on a very part of yourself? You could cut me open and see *Eleanor* and *Maggie* tattooed down my breastbone—the words intertwined like the blazing colors on a rock candy stick. No, if anything my relief was an admission of failure. Something had gone wrong with our ability to get through to her after whatever the hell happened that night. We had to let time take its course and hope damn hard that it would wind Eleanor back to us both.

You went through the motions of preparing for her leaving home with such patience. In the months following her last exams, Eleanor became an increasingly distant lodger. There were whole days, beautiful, sunny days, that summer she turned eighteen when she wouldn't leave her room. While I worried she wouldn't get out of bed to make it there, you lined up crates in the hallway with military precision: bedding, stationery, kitchen equipment.

The drive up to university was excruciating. I can't imagine you have forgotten that. After fifteen minutes of asking if Eleanor was excited, nervous, had she forgotten anything, I settled for a blast of Magic FM loud enough to kill the awkwardness. When we arrived at her halls, we zipped into motion, trailing the boxes up to her new room. There was strictly no talking, to other students or to their equally burdened parents. Once everything had been unloaded, we stood in our isosceles formation, Eleanor ahead, the two of us huddled together behind.

"Well, shall I make the bed for you?" You are relentlessly chipper, but I can sense tension at the corners of your mouth.

"No, it's fine, Mum." Eleanor's back is to us as she surveys the families jostling for parking outside. You are already wrestling the lid off the plastic bedding crate.

"Really, Mum."

"Please, darling, I'll feel so much better knowing you have a nice fresh bed to get into tonight."

The fitted sheet is out and you are off.

"Saves you having something to worry about when you get in from your first freshers' party." I am trying to keep the show on the road for just a few minutes longer.

I walk to the window, where Eleanor is plucking threads from her frayed jumper sleeves, wrapping the longest strands around her index finger until the flesh between them bulges. I place a hand on her shoulder blade, lightly. She recoils. I am glad you are too entrenched in the duvet cover to see. Eleanor turns around again sharply.

"Really, Mum, that's enough. I mean it. You can go."

"Darling, I've only done one pillowcase."

"I only sleep on one anyway."

You let the spare case you are holding drop onto the bed. I can hear my heart pounding, or is it yours?

"Right then, we'd better be off, Maggie." You are looking at the carpet, an industrial taupe stained with years of student debauchery. I am cautious of moving you too quickly in case the tears have started.

In that moment, I hated Eleanor. Hated her for being so cruel. Hated her for what she did to you, how she cut you to pieces and made no effort to stitch you back together again. Left you with more holes than the sodding colander we had lugged the whole way up there. What sort of father does that make me, to admit that? One strung out by love and clinging on for dear life to the very end of his tether.

I approach Eleanor. I've never been effusive with physical contact; instead I give her arm a firm squeeze, hoping it will encourage her to go and hug you. You look up, your eyes glassy. For once, Eleanor performs.

"Thanks, Mum," she mumbles, "for this." Eleanor gestures in a vague semicircle.

On the car ride home, we return to silence. Every so often I glance across and catch you in my peripheral vision. You are looking at your lap, head bowed. When we pull up outside the house it is dark, the October chill already settling in, but neither of us makes a move to go inside. The fan heater rattles out its last gusts of musty air as the engine cuts. I take my hand off the gearstick and reach for yours.

"We have done all we can, Mags. We have to accept that."

Silence.

"I can't. She's my daughter." There is a wobble in your voice.

"She's mine too."

"I know. I didn't know it would be so hard. That she would be so hard."

All those years when it was just us two, when we thought it would always be just us two, that had been enough for me. Would it have changed anything if I had told you? If I had explained that I had never factored in a third, the nativity plays and parents' evenings and first boyfriends, or lack thereof. I'm not sure I could have risked you walking away to find that someone who wanted more, who wanted all that. I realized in that moment, the car windows steaming up from the cold, you had thought of barely anything else, even in the early days. It is one thing to have a dream realized, quite another to have it play out as a nightmare.

"Let's get inside, Mags, it's getting cold. I'll get us some soup."

That night we ate from the bowls my sister had given us as a wedding present. They were dusty blue, with a pair of lovebirds on them. A little twee, but you were attached to them and I loved the joy they brought you, the feeling that I was somehow a part of it. I washed them first, as they had been accruing dust over the last eighteen years. We only had the two.

Chapter 12

For the first few weeks after we dropped Eleanor off at university, we didn't hear a peep from her. I could see you checking your phone first thing in the morning, last thing at night. Every couple of minutes in between. I told you this was what we should expect, it was a good sign! Surely she was making friends, missing lectures, losing her keys—normal student behavior.

Only, we'd known since that summer two years back that she wasn't a "normal" teen. She was withdrawn, and when we could draw her out, she was irritable and permanently on edge. On the edge of what? Well, we never knew. Do you know, Mags, I often dreamed of a hybrid Eleanor? Her spherical toddler's face fused onto her teenage body, all angles and uncomfortable poses. That mind buzzing with curiosity melting into something bigger, some vast force behind it all, wasting away before our eyes. I would wake in the morning and immediately check my phone as well. Nothing from her.

I told you not to text her, not to bother her. In reality I was terrified of how you would respond if she didn't reply. I texted her, though. The odd How are lectures? Bought any fruit and veg yet? I was quite used to going unanswered. And what could we do about it anyway? We couldn't go to the police over our errant student daughter, though God knows what they would discover if we did. It would be so melodramatic. Besides, what would we even say? *Our eighteen-year-old daughter is ignoring our texts. We're worried about her.* She was an adult now, in the eyes of the law, if nothing else. They'd laugh us out of there.

If I'm really honest, Mags, I wonder if this was just another way for us to avoid acknowledging what was really going on? To delay the inevitable conclusion that now seems so achingly apparent: you were right; we were losing her.

December rolled around and, along with the habitual flurry of round robins and drinks-party invites, we got the call from Edie asking if the three of us fancied coming to hers, like the year before. As soon as you hung up, I knew the weeks of burying our heads in the sand were over.

"I need to know that Eleanor will be coming home for Christmas." You haven't moved from the phone cradle.

"Of course she will. Where else would she go?" Even as I say it, I feel doubtful.

"Frank, you need to go visit her."

"Me? Why? Surely we go together."

"She doesn't want to see me, Frank. You are better at this; you know how to handle her."

For the last two years I have approached parenting like a round of roulette, with the same nauseating sense that each turn was spinning me ever more wildly out of my control, and now this? I have tried all my chips—kindness, concern, earth-shattering fear— and none of them have brought me any luck. I look at you, the grand master, trembling beside the landline, and even now I can't bring myself to believe you are as at sea as I am. It is you who has this wrapped up, Mags, not me.

"It's nearly the holidays, and she won't want to see me either." I am aware that my excuses sound hollow, insincere.

"Please, Frank." You fix me then with a look so blatant in its desperation that I know I have no choice. I wrap my arms around your waist.

"Fine, tomorrow. I'll go tomorrow."

"Morning?"

"Yes, in the morning. Just . . . let me get a few things sorted."

The next day you have left for your rounds before I am up and breakfasted. On the kitchen table, there is a note in the red kitchen planner, in the ruled notepad section that sits to the side of the shopping list. You wish me a safe journey and ask me to bring the bag in the hallway. As I head out to defrost the car, I take a look at what you have packed for her: a scarf, hat, gloves, and, at the bottom, one of those mini portable heaters, the sort that burn through a lot more energy than they give out. I imagine you painstakingly selecting one that will fit under her desk, keep her feet warm as she works. I feel broken before I have even left the house.

I drive fitfully on the way up, chopping and changing lanes in the way you hate. I don't stop at the services. Throughout the whole journey, I feel the same foot-tapping urgency I had in the delivery suite at Eleanor's birth, only this time I have even less of an idea what to expect.

Outside the halls, I try to remember which window is hers. With all the curtains drawn it is hard to tell. I am cautious about spending too long staring up at the first-year rooms lest I get mistaken for a Peeping Tom and instead make my way to the entrance door, which some late-night partygoer has propped open with a twelve-pack of Carling, a couple of cans of which remain, remarkably, untouched. In the foyer, a few pigeons are pecking crumbs from the crenulated ridges of the ribbed carpet, their beaks peppered with loose fluff. I am thankful you weren't there to see that, Mags, really I am.

There is a board that lists the names of the students and their corresponding room numbers, and I am relieved to see Eleanor is still on there—43. I take the stairs, unsure which section of the local bird population I'll find in the lift, and pause for a minute to catch my breath when I reach the fourth floor. It's just gone eleven, but there is little sign of life here yet. I could wait. For what, though?

I knock, loud and crisp, hoping to convey a little authority. Or at least enough to wake her. After a few seconds I hear the creak of bedsprings and the sound of the key turning the lock on the inside. I am met by a young girl, bleary-eyed and disorientated, with the same dark circles as Eleanor, the same messy bedhead. Only this is not her.

"And you are?" Her voice has an accent I struggle to place.

"I could ask you the same thing."

The standoff is turning nasty rather too quickly, and I realize my mistake. I need her help, her intel.

"Sorry, I appreciate this must be a shock, me arriving unannounced. My daughter is Eleanor, Eleanor Hobbs? This was . . . well . . . is her room. It says so downstairs, on the board? Do you know her?"

"Yes, Nell had the room before me. She found somewhere else to live. This is now mine." Her vowels are sharp and clipped in a way that gives the impression that she wants me gone. Quickly.

"How long have you been here—in this room, I mean?" I slip my foot against the door frame as subtly as I can. I can't afford to be blocked out.

"Three weeks now. Nell did my course. She knew I needed a cheap place and offered me this, no rent till end of the term; then I will take over."

My mind is spinning. Nell? Somewhat ungenerously, I wonder why she hasn't told me we are bankrolling her friend's accommodation, even if she didn't mention her new identity.

"Look, I need to go soon. Lectures . . ."

"Yes, yes, I completely understand." I gather myself. "Look, do you know where Eleanor might be? A particular bit of town? I need to get hold of her—today." I flash her a look that I hope reads as urgent. I would take desperate if I had to.

"I haven't seen her in a while, but most students go to Moss Side." Then she adds, almost as an afterthought, "It's cheap."

"Thank you, really, thank you." She is beginning to edge the door shut, her impatience palpable. "If you hear from her, hear any more, will you let me know?" I root in my pockets and find a crumpled receipt. "Do you have a pen?"

I detect an exasperated sigh as she turns to fetch one while I hold the door with the sole of my shoe. When she returns, I scribble my name and number on the back of the receipt and hand it to her, leaving the pressure of my thumb on her palm for just a beat too long. I want her to feel my fear. I want to share it with someone, anyone, in case that will lessen it somehow and give me just a few more inches in my tightened chest to breathe freely, like I used to. Before Eleanor. Always before Eleanor.

"Please call."

The door shuts, and I barely withstand the temptation to crumple against it. *Where is she?* I touch the home screen on my phone; it lights up with email notifications from work. Nothing from you. I can see you at the surgery, your mind anywhere but on the young mums needing postnatal care, fixated on your own baby, miles from home, fighting every urge to call, to text, to scream at me to bring her home.

Back in the car, I consider my options. I could try the student accommodation services. Surely the university must keep track of these things? But even if they did, would Eleanor ever forgive me for getting them involved? While I wrestle with my conscience, I google Moss Side and find myself distinctly concerned. I am looking in a haystack I couldn't be more unfamiliar with and for a needle that doesn't want to be found.

Even with no leads, I decide to start by following the satnav to the first address it suggests there. The streets are busy: a mum struggles to push her pram up a hill while the two tots behind her narrowly avoid a mobility scooter coming in the opposite direction; across the street, a group of teenage boys slouch against a wall, a jumble of limbs they are still growing into, their eyes flicking between their phones and the busy intersection I have just come from. I park, lock up, and begin to head toward them.

"Excuse me?" I approach a boy on the edge of the group. He is engrossed in whatever is on his screen, and it takes a second or two for him to look up.

"All right?" He is younger than I had guessed from

the car, a mound of angry red spots flaring across his forehead, a downy dusting of hair on his upper lip. The rest have clocked my arrival and begin to look in my direction. I feel like a Victorian curio dropped onto the street.

"Yes, yes, thank you. I'm looking for my daughter."

"You got a picture? Maybe Benny here knows her?" They snicker. The one I guess is Benny administers a painful-sounding thump.

I fumble for my phone in my shirt pocket, bring up the photo app. It suddenly strikes me that I don't have anything recent, nothing from the last few months. I trail back through the images of the lab refurbishments, you among the succulents at the garden center, the odd badly angled selfie of us both. Finally, I find one of Eleanor. She doesn't look all too pleased about being photographed makeup-free and still in her pajamas, a half-empty glass of Buck's Fizz in her hand. Last Christmas, according to the date. I am struck by just how vulnerable she looks, a child with the weight of adult worry etched under her eyes.

I turn the screen to face them, braced for a flurry of inappropriate remarks. Clearly, they think better of it.

"Sorry, I haven't seen any girl like that." They turn their semicircle inward again by a fraction.

"Thanks anyway," I mumble, tucking the phone

back in my breast pocket, keeping some part of Eleanor safe and close to me.

I peer into the houses where the curtains have been drawn or never existed in the first place. I imagine handing out flyers, leaving my name and number in all the local shops. I try to quell the thought. It would hardly be appropriate to launch a missing-person campaign for a girl who is only missing from our lives.

At the top of the hill, I stop by the corner shop. There isn't much on the shelves and what there is has been pushed toward the back, giving a look that is more postapocalyptic than minimalist. I pick up one of the two bottles of sparkling water and wonder just how long it has been there. The man behind the counter slides off his stool to serve me, and I hear his knee click as he stands.

"Sixty pence, please."

I hand over the cash and bring out my phone at the same time.

"Could I ask you something?" I continue before he has a chance to stop me. "Have you seen this girl? Eleanor, or Ellie, Nell maybe? She's my daughter? We lost touch." I am struck at once by the gravity of what I have just admitted and, at the same time, its sheer understatement.

"Pass it here." He sits back down and produces a pair

of glasses from behind the cigarette cabinet. He tucks them behind his ears and keeps one finger on the bridge, bent badly out of shape, as he zooms in on the image of Eleanor. I can feel my heart rate quicken as he zooms in. Clearly he has been here before.

"Yes."

I gulp, and my tongue sticks momentarily to the roof of my mouth, thick and fuzzy from the sleepless night before.

"Here?"

"She comes in to buy stuff. Alcohol, cigarettes, pasta. She must live nearby."

"And is she by herself?"

"Usually. Sometimes with another girl."

I am unsure what else I can ask but am anxious about losing this sole link to Eleanor. My link to finding her again. The bell above the door rings to announce another customer, and I realize that my time is running out. He senses it too and leans forward over the counter, one elbow propped against the chewing-gum stand.

"Look, I'm a father too. I know how we worry, even when they fly the nest." His other hand reappears. In it there is a worn A5 notebook with a pencil dangling from the bottom. He opens it at the page marked by the string and begins to run his index finger through the faintly marked lines. "What did you say her surname was?"

"Hobbs." I hope she hasn't renounced that too.

"I shouldn't be doing this," he mumbles, "but we worry. Being a parent—worry, worry, worry."

I smile weakly, aware that the next customer has just begun queuing behind me.

"Here she is—Nell Hobbs. She keeps a tab."

For a second, I am confused by what sort of shopkeeper allows students to keep a tab. I quickly suppress that thought; I couldn't be more grateful that he does.

"Take a picture of the address. Can't say it's a real one, or that she's still there, but it's worth a try."

I do as I'm told, overcome with a sudden urge to reach across the counter and hug him.

"Thank you. Thank you so much."

"On the house." He slides a Mars bar toward me. "Good luck."

The address isn't far, thankfully. There is something rather grand in the long, luxurious vowels of Albemarle Street that its appearance doesn't live up to. The wheelie bins cluster together, some still standing, their lids blown open, while others have fallen, spilling their innards on the pavement like a group of neighborhood drunks on the way home from a night out. In front of most of the houses there is a collection of junk—a discarded mattress here, a TV with a punched-in screen there, a microwave with the cable ripped out, a jagged hole in the plastic casing at the back. I try not to think how much force that would have taken.

Number 174 is at the end of the terrace. The grass could do with a mow and the patches where the moss hasn't taken hold grow wild and unruly, catching crisp packets and cider cans. I feel I could learn a heck of a lot more about Eleanor's diet from her front lawn than from the number of meals she has endured with us this past year.

A twitch in the lace curtains on the second floor registers in the corner of my eye. I have been so fixated on tracking down Eleanor that I haven't given any thought to what I will say. One hundred and fifty miles is a long way to come just to extend an invitation to enjoy a bone-dry turkey and a series of increasingly tenuous cracker jokes. I suddenly realize I have left the heater in the boot of the car.

"Dad?"

It is not so much a greeting as an accusation. I step up the path and see that she hasn't taken the chain off. I don't imagine I will be asked to stay for tea.

"Eleanor, hi! How are you?" I inch closer, hoping I haven't come all this way to have the door slammed in my face.

"How did you find me?" Eleanor is clearly shocked, but there is some other emotion at play beneath that that I can't quite put my finger on. Before I can work it out, she pulls her sleeves down over her palms, wraps her hands inside her sweater. I have seen her do that a hundred times before: as a child getting chilly at the bus stop, as an adolescent increasingly on edge.

"Oh, you know, that degree does come in handy." Perhaps not a time to be joking. She seems distracted, distant. "Look, darling, I have some things from Mum in the car. I can go and fetch them—"

The words are barely out of my mouth before I am cut off.

"No. No. I'll come with you."

The door clicks shut, and I can hear the snatch of keys behind it, a vague call up the stairs. A minute later and Eleanor emerges. She isn't wearing a coat, but I restrain the urge to say anything. I offer her my scarf instead and flush warm with delight when she accepts. For the first time in a long time, I feel like a father again. Providing. Being acknowledged by my child as something more than a nuisance. Maybe it isn't too late to get us back on track?

I walk slowly, trying to eke out the journey back to the car. I'd walk to the end of the earth barefoot if it would buy me more time with her.

"So, Ellie, how is uni going?"

"Fine, yeah, well, I suppose." I try to catch her eye, but she resolutely avoids meeting my gaze. Instead, she looks down at her battered trainers, a nineties trend I could have sworn had gone out of fashion, only to boomerang back with an extortionate price hike a decade later.

"And you're living here now?" I try out a tone I hope is encouraging rather than judgmental.

"Yeah, suits me better, I've got some friends here. Different unis." Her voice is quiet and it quivers slightly, as if getting the words out is a strain in itself.

"Well, that's great, Ellie. I remember that I didn't make any friends my first year at university." I can sense the silence about to settle. "And the first term must nearly be over now?"

Eleanor nods. She is smart enough to know where this is going.

"So, we'll be seeing you at Christmas then, I hope?" We've reached the car and have come to a halt. "Your mother would love to see you, Edie too. And me." I am standing with my back to the driver's door, as if I am terrified Eleanor will hop in and zoom off forever, license or no license.

"I'll see." Eleanor is still analyzing her trainers, and her hair hangs forward, a mess of curls and the odd matted knot, obscuring her face. Looking at her straight on, I am struck by how much she seems to have shrunk, her tracksuit bottoms hanging off her as though she is a child playing clandestine dress-up in her parents' clothes.

"Eleanor, please." I reach out and tilt up her chin. I expect her to flinch the same way she had the morning after the dinner party and every time I'd tried to hold her since. Nothing. There is something so infinitely re-assuring in that brief moment of touch. I want to bundle her in my arms and never let her out of my sight again. I cannot tell if I am imagining it or if it really does seem that, for a split second, she might throw herself against my chest of her own accord. Every muscle in her body seems to have been pulled tight in the effort to keep her distance.

Eventually, I step back, wary of pressing my luck. Her eyes seem larger, the sockets scooped out in purple hollows. Tears are brewing. Quickly, she draws up a sleeve, looped loosely over her hand, to blot them away. In the ferocity of the motion, the misshapen fabric

182 · ABBIE GREAVES

gapes, and the inside of her wrist, feather thin, escapes. Red raw against the translucent skin is a network of interlocking scars. Among them, her radial artery pulses short and shallow.

Eleanor realizes what has happened and pulls her jumper down in a flash. I am left staring at her worn sleeve ends like a child bereft at the end of a magic show. *What the hell was that?*

"You ought to get going." Gone is the tenderness of a moment before. Eleanor straightens up, all the time keeping her hands balled into fists so tight that her nails must be cutting into the flesh beneath.

"Eleanor?"

"Please, Dad."

Do you know what, Mags? Eleanor didn't even stay to wave goodbye. She walked off there and then. No momentary bend of her head for a goodbye kiss. Not a single glance over her shoulder. It is always the smallest things that cut the deepest, the splinters that wriggle their way so far into the wound that you have no chance of removing them.

I am a mile onto the motorway when I start crying. I pull over at the first services and squash your bag of gifts into the nearest bin. The plug on the heater falls out of the cheap cotton tote, and its plastic casing chips against the metal can. None of this can fix it; not a visit or a vest or whatever other token of our endless devotion. She needs more. She needs help. The sort of help parents can't provide.

And that is when it hits me. I could lose her, that part of my heart I never knew I had or would be lucky enough to find. That tiny ball of cells—yours and mine—that had given my life a whole new meaning.

With new resolve, I fumble for my phone in my jeans pocket, my hands clawed from the cold. I open the search engine, type in *self-harm* (give or take a few rogue letters), and find the NHS site. I manage to copy the link into my thread with Eleanor. I check once, twice, three times that this is going to Eleanor, not you. Underneath I type: Please, I love you.

I should have told you, Mags—what I saw, how I felt. I didn't have the words. But even if I had? What good would that have done? What use would they have been? I had to protect you too.

Even now the words still aren't enough.

Chapter 13

I am woken by firm pressure on my shoulder.

"Hey, Frank, you're drifting off," Daisy says, stepping back from me and heading to adjust the drip on Maggie's left arm.

"Shit. What time is it?"

"Seven in the morning."

"Shit."

"Hey, hey, now, don't be so hard on yourself. It's tiring, all this. You've been here three nights now. It's your body crying out for a break. But I thought you'd want more time before . . . well . . . before Dr. Singh gets back."

So, Daisy knows too. Half the hospital must be peering in at the man on this most borrowed time.

"He told you."

"Hmm." Daisy releases a small, closed-mouthed hum that gives nothing away. The answer is written in her inability to look me straight in the eye.

"How long before he gets here?"

"He's usually in at nine, but I can try to stall him a bit longer."

"Thanks, Daisy."

"Not a problem."

It is all too much to take in. I slump forward into my palms, raking my fingers through the little hair that, miraculously, has not yet receded at my temples. Two hours before the doctor is back. Two hours before I need to make a decision on what happens to Maggie.

"That story of yours, whatever you had to tell her, wrap it up. You've got this, Frank." Daisy waits to see that I am sitting up, not at risk of dropping off again, and then heads out the door.

I force myself to stand up and shake my arms out. Two hours. That's all I have left. A lifetime together, and now we are teetering on the final meters of the tightrope of time. *How have I not managed to spit it out yet?* In the darkness, I bump heavily into the hard plastic edge of the bed frame and swear under my breath. Even after nearly four days, I still find it hard to comprehend that Maggie isn't asleep, that she won't wake up any minute at the slightest of noises.

"Looks like my time is running out here, Mags." I attempt a chuckle that comes out more macabre than I had intended. "We never did talk about this, did we?" I gesture at the room, the panoply of humming machines, the sanitizers affixed to the walls. What difference would it have made, anyway?

"I'm going to fight for you, Maggie. Even if you think you are done. We can't leave it how it is."

I wish I could open Maggie's eyes, to see if there is some belief in there, if she can still find it in herself to trust me. The cardiac monitor on her left side beeps the hour, and a new bar of readings begins.

"I'm sorry, Maggie, but we can't leave it here. I've been in pieces over this. I opened my mouth to say it a million times, and God knows you must have noticed. I thought maybe once the shock had worn off it would be easier. But that never happened. It just got harder and harder, Mags. I told myself I had time to find the right way to say it. I wanted a way to tell you the truth without risking you leaving me . . ."

My voice breaks into the short, shallow heaves that signal I am about to cry. How I haven't done so more is a miracle in itself. Only I can't afford to lose this time. I try to slow my breathing and shake my head, my neck stiff from three nights on a camp bed.

"They'll be here soon, the doctors, and they want to talk to me, about decisions and next steps, and whatever they are, Maggie, I need to tell you this now . . . About . . . the silence, about why. Just please, Mags, remember I'm sorry.

"Please come back to me."

I spent the whole drive back considering what I could tell you. Did I admit to having seen Eleanor? Or say I had missed her at lectures, that I had left a note? I had already resolved to lie. I'm sorry to say this, but if I'm honest, I never even thought of it that way. Not even as a white lie. It was to protect you, when you needed it the most. And hadn't I promised that to you, in the registry office, the two of us shivering in our cheap garments, no idea how the vows would pan out?

Thankfully, Eleanor had already come to my assistance. You were at the front door before I'd had so much as a chance to lock the car.

"Evening!"

"What's all this for?" I am delirious with confusion. The events of the day flash before me: the latch on the door; Eleanor's rush to pull down her sleeves and get me out of there; how close I came to collapsing at the service-station forecourt; how close this all was to falling apart.

"She called!"

I try not to show my shock. Fortunately, you are too delighted, too relieved, to notice. You have already headed back into the kitchen to stir whatever is bubbling on the hob.

"She said how good it was to see you and that she has moved." I open my mouth to answer but you are off again. "That she's sorry she hasn't replied to us, but the signal is very patchy there." I think of the full signal bars I'd had on my phone; how quickly the satnav had loaded. Clearly Eleanor had resolved to be creative with the truth too.

You are out of sight from the stairs where I am sitting, busy doing battle with a knot in my shoelace. There is a giddiness in your voice that I haven't heard in months, years maybe. I am terrified of how quickly this could be extinguished by just one wrong move on my part.

"So, how did you find her—if she's moved?"

I am glad I am far enough away for you not to see the panic flit across my face, my cheeks flushing and my mouth dry as I spit out the first explanation that comes to mind.

"The girl in her room."

"What about her?"

"She was very helpful. She was a friend . . . She gave me the address."

"Lucky she was in then, eh?"

"Quite."

"And we talked about Christmas, but she's away with friends. Did you meet them? Frank?"

"Oh, sorry, Mags. Just give me a second." I wiggle my foot free and head over, pretending to look at what is for supper. I cannot meet your eye.

"So, what were they like, Eleanor's friends? The ones she's living with?"

"I didn't speak much to them, really."

"Oh." You look crestfallen. I have burst your bubble, unwittingly, and feel myself scrabbling to contain the damage, using reserves of energy I thought I had long since spent, somewhere off the M5.

"You know what she's like—'Dad, stay in the car!' 'Don't say anything!' Really, I'm used to it." I wrap my arms around your waist and nuzzle into the curve of your shoulder. "The house looks spacious. I suppose she wanted a bit more freedom than halls. They do all rather live on top of each other there."

"And she looked well?" You spin round to face me,

and I can feel your eyes boring into mine, as if you will find Eleanor's reflection in there, just so long as you look hard enough.

"Yes, same old, same old. A little tired, but . . . that's freshers' term for you, I suppose."

I bend down to kiss you, and for the first time in years I close my eyes as I do so. I don't know what they will give away.

Eleanor had averted danger once, but regular service soon resumed. We were being cut off, slowly but surely; we knew as much even if we couldn't bring ourselves to admit it out loud. Do you remember when she was little, just toddling, and we wouldn't have a second to ourselves? The minute we were out of the room, to the kitchen, to the bathroom, she would be stomping after whichever one of us it was, dragging Jeffrey the bear behind her. I would have done anything to have that back, Mags. That closeness. That connection. That sense she still wanted us. Looking back now, I feel so selfish for wishing she would grow up faster, so we could have a second of peace and quiet. When she did, I couldn't be at peace without her.

She called sporadically, although there was so much silence on the line that I often wondered why she bothered. Was she reaching out, do you think? In some long-winded way? We would ask, in turn, as the phone passed between us, *Are you sure you are OK? You can always come down here for a weekend, you know that, don't you? I'll drive you back as well . . . Here, talk to your mum, darling.* With every stream of fabricated engagements that would stymie our attempts to visit, I could see the way you cradled the phone with such tenderness, cupping the plastic with both hands as if you were holding Eleanor as a new-born all over again.

When she did return home in those first two years of university, we never received much warning. Sometimes Eleanor would ring for a lift from the station; other times there would just be a ring on the doorbell. That was the cruelest part, the not-knowing. I couldn't bear to watch the way your face would light up at every unexpected call, the hope in your eyes, the way you would take a deep breath as if to open up the chamber of your heart to create just that little bit more space for love. I can imagine only too well what debilitating disappointment greeted the double-glazing salesmen and Jehovah's Witnesses in our neighborhood.

In the November of Eleanor's third year, salvation came early. It must have been the first week, as there was a strong smell of bonfire in the air. Either next door was feeling festive or they had a lot of evidence in need of urgent disposal. We nearly didn't hear the doorbell over the sound of fireworks from the park down the road.

"Frank! That's the door!" You are surrounded by piles of bills and the file boxes from which they emerged. The shredder burbles at your feet. "Frank!"

I don't need to ask what the urgency is. We have been living with it for years.

"Yes, yes, I'm going. Calm down!"

Even with my reading glasses I can see it is Eleanor. It is her size, her restless shuffling from one foot to another, the fact that her finger is poised to ring the bell again but hovers just an inch away.

"Eleanor! You're home."

It's been over three months since I last saw her. She was here for a night in July, visiting friends before heading back up to Manchester, where she had a summer job. She arrived late, left early. Like every visit since she left for university, it was so short that it was impossible to draw anything out of her. Nothing important, at least.

Maybe it is the arrival of winter, but the Eleanor on the doorstep now is the palest I have ever seen her, positively ashen, all the color drawn out of her. As if to compensate, there is a swipe of cherry-red lipstick across her mouth. I wonder if she did it on the bus; the blurred edges don't quite match up with the pale curves of her own lips, and there is a smudge on the bottom of her top left tooth. It doesn't do much to distract from her pallor.

"Yeah, I'm back. That OK?" Eleanor looks down at her feet, kicks the front step. For a second, I am overwhelmed with a desire to tell her off, to remind her that we didn't pay for scuffed shoes. That part of parenting never disappears, does it, Mags?

"Yes, of course, Ellie, come on in." I reach out to take the duffel bag that she is struggling to manage with both hands. She is wearing fingerless gloves that seem to accentuate just how little flesh there is. Her hands give a slight tremor as she passes her bag over. As she steps inside, I see her eyes flick, almost imperceptibly, over her shoulder. I wonder who might be outside. I wonder if this has become a habit too.

Eleanor barely reaches the hallway before you are out, released from the burden of household bureaucracy and bundling her into your arms. She doesn't reciprocate. Not obviously, anyway, not with arms outstretched or by leaning into your neck. She doesn't shrink back, though, and I feel the relief course through me.

Over dinner, I am grateful at how you manage to carry the conversation, to generate some sort of flow with even the most reluctant conversationalists. I find myself looking for signs that things are on the up, that what I had seen was a one-off. I stare so hard at her sleeves that a pain starts up behind my eyeballs.

"So, Ellie, do you know how long you will be staying?" I have always been one for absolutes, as well you know.

"Frank! What a question to ask! Eleanor has barely arrived."

"Not that we don't want you here," I scramble, trying to fight against the tension that is encroaching around the table. "You know you can always stay as long as you want. It's just so we can make plans, maybe take some time off?" I meet your gaze and am glad to see that you are smiling again, nodding.

Eleanor is pushing the carrots around her plate, and I am reminded of how she used to hide her vegetables under her knife and fork as a child, lining the sweetcorn up in two perfectly straight columns just to get down from the table.

"Any idea, Ellie?"

"I was thinking a few weeks."

In the corner of my eye I see you flush—with delight? Fear? I can't tell.

"Oh, Eleanor, that would be marvelous." You are overcompensating, reaching over to touch her as if to check that this is for real.

"What about your cour—"

"I'm sure you need a break from all that hard work."
I am not sure you have ever cut me off with such decision before or since.

"Thanks, Mum," Eleanor mumbles, stretching out her hand toward yours.

That night, when we are as sure as we can be that Eleanor is asleep, you finish my question for me.

"What about her course? About university?"

Even though we have gone months without seeing her, you still meticulously mark her term dates in our three-way family calendar, the sparsity of entries in the Eleanor column only serving to remind us of how close the hinges on our triptych are to falling clean off. I roll onto my side to face you and brush the stray hairs out of your eyes.

"Let's take each day as it comes." I am close enough to feel your breath warm my collarbones. Your bottom lip quivers, and I stretch my neck to kiss you, to still you.

The days themselves were stilted; the more we reached out, the more she pulled away. I mentioned it once—what I had seen, up in Manchester. I asked if she had spoken to someone, like I'd suggested. She told me she had. There was a free service up at the university. It was fine. She had sorted it. It was all in the past. The whole time she was speaking, she was fiddling with the tassel on a cushion, twirling it endlessly around her index finger. She didn't meet my eye. Now, after everything that has happened, I wish I had pushed more. Pulled up her sleeves, demanded some incontrovertible proof that this wasn't just another way to get us off her back. But then? I was just grateful to have her home for more than twelve hours. I returned to the living room and our own round of family charades: Eleanor in her room, door closed, pretending to work, us downstairs, door open, pretending to read, alert to her every movement.

In the end, Eleanor barely made it through five nights. She left before supper on the sixth day, which I could see killed you. When I returned from the station, the stroganoff was in the bin and you were in bed. I crawled under the duvet, fully clothed, my shoes still on. You buried your head in its spot, pressing your ear against the coarse wool of my jumper.

"What if she gets hungry?"

I was too late to save your bottom lip that time.

I had long suspected Eleanor's studies had fallen by the wayside, but somehow I couldn't bring myself to voice my concerns, not even to you. Still, when, shortly after her abrupt departure, Eleanor texted to let you know she would be deferring her final year, getting some "real-world experience," it took a feat of willpower for me not to phone her and tell her in no uncertain terms that it was a terrible, terrible idea. Not that she would have picked up, I suppose.

It killed me, Mags. That. It wasn't about the money, how it looked to other people. It was her bright brain, all those stellar school reports—*Top of the class! Firing on all cylinders!*—the intelligent questions and the curiosity and our evenings on the patio discussing why everything was the way it was. It was the last dregs of all this pouring down the drain.

When I held her that first time, her tiny, wrinkled fist clutched around my index finger, all I saw was potential. She could be anyone, do anything. I told myself I would do anything in my power to make that possible.

And now? I had no idea if any of this was salvageable. While I agonized over what else we could do, you replied by text and told her that we supported her "no matter what." I wasn't consulted on that. I don't blame you—finding the right words never has been my specialty.

From then onward, there was even less regularity to when we saw Eleanor. We discussed an intervention. Multiple times. At first it felt so farcical saying that word, in the kitchen, hushed over supper, or sitting side by side on the sofa, cowering behind the *Radio Times*.

That's denial for you. And once we broke through that and accepted it as our only option? There must have been half a dozen occasions when we had steeled ourselves for it, only for our resolve to go out the window the moment Eleanor appeared on our doorstep, both of us desperate to hold her and touch her and confirm in her physical form—the shredded jumper, the messy hair—that yes, she was still among us. Distant, different, yes, but still there.

Eleanor's twenty-first birthday came and went without fanfare. It was the August after she should have graduated and she was still in Manchester, cagey about the work she was doing. Something in an office, answering phones, admin, "that kind of thing." We sent a present, a necklace consisting of a fine chain and a slim disc of gold. We'd had her initials engraved on it, along with her birthdate. On the back, *Love always, Mum & Dad.* You had gone to all the trouble of getting the package tracked, insisting on sending it first class. A week later, the parcel came back. The recipient was no longer at that address.

I remember the first time Eleanor came home on a comedown. Or the first time it was obvious, at least. It was only two months later, and the necklace was still in its navy cushioned box on your bedside table, the packaging long since crushed at the bottom of the bin. She arrived just after supper when you were in the bath. God, I was grateful for how long you spent in there then, Mags. You didn't need to see Eleanor like that, really you didn't.

Her nose and eyes were streaming, which she blamed on the pollen, even though it was October and the pollen index must have been on the floor. Her pupils were large, like an owl's, glazed and lost. There was a slick of moisture across her forehead, the sort you get with a fever, only she hadn't mentioned she felt sick. Before you went to bed, you cranked the heating to high, and still she was shivering as I watched her from the living-room door.

"It's good to see you, Ellie," I say to her back as she fiddles with the remote. "How are you feeling?"

"Fine."

She doesn't turn round, so I go to sit on the armchair, forcing myself into her eyeline.

"But, Ells, you don't look it." I steel myself. "What have you taken?"

"Does it matter?"

"Yes, Eleanor, there is nothing that matters to me more."

Eleanor turns off the TV and, briefly, meets my eye.

"I'm an adult now."

"I know. It doesn't mean we don't care."

"I can do what I want." Eleanor's eyes flare. She's prickly. Instinctively, I want to back off, but I've already got this far.

"Yes, but your mum and I worry about you constantly. We want to help."

Eleanor looks as if she is about to speak, only it's a yawn that comes out, the sort that seems to reset her jaw and looks as if it could swallow me whole.

"Eleanor, please. What can we do? We can get you help. You can stay here as long as you want. We can . . ." I am exhausting my store of ideas, all of which seem vaguer out in the open than they did in my head.

There is a silence and then—"It's my life, right?"

I nod because, well, she is right, isn't she?

Eleanor leans forward on the sofa and begins to thumb one of the array of cacti that sit on the coffee table, testing her pain threshold on one with long, thin spines. That particular specimen has lasted since one of our earliest dates together. I try to channel some of its tenacity.

"So, I can lead it how I choose."

"Eleanor—not like this!" The last word comes out as a hiss. I am wary of disturbing you, of you coming back down and facing a scene. "Please, Eleanor, we love you."

The trump card. The one I'd hoped was so blindingly obvious I wouldn't need to play it.

"I know you do. I don't deserve it. I'm bad. I messed up. I'm not what you wanted from your only child. I know all that."

"That isn't what I meant at all." I reach to touch her arm, just above the elbow. Under my palm, her whole bicep shakes, the muscles in spasm.

"We love you as you are. But we want you well again, Eleanor. What did we do wrong, huh? Just tell me so we can fix it. We would do anything for you." I am whispering, in fear of my own daughter. It is one thing to imagine you have a problem and quite another to have it confirmed.

"Nothing," Eleanor breathes, meeting my eye. "It's just me that went wrong."

I don't have the chance to ask more. Before I know it, she is on the move, snaking past me. For a second, she hovers by my side, close enough for me to reach out and touch the spot on her forehead where her baby hairs have never quite grown out. I am too scared to stand and kiss her there in case she bolts.

"Night, Dad."

The next day she was gone. You didn't even have the chance to give her the necklace.

After that, we began operating some sort of halfway house. Or at least that was how it felt to me, putting her up when she was between places, low on funds, high and erratic or suffering the aftereffects. I never knew how much you caught of the interactions between Eleanor and me, usually snatched during the moments when you would be taking a bath or popping to the shops for supplies.

She would never demand money, not in so many words, but the absence of overt pleading didn't stop it from feeling as if she did: "My rent is due and I'm short." "My phone broke." I never found the energy to query these things, preferring to save my energy for asking the important questions: "Are you OK, Eleanor? Do you want to talk?" She'd shake her head, numb, like a child rudely awoken from a nap. She was vanishing before us, Mags. The lights were out, and there was no one I recognized at home. All I wanted was to hear that she felt something, anything at all.

When I slipped crisp twenties into her hand, defeated and terrified by the thought of our daughter in need, evicted onto the streets, going hungry, I needn't have reminded her not to tell you; the notes had barely left my hand before they were folded and stuffed in her pockets. The worst of all? "The train fare wiped me out," as if visiting us was the real problem here.

Having seen what I'd seen—was it reckless of me? Maybe, Mags, but how do you turn away your only child coming to you in need? I like to think you would have done the same. The same instinct that compelled us to feed her when she cried out for it was now feeding her habit instead. I hoped it was a phase, for your sake, for hers, for my bank account. You tell yourself all manner of things to reconcile yourself to a bad decision. To keep that most invaluable part of you—your own genetic code—in your life, even in some diminishing form, you would do anything. You must know that too.

The whole time I was thinking: *This is not happening to me. This should be happening elsewhere, to someone else's family.* We had a comfortable home, an excess of love to give. How the hell had this happened? I judged myself, Mags. I should have taught her better, showed her the right path. Even when I thrashed one out for her, nothing would get through. The clinics, the meetings, the retreats—no-shows.

I suppose what I'm trying to say, Mags, is that we never knew with Eleanor. We spent five years after she dropped out of university without a clue—when we would see her, how long it would be until the next time. And in the meantime, we were just about keeping afloat, while Eleanor did what she had to do. That was the agreement, right? She had to hit rock bottom.

Because without it, in free fall, there was nothing to check her. She needed that jolt. That slamming realization that this had to stop. We would wait for as long as that took.

I began almost to welcome the moments when she would take her leave of us. I hated myself for that. But then I would see you crumpled there, in the hallway, pawing at the carpet on the spot where she had just been as if it could give you back more than your own daughter could, and I understood why—or I nearly did. My heart was being torn in two, and there was no adhesive I could find that was strong enough to close the fissure.

This isn't a justification for what I'm about to tell you, Maggie, for what I did. No, there is no justification for that. Trust me, I've tried to find one. I've been trying to tell you this all along—what I did, what made me close off . . .

They told me to go slowly; they said it would help you if I didn't just blurt it out. But I can't get out of it now, can I? I've avoided telling you for so long, and it's nearly killed you in the process. I never meant for this to happen, it's just that . . . Maggie? Maggie, darling, can you hear me?

A nail presses into my palm, a short, considered jab. Sharp enough to leave an indent.

"Help! Daisy!" I don't want to lose this moment, not when I have come so far. Not when the words, the very explanation of my silence, are dancing on the tip of my tongue. But I can't lose Maggie either. I hit the buzzer that winds down from the side of the bed two, three, four times in my panic and pray desperately that it works.

"Daisy! Help!"

Chapter 14

I hear her before I see her, outside the door, her rubber-soled shoes flapping against the floor like whips.

"Aye, Frank, I'm here, what is it?" Daisy looks at Maggie before she sees me, still hunched over the button as if it will blow at any second. She notices the quiver too. She pages for help and immediately sets about tapping at Maggie—her wrists, her feet, her neck. All of a sudden it is as if my contribution never mattered at all.

I always did say Maggie had a knack for timing. *How is this possible?* I needed, what, five more minutes? I wish I had just cut to it. I see my chance, fleeting, running off into the distance, too far away for me to gain back that ground. I can't say it here, not now, not with an audience. *Can I?*

"Daisy, what's the situation?"

A flurry of consultants arrive, headed by Dr. Singh, his white coat billowing out behind him. Daisy responds with an array of numbers—too high or too low or too alien for me to make any sense of them. After so long with just my own voice, the noise feels grotesque, ungainly in the small intensive-care room.

I stand up and back toward the window as they approach Maggie, brandishing an array of implements and devices in front of her like aggressive sellers in the final minutes of a flea market.

"Frank, she's gonna be OK, just like I said." Daisy has managed to extract herself from her colleagues and has moved so that she is partially blocking my view. "You've got to be strong for her when she comes round. She's going to need you."

"I haven't been, Daisy. I haven't been strong for her at all." It is all too much. The room, the people. I can feel the sob rising in my throat, and Daisy senses it too. Her sixth sense—compassion.

Daisy nods in the direction of the door. "We've got this. I'll take good care of her, I promise."

I don't move.

"You did your bit, Frank, but now you have to trust us. Come on." I don't want to leave, but I am being steered out. Daisy places her hand on the small of my back in an attempt to shepherd me toward the exit and away from the freight train of terminology speeding through the room.

"Daisy, I can't. I didn't finish. There's something I have to tell her. The one thing I came for—"

"You have to go. Really. Please, Frank, don't make this difficult for me." She is firmer now. I know I must look like a madman, blathering away, distracting necessary resources.

"I have to tell her why I stopped talk—"

"Frank, please, you can do this later. When she's well. Just give her a kiss goodbye; you'll see her again soon."

There isn't space in the wall of backs. *Can I even say it in front of an audience?* I can kid myself as much as I like, but deep down I know I am not that brave a man.

One of the nurses dashes out into the corridor, and I manage to slip into her space, right by Maggie's head. I bend down until I am almost squatting, my head level with hers. Both knees click, and I can see the doctor's attention turn toward me and his colleagues following suit. I press my lips against her cheek.

"I love you, Maggie."

His Silence

Chapter 1

It was Frank's text that set Edie off. From the empty spaces between his understatements, she knew instinctively what Maggie had done. She has known Maggie for even longer than Frank has, and for the last few months she has expected this. She tried to get through to Maggie, to them both, but it was impossible. The curtains were closed, the doors locked, and they never answered the bell. It reminded her of the pictures in her school history textbooks of the quarantine zones set up to contain cholera in the 1800s. But there is no sickness like that of a mother desperately trying to reach out to her only child.

At reception, she tells them she is Maggie's sister. A lie, but a forgivable one, if such a thing exists. She is directed down the intensive-care corridor, but they haven't given her a room number, assuming she must have it from another member of this most imaginary family. She sees a man with his head between his knees and is drawn to him like a moth to a dying flame.

She doesn't say a word when she reaches Frank. Instead she rubs her hand slowly up and down his back. It reminds him of what Maggie used to do, but there isn't the same comfort in that linear motion as there was in the perfect circles his wife would trace. After half an hour, maybe a little less, the nurse comes out with a blanket. It is the same one that Frank has slept with for the past three nights, but she has folded it so it is almost as good as new. Together they prop Frank up so he can rest his head on Edie's shoulder and his knees are free for the blanket. Every muscle of his body is trembling, even with the woolen covering.

In the doctor's office, the prognosis is directed at Edie, despite the fact that she has only just arrived. He apologizes for not being able to provide a full update earlier, but his attentions have been focused on stabilizing Mrs. Hobbs. Maggie is being woken, slowly, with the help of their catalogue of increasingly serious-looking technology. There will be a whole team of doctors continuing to work on her for the next twenty-four hours—visitors *strictly* prohibited, he's afraid—so they need to head home until the following afternoon at the very earliest. The period until then will be critical. Of course, if there is an urgent development, someone will call.

Edie has to drag Frank back to her car. He is like a child playing dead. It is as if the fight has gone out of him, but she doubts that can be true. Frank has always been ferociously loyal to Maggie. If there is anyone with the sheer force of devotion to safeguard a recovery, it is him.

At the house, Edie rummages in his pockets for the keys, which feels a rather obscene thing to be doing to your best friend's husband, even in the circumstances. She takes out his phone while she is at it so she can charge it and make sure he has no excuse for ignoring her calls and texts again. Once she has the door open, Frank finds his own way to the sitting room, his gait uneven, as if one leg has somehow shortened during his hospital stay.

Edie heads off to the freezer to find something she can reheat for him. Frank has always been skinny, one of those men who never quite fill out their beanpole teenage self, but now he is positively concave, every bone in his upper body jutting into her when he sat with his head on her shoulder in the hospital.

She sets a dish of nondescript casserole in front of him and offers to stay. She really means it. She is Maggie's friend, but she has always liked Frank. He was good enough for Maggie, perhaps too good, and she cannot stand to see him like this. No, he doesn't want the company. There is a mumbled thank-you and then he looks out the window so that Edie doesn't see him cry. This is not her cross to bear, much as she has tried to take some of the weight.

When Frank is alone, when he has heard the car door shut and seen the reversing lights flashing in the glass, he stands up and heads to the door. On the way, his eye is drawn to a photo of the three of them, in pride of place on the mantlepiece. In it, Eleanor is dressed as a dinosaur, a costume he'd bought for her fourth birthday. It was hot, and they all came home light-headed and rosy-hued. It feels like yesterday, so recent that, subconsciously, he reaches up to touch the back of his neck, as if there is a burn still radiating its heat.

It's all too much, and he turns the photo facedown. Frank stumbles through to the kitchen; he wanted to go in there the moment he arrived back, but it was something he had to do by himself. He is struck by how normal it looks, aside from the chairs strewn about in the paramedics' frenzied attempts to keep her alive. There is the usual tidy collection of food waste, a glass, an abandoned tea towel.

He takes the seat where he found Maggie, almost

expecting it still to be warm from her body, with all the will of a man entrenched in his habits and crazed with grief. He wants to relive her last moments here. He wants to know what she was thinking. Some of it he already knows, however much he has tried to suppress the thoughts—the feeling of having been let down, of being alone and desperate to speak to him. For some people, their pain is a space to retreat into; a slow-setting solitude away from everyone and everything else in life. For others, it is an itch that triggers a cease-less need to speak. If Maggie could just . . . could just have . . . verbalized it all—wouldn't that have offered some sliver of relief?

It is whilst Frank is lost in his reverie that his hands drift over the vinyl tablecloth. He picks up the brightly colored stone that is weighing down the bills. It is oddly familiar, but at first he can't quite place it. Then he turns it over in his palm; on the base the word MUM has been painted, the wobbly letters painstakingly drawn out in different sizes, a faded pencil guide beneath. It is enough to sear, and he drops it back on the papers, instead running his fingertips across the red leather planner that has been sitting on the table ever since they bought it together over a decade ago, in a tiny stationer's shop in Paris on one of the rare trips abroad that they took, just the two of them, after Eleanor was born.

It is a beautiful book, even for a man with no head for aesthetics. In the main, it is a journal, thick A5 pages with faint lines like the sort snails leave on the paving stones after the rain. On the right, there is a narrow section for lists, barely three inches wide. At the recommendation of the shopkeeper, who took himself terribly seriously, they'd had Maggie's initials embossed on the front, even though it had felt like an indulgence.

Frank has never been nosy. What would be the need? He just wants to feel the last thing her hands held. Prior to this week, the planner has only ever been used for perfunctory household matters. Lists, mainly, the odd page torn out to leave a note for whoever had come to fix the sink. He opens the book, expecting to see the last shopping list. Instead he sees his name. He shuts his eyes and opens them again, blinks heavily a few times, like they instruct you to do at the optician's. A bead of sweat drops from his forehead into his eye. He rubs it, blinks, looks again.

Frank.

She wouldn't leave without saying goodbye. Why had he ever thought that was a possibility? Perhaps because he hasn't had a chance to think, besides keeping Maggie alive, that's why.

Frank.

Those five little letters should bring relief, but in

reality all Frank feels is panic. He has spent the best part of half a year dwelling on what he has to say. In the churning cesspit of his mind he has managed to forget that maybe, just maybe, Maggie had something to say too.

Something every bit as urgent.

He begins to read.

Seven days to go

Frank, how long do you think it would take you to realize I wasn't speaking to you? You never have been the most observant man on the planet, so, what, say a day? Two, tops, if you were engrossed in some particularly important project, I'd say.

It took me a week, if I remember correctly. I had an inkling before then, sure, but that was when I knew for definite. Quite remarkable, huh? Then again, no one has ever described you as verbose, nothing even close, and after forty years of marriage, there is so very little that requires us to speak. I know you by heart. Better than the back of my hand—silly phrase that, anyway. Some days I feel as if we have spent decades rehearsing a day-to-day dance that we perform, each action and decision and movement honed to perfection.

I suppose that says a lot about what happened

to our relationship, when Eleanor began to spiral. I often wonder whether, if we had spoken more when it started, when we began to realize this wasn't a phase, that it was something deeper and darker and so much more unsettling, we could have avoided all this. On the other hand, I of all people know that it is so much easier not to speak about something than it is to tackle it head on. Is that what you are doing now, Frank? Is it?

The day I clocked that you weren't speaking to me, I told myself I would give you six months. It was after Edie had been round and, instead of making our supper, I took every last item in the fridge and smashed them all on the tiles at my feet. When you found me, sodden with sauce, mid-destruction mission, I screamed at you. You can't have forgotten that.

Why? Why? Why won't you speak to me?

It was the first time I verbalized it.

Why?

I hated myself for wailing. I never wanted to be that wife. The shrill harpy with the nagging and the whining. I hated myself so much for that, but I couldn't hold it in.

Why?

Something about the noise managed to hurt my
ears after a week in the quiet.

Why?

How many times did I ask that? Ten? Twenty?
And each time—nothing from you. Not verbally, at
least.

You ran me a bath, silently. I sat on the edge of
the tub, watching as you tested the temperature with
your fingertips and fiddled with the tap accordingly.
I studied every motion in your wrist and the way
your eyes wouldn't move from the flow. I wanted a
clue. Did this go beyond the obvious? If not, what
the hell was it, Frank? I couldn't stand to have you
retreat from me too.

You dried me off, and I felt myself go limp in
your arms. I was so exhausted, by everything, and
I thought that I had finished myself off with my
outburst. Then, when you tucked me into bed, I
found just enough energy to grab for your hand.
You always did say that I never ceased to surprise
you. I hoped I could get through to you then, that I
could press my message into your palm somewhere
between your heart line and your lifeline.

It was so tender, holding hands like that, and
so like the old days when things were happier and

easier that I began to cry. I cried so much that I
was sick, right on the pillowcase. I couldn't move
to change it. You came round to my side of the bed,
propped my head up with one arm, and disposed of
the wet bedding with the other. I thought you might
say something then. *Don't,* perhaps. Even being
chided like a child would have been better than
nothing.

Silence. With your arms around me, I told myself
I would give you six months to find your voice.
That would be enough, surely. In the face of forty
years of marriage, what is six months? The blink
of an eye. A long, torturous, stinging blink. But a
blink nonetheless. And if six months wasn't enough?
Well, I didn't think I would have to deal with that
possibility.

And yet here we are. Five months, three weeks,
and still nothing. I can't do this anymore. I said
I would never leave you; I must have said that a
thousand times over the course of our marriage. I
meant it every time. But I never imagined it would
come to this.

Now we are into my last week, the last seven
days I promised myself, and I know that I cannot
go without leaving a clean slate. Or the cleanest one
I can manage under these conditions. If you won't

reach out to me, I can still find a way of reaching out to you.

There is so much I always meant to tell you but somehow never could—my confessions, Frank, if you will. These are my secrets, everything I couldn't say over the course of our married life. There are reasons why I didn't tell you at the time, you'll see that, but if it boils down to just one thing, it is this: I didn't want to lose you. I don't want to leave you now either, but it's better this way.

I hope you can absolve me with that huge heart of yours. If not, then at least you can see how much I loved you, with everything that I am.

Chapter 2

F rank's hands are trembling. His fingers are beginning to cramp from holding the book so close to his face. He doesn't trust his varifocals, not at the best of times, and this certainly does not constitute one of those.

For ten years, since they came back from Paris, he has never so much as looked in that book. He assumed Maggie was using it for household matters, and that was never his domain. Not that he thought he was better than that; it was just that Maggie handled all those matters so efficiently, without the clowning Frank always seemed to bring to everyday tasks.

Now he could curse his own maddening obliviousness. What if he had looked in the book earlier? If he had caught her writing in it last week instead of trying to numb his brain with computer chess or the fiendish sudoku? Things would be very different indeed. There's no doubt of that. He would have flushed every last pill and razor and blade down the toilet and not slept a wink. He would not have taken his eyes off her, not even for a second.

He traces his fingertips over her script, so small, so neat. He imagines he can feel her fingers there. Tiny, fragile little things, in recent months the nails bitten down so short that the flesh had grown like protective roofs above the stubs. Slowly, he gets onto his feet and heads up to their bedroom with the red leather planner in his hands. He cradles it like a baby, though it is a long time since he has had one of those.

After forty years, he'd felt he had finally come close to pinning Maggie down—her contradictions, her contrariness, her shifting moods—the result of some random biochemical generator that he had invested decades of research into. And now? *Confessions.* He feels that the equipment was faulty and not a single piece of it has given readings that go into quite enough depth. Everything will need recalibrating.

He knows he is not the man to talk. His hypocrisy is shameful. He thought he was the only one with a secret, its bulk so heavy he has been unable to think of anything else. His mind flashes back to the moment at her bedside when he came so close to finally admitting what he'd done, how he had let his family down. His hand shaking on the white sheet, his eyes fixed just above Maggie's oxygen mask for any sign that she was registering what he was about to say. *Maggie?*

Six days to go
So where were we, Frank? My confessions, yes.
It sounds so terribly Catholic, doesn't it? I've
never really flirted with religion. In fact, that
was something that drew me to you. You had no
need for higher powers, just facts and reason.
Solid ground for me to stand on—stability, at last!
Solid ground for a marriage too. Or so you would
think. That said, I have always liked the idea of
the confessional; some kindly, balding priest on the
other side of the screen, primed and ready to wipe it
all away with just a few incantations and a donation
to the charity tin. I am not sure this will be so easy.
   I am, unfortunately, a serial liar. It's not nice
to write, harder yet to live with. Did you notice,
Frank? Did you? Part of me hopes so, so this
won't be as much of a shock. Part of me hopes not,
otherwise my deceits have been in vain. Either way
you will be disappointed and I can never stand to see

that, in me of all people.

I'm not proud of the way I am, but I am proud
of the relationship we have had, and I'm afraid that
my lies have been a part of that. I always see our
marriage like a bike chain, looping through the
years in smooth, predictable circles. But with age
come sticking points, and sometimes a little lie is
all it takes to oil the mechanism and keep the whole
show on the road.

Why? That's the crucial question, of course. I
would trace it back to my mother. I can imagine
you reading this, your eyes rolling up to the ceiling
the way they always did when I mentioned her.
You blamed her for a lot, and for a lot that was fair.
But if there is a straightforward pattern of passing
blame from mother to daughter, down through the
generations, where does that leave me with Eleanor?
Responsible. That's where.

But, first things first: back to my mother.
You never liked her, that was clear. Not when
she came to stay, not when she phoned. Not even
when she wasn't in contact for months on end.
But me? I didn't hate her. I tried once, but it was
so unsustainable. She frustrated me, baited me,
irritated me to the point that I would avoid her calls

for weeks on end, but still I didn't hate her. I only hated what I had inherited from her—that subtle, utterly undetectable ability to lie.

In all our years together, I never found a way to explain that all my earliest memories of my mother are of her with other men. I didn't want you to judge her. You already did, so harshly, and she was my mother—do you know how much that hurt me? I don't judge her for that. Not really. My father was never there, always working, and that was a relief. When he was home, no one could relax. Not so much treading on eggshells as marching barefoot on glass.

"What have you been up to today then, Margot?" he would ask over supper.

"Mum made us stay in because she had friends round."

"Oh really . . . Anyone you knew?"

My mother was never quicker than when she was interrupting me.

"Anna and her sister—one of their friends."

The minute my father looked down at his plate she would shoot me a look that said I was better seen and not heard. Disaster averted. Until the next time, of course.

After that, it never crossed my mind to tell him

the truth about the stream of uncles who would
pass through the house bearing gifts and no genetic
relation to us at all. I suppose you could say lying
became second nature. It became my preservation
technique. Not so much for myself but for those
I loved more than myself. And I'm afraid you fell
perfectly into that category, Frank. I told myself I
would never be like that.

And then one of the first things I ever told
you—a lie. Fresh out of my mouth before I had a
chance to haul the words back . . .

As a husband, Frank has always felt that he has been
winging it. There isn't an instruction manual, more's the
pity, and his own father had passed away by the time he
really needed his advice on longevity, what it takes to
keep the show on the road beyond the early, easier years.
Frank assumed there were basic tenets for a successful
marriage: don't take your spouse for granted, be kind,
be honest. In fact, he should rearrange that. Surely honesty is the first rule.

If Maggie started out with a lie, what else can't he
trust? It is true, at least, that he never liked her mother.
He knows a little about Maggie's childhood, although it
was always like pulling teeth, trying to get her to go into
any real detail on the subject, however much he asked.

He knows that her mother left the family for another man the moment she thought the children could look after themselves, although Maggie—at thirteen—had begged to disagree. He can't say he ever made much progress with his mother-in-law. She would never answer a straight question, though was fond of putting everyone else on the spot. An avoider. He should know. Frank winds back over the six long months when he tried so desperately to keep hold of Maggie, evading the truth of what he had done by not speaking at all—

Frank is jolted out of his reminiscence by a sharp prick in his thumb where he has been resting it too hard on the paper. He looks down at the thin line of red now trailing along the bottom edges of the book. Maggie would be appalled—she was so attached to this planner, even before she repurposed it. He blots his hand against his shirt and watches as one drop spills out, spreading its liquid contents and weaving its way into the tiny, almost imperceptible cotton fibers. Just like a lie, he thinks, reaching out so much further than first thought.

One of the first things I ever told you—a lie.

Frank tells himself that if he was a good husband, he would have some inkling of what that was. In reality, he has no idea. Something about his outfit? A commentary on what he had planned for their first date? He twists the bedside lamp so it shines more fully on the planner.

He'll have to find out the hard way.

Six days to go

I never should have gone on that first date with you, Frank. It wasn't right or fair.

Why? Well, I was attached. Quite seriously— two years in with Guy and all eyes fixed on my ring finger. When I first bumped into you, in the Rose & Crown, it was his birthday and not a very happy one at that. Edie and Jules had told me that I could expect a proposal that Christmas. They said he would finally make it official and put me out of the endless limbo of uncertainty.

He didn't pop the question, obviously. I doubt he was even aware that he should. You men never get it, do you? While Guy was so wrapped up in rugby, his career, his own anus, I was busy being humiliated. Why wouldn't he seal the deal? What was so wrong with me that he couldn't just make the commitment? Was he waiting for someone better to come along? Honestly, it didn't even matter if I wanted him down on one knee or not; all I needed was just to get the whole performance over and done with.

I say this as if he was awful, but that's not fair either. It wasn't as if Guy was a bad bloke. For starters he was very easy on the eye. I know it sounds terribly shallow, but that was the biggest draw at first. He was charming and funny too, the sort of easy, consistent fun that I had wanted as a student, away from home for the very first time. When I was with him I wasn't the third, slightly square musketeer tagging on to Jules's and Edie's coattails. In his company, I was a good-time girl. I didn't care if I was basking in his reflected light, just as long as I could glow too.

The longer we went around together, though, the more everything that initially had been so endearing to me began to grate. His jokes fell flat, I was tired of his one-man show, and he seriously needed a haircut. I wanted to know where we were going, if anywhere at all, but the moment we were alone, he scrupulously avoided any form of serious conversation. I had never seen anyone change the conversation so quickly, and trust me, he wasn't the sharpest tool in the shed.

The thing was, for all my frustrations, I couldn't see a way out of it. He was, by most measures, a catch. Would I do better? Did I really have the energy to try? Deep down, I knew that I was hard to like, let alone love. I have so many edges, sharp ones at that, ones that can't be filed down. There was only so much that I could change about myself, and surely I should settle for someone who was interested enough in me to stick around? If anyone knows how difficult that is to find, it's me.

You saved me from that, Frank. You raised my aspirations, and you took me as I was. I know I didn't make it easy. In your shoes, could I have done what you did? Probably not. You took a broken woman, and you loved her as if she were whole. You didn't try to fix me, and that was your greatest kindness of all.

I'll never forget the moment when I knew that you were it. The real deal. The end of the search I didn't know I was still conducting, somewhere at the back of my mind. It was following our afternoon in the museum. You insisted on walking me back to my bike even though it was freezing and miles out of your way. We'd kissed by then, but the experience had made us both bashful. I was grateful it was dark and so you couldn't see me blushing as we set off back to the surgery to collect my ride home. Every so often your hand would brush against mine, furtively, as if you were testing your own confidence.

I was disappointed when we reached my bike.

"This is it!" I said, or something like that, hoping at the same time that it wasn't true. I so wanted to see you again. I was waiting for you to ask. That was what had always happened before, if things had gone well. The sort of men I knew were keen to lock you in for round two or were entitled enough to assume it was on the cards regardless.

"It's been a pleasure," you said, eventually. Just that. Nothing else. It was as if those few hours were all you could have wished for.

"Will we do it again?"

I was the one who asked. I never would have done that before you. There was something about you that made my mind stop its whirring conveyor belt of anxieties and expectations, at least temporarily. I could do what I wanted, go with my gut. Finally, I could be myself, not what someone else expected me to be.

Up until then, I'd spent so much of my life ceaselessly trying to be good. A good daughter, or at the very least good enough to meet my mother's exacting standards and persuade her to stick around. I went off to college, and then I was determined to be good fun, the sort of person people wanted to make good friends with, someone the guys would think was a good bet. The minute I nabbed one,

I wanted to make sure he thought I was a good investment for the long haul. *Good, good, good.*

And with you? From that moment under the surgery's security light, when I spoke up for what I wanted and to hell with everything else, the whole endeavor went out the window. All I wanted was to be good at love. I wanted to stop sabotaging my one shot at happiness and finally relax into the love of someone so good that I didn't have to try anymore. You were always the better half of this relationship. You are the very best of me.

I know it can't be easy to hear about Guy, but trust me, this is the last you will. He was out of the picture pretty much the minute you walked in. There was just one night, one overlap. It was a few weeks after we met, a drunken fumble after a night at the pub with some mutual friends. It was a one-off, I promise. Only the timing wasn't great. It lined up, Frank. With the baby. The one we lost. You both did.

I was out of my mind with grief when we got to the maternity unit. I was being punished, I knew it; otherwise why did I have to sit there, with the expectant mums, the new mums, the crying and the ultrasound images and a thousand reminders that I had screwed everything up?

It was a relief when I finally got taken in, when the midwife came and got me and anesthetized something. She told me it wasn't my fault, as she set a mug of tea down on the side. She told me these things don't work like that.

"They do for me, though," I said. I couldn't meet her eye. "I did something wrong."

I was inconsolable, Frank. I had to tell someone. Why the baby? Why not me?

I waited for a second or two, then I looked up at her. She didn't say anything, but there was something in the way she reached over, touched my arm, and squeezed it for just a few seconds too long that showed me she knew what I was getting at. I'm almost certain she did.

Do you know what she said to me? *Blame is never that simple.*

I've thought about that a lot recently, what with everything that has happened. I still don't know if I agree.

Chapter 3

In all their years together, Frank has never considered that there could be someone else. Now he feels naive. He places the book on his lap and rubs his thumb and the knuckle of his forefinger across his forehead, gathering the drooping skin there into a mound. Is this what a cuckold looks like? Perhaps he is too old for that label to stick.

He's had colleagues who dealt with infidelity. Some came out and said it in the canteen over lunch, their levels of indignation and anger rising as they railed loudly enough to make everyone else in the room drop their own conversations and lean in over the water jugs. Someone would place a reassuring hand on their shoulder, reining them in again. It isn't decorous to announce yourself as a victim, not when it reminds everyone else just how distant their own partner has been lately. Some wouldn't mention it at all, as if the very word were contagious.

Until now, Frank has rarely given any thought to which camp he would fall into. He has spent forty years either too happy or too complacent to think that Maggie would ever play away. At what point does cheating become such old news that you look petty bringing it up? He does not want to be petty. Not when there is so much at stake. Not when Maggie is lying hooked up to life support and he is the one who put her there.

It still rankles, though. Could he have been the father to another man's child? Probably. He wouldn't have known. And even if he had? If there was fifty percent Maggie in it, then it would be one hundred percent his. He loved everything about her so much that he absorbed it automatically, without so much as questioning it. Loving to a fault. He was that oxymoron par excellence, if it is possible for such a trait to exist.

Frank shudders at the thought of Guy. He has never been the jealous type. There had been plenty of times when they were out—at the pub, on holiday, hell, even at a parents' evening—when men would be magnetized to Maggie, a rogue hand flittering over her lower back. But to think of himself at twenty-six, fast asleep and dreaming of her while the two of them fumbled round the back of the pub kitchens, pressed up against the empty oil canisters, or in her bedroom, surrounded by piles of hastily torn-off clothes? It makes him feel sick.

On the scale of betrayal, where does infidelity sit? High up, certainly. If he had found this out before, he would have been angry. As angry as he has ever been, although, he supposes, he hasn't set much of a bench-mark. But now? In the face of his own deceit, the secret he has guarded for six long months, there is nothing.

Nothing can be as bad as what he has to tell Maggie the minute she wakes up.

Five days to go
I tried to keep her words at the back of my mind
when we got home, through all the long days cooped
up in bed, torturing myself. Time helped, even if it
never fully healed. You did too, although naturally
you wouldn't take a jot of credit for that yourself.
Sometimes, on the days when I felt so guilty that
the minute I got up I wished I could get right back
into bed, it was the sight of your face that made me
put one foot in front of the other and get on with the
day. You delivered me porridge at my dressing table,
a smile made of raisins balanced across the oats.
Hope can rub off, and you had enough for us both.
What do you think of when you look back on

those early years of our marriage, Frank? I hope they were happy for you. They were for me. I loved waking up to the warmth of your body on the sheets and the way that, when you inevitably woke a good half hour before we needed to, you would start subtly coughing because you knew I hated being jolted awake by the alarm. I liked the way you would leave a Post-it note with a joke in my lunch box and always felt the need to repeat it the minute I got home, as if I had forgotten the punch line in the intervening four hours. When you regaled me with it, replete with actions and accents, it never failed to make me laugh. I hate to break it to you, it wasn't so much that they were funny but that you were. I have never known anyone to find silliness in the everyday quite like you.

For our second wedding anniversary, you organized that day-trip to London. Preserved in your memory, I'm sure, and on the wall of the downstairs loo just in case you forget. We did Buckingham Palace, Hyde Park. A scone from a builders' café off Oxford Street because I'm pretty sure that our budget didn't stretch to the Ritz. You insisted we dress up for the occasion, as if the whole city was paved with aristocrats. I let it slide. After all, you looked so handsome in your suit, and with

THE SILENT TREATMENT · 239

my party shoes I gained an extra three inches. All the better to kiss you with. Naturally, they were something terrible to walk in, and by the end of the day my heels were in tatters. At Trafalgar Square, with five minutes to get to the last bus, you threw me over your shoulder and ran for it, heedless of the crowds.

We were wheezing and choking the whole way back up the motorway. You with the exertion, I'm sure, me with the laughter. Talk about making memories, Frank. You were the master. There was unbridled joy with you, and I'd never known anything like it. There was the noise of the world and the ceaseless chatter of everyone in it, but somehow you could drown it all out so that it was just us and a packet of plasters zooming up the motorway in the dark. When you went for the paper the next morning and my arse was front and center in a piece on the "Unprecedented Women's Lib March," even that couldn't manage to put us back in context of the bigger, wider world.

It didn't even matter that money was tight. The end of the month could never come fast enough, but we found plenty of ways to distract ourselves until then. What was it you called it? Fridge roulette? You'd come home brandishing something from the

"Reduced" section, and consult the contents of the cupboards like an auctioneer before the bidding. "Three carrots, sardines, and two croissants— any takers?" God, some of the things we ate! My stomach ached by the time we got into bed, although whether from the concoction or the laughing was anyone's guess.

We did a round of jam for Christmas presents that third year we were married. You can probably still taste it if you lick round the back of your molars for long enough. Lumpy, stringy. A far cry from the picture in the cookbook and even further from my experiences eating the stuff.

"Fucking toxic!" I believe Edie called it, sticking a finger through the greaseproof-paper lid before we had so much as crossed the threshold of her house. As was tradition, she didn't bother to take our coats. She was never one for traditional hosting, was she?

"Frankie boy!" Matt appeared from the kitchen, half a bottle of red in his hand. We'd been at their wedding earlier in the year, a whirlwind affair, and I was at that stage of getting to know him where his constant appearance with my best friend still surprised me.

Your glasses were all steamed up, so I steered you

in his direction. The two of you engaged in one of those male hugs that always involve a disconcerting amount of backslapping. Edie poured me a glass of wine and pulled me into the living room, where she could continue to chastise me for providing such shit gifts.

The chicken wasn't cooked according to anyone's standard of food hygiene, but we had the vegetables, gravy by the bucketload, and enough Rioja to drown the place. We called it a night after Edie started buying hotels in Monopoly, because, let's face it, she is a terrible, terrible winner. The taxi drove right past their place, and as you were jogging down the lane to flag it back, I gathered up our stuff and leaned in for a goodbye hug with Edie.

"Hey, Mags?"

"No declarations of love—I'm too drunk to appreciate them."

"You should be so lucky. No, look, I had something I wanted to tell you."

You were waving from the driveway, clutching your biceps in the universal gesture of freezing your arse off. I couldn't wait to curl up in those arms.

"Make it quick then."

"I'm pregnant."

Their hallway suddenly felt very wobbly. I leaned

against the wall to steady myself and feigned a shoe adjustment.

"Oh. God. Christ, Edie." She hadn't poured her own glass, had she? "Congratulations!"

"I know . . . Well, look, I didn't want you to think—"

"No. No. Honestly, I'm thrilled for you. For you both."

You leaned in through the cab window and gave the horn a bash. Edie shouted something about calling her, getting a date in the diary for us two, as I stumbled along the gravel to the ticking taxi meter outside.

I never did. Call, I mean. Not specifically about that. I feel terrible now. What sort of friend does that make me? I so badly wanted to be happy for Edie. Happy, pure and simple, without that horrible edge of jealousy that undercut everything.

And what did I have to be jealous of, really? We had so much together, Frank. We had more with each other than some people have in a lifetime, and *still* I wanted more. I hate writing it down here because it sounds so very, very ungrateful. We were young, we were happy, we were fun. We would exhaust the mattress until the early hours, but still, when the lights were out and I had my head on the

pillow, finally alone with my own thoughts, there
was always that feeling of something being not quite
right. That is what it felt like to be childless, Frank,
for me. I couldn't bring myself to admit that at the
time. It felt like saying *we* weren't enough. And it
wasn't that straightforward at all.

I hate to say it, but I resented how calmly you
seemed to accept our situation. For you, this was just
another thing you couldn't have at that juncture, like
enough disposable income for holidays abroad every
year or a pied-à-terre in Mayfair. Those things
weren't part of our life now, but if they were in the
future, then great. If they weren't, it didn't seem as
if that would have any effect on your net happiness,
all things considered.

But for me? Well, it was everything, Frank.
That much must have been obvious. It was a daily
erosion, my infertility, although that is not to say
that some days weren't harder than others. On
the bad ones, when I had an itch in my tear ducts,
like the beginnings of a sneeze, I would get up and
go to the drawer where I kept pictures of my own
mother, from the years before she left. You never
caught me there because if you had, maybe then you
would have understood why I spent so long locked
in the bathroom when my period came, regular as

clockwork, every damn month, year after year. I wanted to do it better than her, Frank. I needed to prove that I had it in me to mother, properly. It went beyond competition. I needed to know I had that selflessness in me that she had never had.

Usually I would spend the week that followed throwing myself into trying again. I'm not sure you saw it as such at first, although you must have figured it out eventually. I was so in tune with my body clock, the "fertile windows" and the "conceiving opportunities," that I felt like I only ever had one eye on the other tasks at hand. It's exhausting, Frank, wanting a child. It really is. Then, when the time was up and the bleeding started, I couldn't help the way I would shut down. It was another indicator that my body was failing. Surely this was its purpose, *my* purpose? I wasn't enough to make anything stick around. I couldn't keep hold of my first child, and now I couldn't create a second.

I could see that you were at a loss as to what to say. If you were disappointed, you did a very good job at hiding it, for a few years at least. You brought me back from the brink with assurances that it was "too soon," "not the right time." You assured me, "It will happen when it happens."

When did you stop believing that yourself, Frank? Six years in, maybe seven? I'll never forget the day you made your opinion on the matter crystal clear.

Frank goes to turn the page and a photo slips out from where it had been sitting, obscuring the next lines of text. There is a small tear in the top right-hand corner, where the metal paperclip has caught, so he has to rest his little finger on the edge to hold the image together, pressing down hard to flatten it against the planner beneath. It's pitch-black by now, and the streetlight outside next door has yet to be fixed, the result of a run-in with a wayward teenager's trainer a few months back. In between its flashes, he has to bring his nose right up to the page in order to make out the faded image.

It is not a photo he has seen before. Maggie must be about nine or ten, her hair pulled into two plaits and her face fixed in a smile that looks far from genuine. Frank's eyes gravitate toward Maggie's mother, the slightly stiff way she is crouching down, turning her daughter's torso around so she faces the camera. *There you go, darling, smile for the camera. Nice and pretty now, there's a good girl.* The shot is made all the more awkward by her mother's choice of a pencil skirt in red-and-white houndstooth with an asymmetric edge. She has to strain to bend over Maggie. It always was such an effort for her, the parenting business.

He has never considered it like that—Maggie having something to prove. To him, she never did. She was enough, more than enough, and so much more besides. He'd said that at her bedside, and he would say it again one thousand times. Why hadn't he told her before? He thought he had showed her it instead, with his gestures, the little things. Clearly not well enough, though—that's what she's getting at here, isn't it? He hates himself for letting her down.

More than anything, Frank hates the thought of Maggie crying alone. She was such a social creature, the sort who would see someone in floods of tears on the bus and immediately hurry over to them, hand outstretched with a tissue. While the rest of the travelers studiously scrutinized the passing traffic, the contents of their bag, their own Britishness, Maggie would be absorbed in comforting the passenger crumpled in the corner. *Here, come on now, it'll be all right. No, no, not at all. Misery needs company, that's for sure. Don't apologize, you can tell me anything.*

When it came to her own problems, that was quite another matter. They were very similar in that regard. Bottlers, the pair of them. Frank always knew their childlessness was hard on Maggie, however much she tried to hide it. He could see how much she wanted a baby. Some days, when he'd coax her out of herself with an excursion to the Cotswolds or a picnic by the canal but still something lingered, he knew there was more at play. Now he realizes it was the *need* he couldn't put his finger on. *I needed to know I had that selflessness in me that she had never had.* If only she had said that. He had so many examples at his disposal. The way she loved him, first and foremost.

Frank places the photo in his chest pocket. That way there is still a piece of Maggie with him, albeit one he doesn't recognize. It is odd, now, forty years into their relationship, to find snippets of Maggie that he never knew before, be it a photo or otherwise.

He is coming to realize that there is a lot about Maggie that he never fully understood, a row of blanks in the crossword of their life together that are still empty. Frank stares at the bare rectangle in the planner where the photo had been and the blur of words beneath. He hopes they can help him fill those squares.

Five days to go
It was May. Just after my thirty-fifth birthday and a couple of months after our eighth anniversary. I remember it particularly clearly because there had

been a week of torrential downpours. They always call it "unseasonable" when that happens, but I've seen it so many times that I wonder if they might just need to rethink their seasons. Anyway, it was wet, it was a weekend, and we were tucked up, the double duvet on the sofa and something suitably mind-numbing on the television. Every so often I'd get a foot in my ribs, but other than that? It was bliss.

I tossed you the magazine I was reading, folded back on the page where some minor celebrity was extolling the virtues of life in the countryside.

"The great outdoors. The dream."

"A pipe dream. Darling, you hate the great outdoors."

"But it would be so much cheaper. Better quality of life. Better homes. Better schools . . ."

"Let it go, Mags."

I was still in full flow, riffing on gardens, space, the pace of life.

"We need to accept that it isn't meant to be. Children, for us. Maybe it just won't happen."

I couldn't believe what I was hearing. Where did that come from, Frank? There was such earnestness on your face, but your voice? That was a different matter altogether. There was a chip of something sharper in there, an edge of metal in it that I hadn't heard before. It felt final.

You started calling after me—something about needing to talk, being on the same page. I knew that if I stayed a minute longer it would be over. All of it—our family, our marriage, our life together. In the hallway I pulled on my boots, grabbed the nearest jacket and a set of keys from the hooks. I made sure to slam the door, good and hard. You didn't come after me. To this day, I can't tell if that disappointed me more.

I had nowhere to go and ended up at the park a few streets away. It had stopped raining by this point, but by the time I reached the bench by the play area, my fingers were stiff with the cold. I ran your sentences over and over again in my mind, trying out a million different inflections. What was this "we" you were talking about? *Our* decisions, *our* lives. I had never felt further from you than I did then, Frank. We were singing from two utterly different hymn sheets, and for the first time in our marriage, I wasn't sure I could see a way back to harmony.

On the bench next to me, a woman my age, maybe slightly younger, shifted her weight from one thigh to the other. She still had her hood up

and looked nearly as uncomfortable as I did. After a
minute or two, she stood and I saw it. A bump, eight
months at a glance, causing her coat to stick out in
an awkward diagonal. Fifty yards away, there was a
shriek; a little girl in a blue anorak was flying down
the slide into a puddle, an older boy with the same
dark hair just inches behind her.

In that second, I hated her. I hated myself for
hating her but that didn't change a thing. I hated
how lucky she was, how fertile. I hated that she had
everything I wanted and didn't even realize it. I had
to get out of there, quickly. I didn't trust myself.
Not to what? Run off with her children? Punch her,
kick her, scream in her goddamn ambivalent face
for wanting just five minutes of peace from their
mayhem?

In the end that was what sent me home. I was
petrified of myself. At least with you, Frank, there
were boundaries. When I got in, you came out from
the kitchen and helped me get my coat off. You
didn't say anything—what was there to say? I didn't
want an apology, not when I knew you wouldn't
have meant it.

I wonder now if you sensed how close I was then
to walking? I spent that night running through all

the various ways I could go about finding myself
someone who could appreciate the loneliness of
a twosome as much as I did, only to flip back on
myself, questioning whether that was even possible
at all. Could you advertise wanting children without
sounding desperate? I doubted it.

And besides, what about you? I imagined myself
wheeling the big suitcase out of our flat and into a
bedsit for one. I'm not sure I could have survived the
goodbye. Could you?

A sticky heat rushes up the back of Frank's neck. He
throws his legs off the bed and reaches to push open
the window as far as its old hinges will carry it. In the
process, he manages to knock the alarm clock off its
perch on top of a stack of crumpled journals. Just gone
midnight. He presses the metal casing against his forehead in the weak hope it will cool him down in the
absence of any discernible drop in the outside air temperature. No such luck.

Out of our flat and into a bedsit for one . . . Frank
runs over the words again and again until the sentence
dissolves and all he is left with are a few foreign syllables,
strange to his ear and stranger yet to his mind. No, he
never knew that Maggie wanted out, not then. Not ever,

in fact. Sure, it got hard, far harder than they ever could have imagined, but there was no way he could envisage his life without her.

He thinks of Maggie lugging the wheelie bag down from the attic while he was in the lab or the minute she caught him dozing on the sofa. He sees them both in the porch: Maggie leaning in for a final hug, all the while her upper body tensed to keep that slight remove between them, in that instant more like friends than soulmates. His head swims with the pain. He has no doubt that she would have found someone new, someone for whom children was the be-all and end-all—but him? He would have never been able to move on from Maggie.

Maggie must have planned a million exits over the past few months too, the minutes of obsessive thoughts and relentless anxieties stretching out into infinity day after day, even if Frank was still physically close. Who wouldn't want out in that situation? Someone scared of being alone—that's who. Maggie never walked by a single bed—in a house, in a shop—without feeling sad. It wasn't so much the fear of falling out that got to her, rather the fear of not having anyone there to catch her.

Everyone has their limits, though, and what if Frank had, somehow, in these last six months, managed to tell

Maggie what he had done? Well, then she definitely would have walked. He cannot imagine Maggie being able to so much as look at him, let alone live under the same roof, once she knew the truth.

I'm not sure I could have survived the goodbye. Could you? Frank has barely managed these twelve hours away from the hospital; it is madness for her to have thought otherwise.

"Of course I couldn't, Maggie," Frank mumbles as he finds his spot on the page again.

Five days to go

Luckily for you, for me, for us both, I've never been a quitter. I'm not sure I could have coped alone, and any man I could have found would have lived so very obviously under your shadow. That much was evident the morning after. You brought me pancakes on a tray and cleared your throat, gently, to wake me up. An olive branch, of sorts. They were the fat ones I like too. You sat there and watched while I ate.

I offered you the final forkful by way of acceptance.

"Mags, look, I am sorry for what I said. I shouldn't have said it like that. It's not what I meant, not like that . . ."

I didn't want to hear it. That looks terrible,

written down. But you know what I mean. It wasn't the time to rehash it. I loved you. I wanted things back on track. And besides, I'm not very good in the morning. I kissed you so suddenly that the plate clattered to the floor. In the ten minutes that followed, I remembered how neatly we slotted together, how perfectly you understood what I wanted even before I did. As we slowed down into stillness, my mind was so free of it all—the stress, the pain, the worry—that I could barely remember how we had ended up arguing in the first place.

The air was definitely clearer after that. I didn't want you to feel as if our lives were on hold. It wouldn't have been true anyway. We did more in a year than some couples did in a lifetime. At the weekend, when we had the energy, I loved how you would blindfold me in front of the big map in the hallway and spin me round and round until I had no idea which way was up. You'd pass me the marker pen, I'd jab it on the paper, and off we would go to wherever it had landed, a backpack between us. We saw Glasgow, Bristol, the South Downs and the Fens, the whole length of the Norfolk coast. We did Birmingham, Manchester, Newcastle, and, my favorite, Margate. We went up and down the length of the country seeing every sight imaginable and still there was only one face I wanted to see when I woke up. Any solution had to involve you. That I was absolutely clear on.

It didn't take me long before I started thinking about adoption. We didn't have the money for any expensive treatments, and besides, I liked the idea of being able to help a child in need. There were plenty of materials available at work, and on more than one occasion I brought them home, stashed at the bottom of my bag. I could have sworn you must have been able to sense them burning through the leather. All the way home, I would run through how I would present them to you over dinner, the pamphlets tucked untidily in my skirt pocket as if they had just fallen in there.

Every time the moment materialized, I lost my nerve. I can't put my finger on why exactly. If I had to, I'd say it was the fear. What if it came out wrong? What if I made you feel that you, that *we*, weren't enough? I couldn't stand to see you upset, especially not at the end of a long, hard day. I told myself there was always tomorrow, the day after that.

Then, in the midst of it all, you drew a line in the sand. It was a Sunday night, and I was late back from some training course or other, wheelie suitcase in tow. You met me at the door, which wasn't unusual in itself.

"Been waiting on the doorstep all afternoon, have you?" I said as I reached up to kiss you.

"Something like that. Hey—not so fast." You put an arm across the door frame to bar my entry.

A scarf dangled from your hand. You took the suitcase and pushed it into the hallway behind you. We were going through the familiar performance with the blindfold, so, naturally, I was thinking about our next jaunt.

"I'm just back through the door—can't I have a rest?"

"We're not off anywhere, I promise. All right, this way." You held my hand, guided me over the step in the porch. "Straight on, left a little now. Farther. Yes. Keep it coming."

Everyone knows the layout of their own home, so I'm afraid it wasn't as much of a surprise as you might have hoped, Frank. It was clear after just two or three steps that you were leading me to the spare room, the one place I avoided at all costs. It was going to be the nursery.

When you opened my eyes, I was standing slap-bang in the middle of a room transformed.

The piles of rubbish had gone, and it was freshly painted, a vibrant egg-yolk yellow. The floor still smelled addictively like varnish, not that you could see much of it. Every inch was covered in succulents: great green spines and plush, velvety leaves, arrays of buds and points and strangely ridged stems. Along the windowsill, you had collected all the cacti you had given me over the years.

"Short and spiky, huh?"

I stepped away from you to examine the detailing on a terra-cotta pot in the corner of the room, trailing my fingers over the carved Aztec pattern that circled the rim.

I was about to open my mouth—to ask about the cost, how long it had taken you, the planning, the potting. Before I had a chance, you sidled up behind me, placed your hands on my hips, and answered all my questions in one.

"It doesn't matter," you said. "*You* are what matters. I thought it was time that we acknowledged what we have lost and what we can't have. I don't want us to hide it anymore."

And then I saw it—the mobile—the network of fragile paper birds that was the first and only thing we bought for the baby who was never meant to be.

Do you know, Frank, I thought you had disposed of it?

I was a woman transfixed. That night, I made us sit and eat our supper in there on the picnic blanket. When we'd finished, I propped open the window to get a breeze in and we lay flat on our backs, hand in hand, while the birds danced above our heads. We didn't need to say anything. It was the sort of contentment that there just aren't the words for.

I want to thank you for that here, in writing. You went out of your way to make me feel wanted and worthy. To make me feel like I was enough, with or without functional ovaries. I didn't return the favor. Not because I didn't love you, Frank.

No, it was never that. That was never in doubt—I felt that love pulling at every joint in my body. It was because my infertility weighed more. I hope you have read this and have felt just how badly I wanted a child to stanch that gnawing emptiness in my stomach that even you and your green fingers couldn't fill. Please bear that in mind. What I'm about to tell you looks ungrateful. That's putting it mildly, I suppose.

Disappointed, that is what Frank feels. In himself, of course. Just because he had come to terms with their childlessness, it didn't mean Maggie had. What was he thinking, sticking a job lot of cacti in the spare room and hoping that would cure her pain? He still remembers how excited he was at the nursery, picking out the plants, loading them into trays, and handing over his card at the till. Why didn't it click that an indoor conservatory wasn't going to be enough?

Frank has never had good instincts. He supposes some people are just not born with them, although he has yet to uncover the genetic reason why. It started at school, where he struggled to make friends. He got there eventually, but at the start of term, whenever he met someone new, he just didn't have the knack of making easy conversation. He went in too hard, asking the sorts of big questions that a bunch of kids with marbles don't want to hear.

It didn't get any easier the older he got. Frank has endured a hundred stilted interviews over the years. He has counted down the minutes of painful small talk at work Christmas parties, willing the soggy sausage rolls over to his huddle just to have something to speak about that wouldn't sound too eager or too standoffish or even too odd. But with Maggie? He thought he'd finally had the instinct business nailed. To this day, he has thought of that garden as one of his finest hours, the sort of grand romantic gesture that he secretly hoped she would boast about to Edie and her colleagues.

It has always been his job to look after the plants. There was the logistical nightmare of dispersing them throughout the flat once Eleanor was born and the room had to return to its initial purpose. Then, after they moved to the bigger place, the cacti were spread out across the various rooms, some tucked away in nooks that were easy to forget, but still Frank remained diligent with the watering. A few years ago, for their anniversary, Maggie even bought him a novelty indoor can for the purpose, painted with Frank's name in big, looping cursive. Every week he would wander through the house, can in hand, and check their hydration with his finger pads, wiping down any excess dry soil with the handkerchief in his pocket.

Frank has kept this up even in the silence. In fact, he wouldn't be surprised if this was what he had been doing five days ago while Maggie sat scribbling above his head, the plants thirsty from the heat. He couldn't stand to see the leaves, once so fleshy and full, wither and turn brown. Maggie would hate that, and he, in turn, would hate for her to think that he had let his great romantic gesture wilt.

Now he knows even his best horticultural efforts have fallen short. It's time he stopped living with his head in the clouds and paid attention to what is right in front of him.

Five days to go
About six months after your gardening triumph, you went on your sabbatical in the States. All that effort on your part and still it only took a day to gather my resolve. I had been keeping the application papers at the back of a file, slid between the photos and the booklets on bonds. The whole thing was fairly painless. My only hesitation was over your signature—should it have been a bit smaller?

I was quite surprised by how quickly we were contacted, but I suppose we were just what they wanted. Middle-class values, a stable home, and the perfect gap for a child. I cleaned the house from top to bottom. I dusted off the images of our godchildren that had been accruing in the cupboard under the stairs, framed them, and made sure they were in the eyeline of the sofa. I'm sorry to say that I locked the spare room, with its abundance of herbaceous health and safety hazards. By the time the doorbell rang, my head was spinning from nerves or from the surface-cleaner fumes—I couldn't tell which.

"Mrs. Hobbs?" The smaller and skinnier of

the two women at the front door stepped forward, extending her hand.

I gave them the warmest smile I could muster and beckoned them in. They introduced themselves as Grace and Mary—very biblical, I remember thinking. If ever there was a time for salvation, this was surely it. I could see them evaluating the steps up to the living room, the lack of a handrail.

When they were settled on the sofa, they both produced clipboards and wriggled their Biros out from underneath the hinges.

"Will Mr. Hobbs be joining us?" Grace asked.

At least they were cutting to the chase. I made your excuses as best I could, all the time watching as the muscles in her face tightened.

"Normally, we would expect both potential parents to be present."

I went to apologize, but Mary cut me off, angling her body toward me and almost blocking out her partner in the process. I liked her immediately.

"So, Mrs. Hobbs, tell us a bit more about why you and your husband would like to adopt."

I was glad you weren't around to hear me put words into your mouth. I reeled off the usual answers—the desire for a child, to share our home, our resources, our time. When I touched on the miscarriage, I could feel my voice flaking.

"I was pregnant not long after we married, but I lost the baby at four months. It was very traumatic . . . mentally, physically too. We tried again, a lot. But we were told that what had happened would make conceiving naturally pretty much impossible."

Mary reached over and touched my hand, stilling its insistent fidgeting with a loose thread on the seam of my jeans. I could feel her keeping that same tenderness as we moved through a series of practicalities, a tour of the flat. I could tell the interview was wrapping up when we made our way back to the living room and neither of them sat down.

"So, Mrs. Hobbs—"

"Maggie, please."

I wanted Mary to see me like a friend. I wanted her to feel she would move mountains for me. She sure as hell would need to.

"In terms of the next steps, we will be following up on the references you provided. We have down here Edith Carlisle, Julia Allen, and Francesca Hobbs—is that still correct?"

I had taken a bit of a risk putting down your sister, but I had hoped they would be too stretched for time to follow up with someone with an Australian dialing code. Besides, the two of you rarely spoke.

"Well, we will need to meet your husband and speak to him too." Grace handed over a card. "If you could get him to give me a call when he's back, I'll fix up a time for that."

That was the end of that, then.

I lost track of the sleepless nights I endured that whole time you were away, running through every possible permutation of how on earth I could explain this to you. I was halfway through an adoption procedure and had forged your agreement. *Just testing the waters?* I'd gone a bit far for that. *Doing the hard work for you?* Parenting doesn't work that way. In retrospect, I can see that, in the end, it was me who held us back and that you were just the excuse. That looks so awful, written down. I soon realized it wasn't so much *a* child that I wanted as *our* child.

I know they checked our references; Jules and Edie called to wish us luck. Nothing from your sister, though. Not to me, at least. Did she call you, Frank? But then the betrayal was so heavy, surely you would have said something. Wouldn't you? In this silence, I have begun to question everything I thought I knew.

I hope you are angry rather than upset. You are so slow to anger—you always were. Your default is upset, and that is always so much worse. Nothing hurts me like the sight of you hurting. I have tried to explain what childlessness meant to me—more than an inconvenience, more than failure, more than wanting someone to lay flowers on our graves. It was all I was back then.

Can you understand that? Can you really? Please try to, Frank, because I think it will help with what comes next.

Chapter 4

Over the past six months, Frank has had more than sufficient opportunity to mull the passage of time, the way it slips by like a black cat in the night. Birthdays. Anniversaries. Christmas. Those odd made-up holidays that Hallmark has gotten rich on that he never managed to keep track of. Repeat.

Now he is forced to think of everything that slipped by over those years. He is aware that he is not the most perceptive of men. Maggie used to buy new outfits and model them up and down the stairs, waiting for him to clock. "Is that new, darling?" he would ask at last, after copious throat-clearing on Maggie's part. But this? He must have been blind not to have noticed.

Frank stands up from the edge of the bed and goes to the window, pushing it open as wide as it will go. Diagonally opposite, they have been too tired to close the curtains. Frank can make out the father of the family in a baggy football shirt and tartan pajama bottoms, trying to soothe a wailing, wriggling baby on the stairwell. He looks frazzled, but his tenacity is admirable. *The things we do for our own flesh and blood, eh?* Limitless.

Adoption would have been quite different. But would his feelings have been the same? Frank hopes so. He tries to think of how that conversation would have played out, if Maggie could have plucked up the courage to show him those leaflets instead of shoving them into the admin drawer of no return. He likes to think he would have responded well, maybe even enthusiastically. But then he is not so sure. It isn't just Maggie with a fear of the unknown.

The alarm clock on his bedside table gives its electronic tut as the digits reset to 03:00. What he wouldn't give for a fresh start himself now. He hasn't thought much beyond getting back to Maggie the minute he is allowed in again. He'll tell her then, no excuses—what he did, why he shut down. And then? Well, there is no second part to his plan.

What comes next. He is not sure that he wants to
know, but he can't stop now.

He turns the page.

Four days to go

Do you know, Frank, that I didn't even realize I was
pregnant with Eleanor until eight weeks in? Now that
I was over forty, things weren't as regular as they used
to be. I was exhausted, bloated, but nothing out of the
ordinary. Maybe a little fuller in the face and feeling
awful with it—slamming headaches and a niggling
pain in my lower back that wouldn't budge. It was
one of the younger practice nurses who mentioned it.
That irked me. Just qualified and suddenly turning
her diagnoses on her supervisor.

It had been nearly three years since Grace and
Mary's visit. In the soul-searching that had come
after, I had managed to catch sight of a future for
us that didn't involve children. A happy one too.
I put our application on hold a month or so later. I
sent a nice email to Mary, and they must have been
used to it because there was no fuss, less rigmarole
to putting things on pause than there had been to
start them up in the first place. She even left me
her direct number, in case I ever wanted to talk
anything through.

So, for the first time since we were married, a baby wasn't at the forefront of my mind. I suppose that was why, at first, I could laugh at the nurse's suggestion. Unfortunately, suspicion is never that easy to shake for good. Another four weeks went by without a period, and that was enough to send me home via the shop. As I handed over the cash and pocketed the two-pack of tests, I wondered if the girl on the till assumed they were for my daughter. I left before she could even print the receipt.

The minute I got in, I locked myself in the bathroom and took the two tests in succession. Sixty, one hundred and twenty, one hundred and eighty Mississippis passed by. I went up to two hundred just to be sure. When I finally allowed myself to look at them, there were two blue lines neatly spaced in the window of each plastic stick. All those years hallucinating them and there they finally were— undeniable.

I didn't stay there to stare at them, much as I could have done. I used a whole loo roll to wrap them both in before putting them in a plastic bag and looping the handles into a tight double knot. I even went to the trouble of dropping the package in the bin four doors down. By the time you arrived home that evening, it was as if nothing had happened.

I knew I couldn't tell you until I had it straight in my own head. The thing is, though, I'm not sure I have ever been straight in the head since that moment in the bathroom, dual blue lines dancing in front of my eyes. This was what I'd wanted; what was there to get straight? Plenty, Frank, plenty. I was too old for starters. Sure, I saw women my age at the surgery for their prenatal checkups, but for the most part they already had a few kids under their belt. Even if they didn't, had they been through the same wringer? Fifteen years of trying and fifteen years of failing. If I hadn't carried a child to full term at twenty-six, light and tight and energetic, what hope was there for me now? I was scared, Frank, so scared. We were in this together, but somehow I felt so alone.

That night, as you lay snoring to my right, I assessed you with a whole new purpose. I looked at that cushion we had bought for your lower back after the escapade with the slipped disc. We'd laughed at the time, hadn't we? I spent the week after the X-ray calling you "Granddad," with that unspoken assumption that probably no one else ever would, not after so long with no success. I examined your hands, the skin between your fingers flaking and raw from the washing-up—all those years of hard marital labor, and to think you were unaware that this was just the start.

More than anything before, this felt like my biggest betrayal. I was carrying a child, *our* child, but I couldn't risk telling you before I knew I was too far gone for there to be any sort of meaningful discussion about what we would do. Try as I might, I couldn't imagine the word "abortion" coming out of your mouth—it was too hard, too final. If you had scrupulously avoided it three months into dating, would you really reel it out now? Even if I couldn't envisage it, I didn't want to risk it.

If I'm entirely honest—and what is the purpose of this whole exercise otherwise?—I didn't want to have that discussion because I didn't know how I would respond to your questioning. I had spent years wanting this so badly I had thought of barely anything else. And then it happened and suddenly I felt unsure. I was excited, elated, but that wasn't the whole picture, not in the way it seemed to be for everyone else.

Could I mother? Did I even know how? It wasn't as if I had been set a good example. I hated my own contrariness, my mind's complete inability to just settle and accept that everything would work out fine. Now I wonder if it was a sign. That sounds terribly spiritual of me, but you know what I mean. Maybe there was something, somewhere out there, trying to tell us, Frank, about Eleanor?

I must have been desperate because I ended up calling Mary. She had probably just given me her number to be kind; I doubt she expected me to use it. One lunch break, though, it all got too much, the weight of not telling you, of not telling anyone. The weight of my own uncertainty. She picked up on the first ring.

"Hi, it's Maggie Hobbs. I submitted an adoption application a few years back. You gave me your number . . ."

There was a disconcerting pause while I imagine she tried to trace me.

"My husband wasn't at the first meeting," I added.

"Of course. How are you?"

"I just wanted to let you know that I'm expecting." The words fell out far faster than I had intended. I suppose that's what comes from phoning on a whim. "I'm going to be a mother."

She was so thrilled, Frank, and that was just what I needed—that unequivocal, unreserved, unmitigated delight that I hoped would rub off on me. With her enthusiasm still fresh in my mind, I got myself registered with a doctor farther out of town and booked my first scan for the end of the week. It was a Friday afternoon, and it seemed safe enough to call in sick at work.

It was still too early to find out the gender, so the whole thing felt more like a formality, or that was what I told myself as I filed into the waiting room, one of only two women sitting solo, without a partner or parent fussing over their every move. I missed you then, Frank. I wished that things could have been even a bit more straightforward for us.

"Is the father in the picture?" the midwife asked as she smeared the ultrasound gel across my stomach.

"Yes. My husband's away, unfortunately, at a conference. Obviously, he's sorry he can't be here." I couldn't believe I was rolling out the same line I had to the adoption services, only this time you were barely twenty minutes away in the car.

I was so worried about what she thought, about whether the lie was flashing across my face, that I hadn't even been looking at the screen, where a grainy image was shifting in tiny, incremental movements.

"Congratulations, Mum." In the background, the printer whirred and chugged its way into life.

A minute later and I had a photo of our future balancing on top of my handbag.

I told you that night. I was going to wait until Jack and Sarah had gone, but I didn't trust my own resolve. Somehow having the image tucked in my back pocket made it all so much easier. It was concrete, the backup I needed if you expressed so much as an inch of doubt. In the end, you didn't. You might have been surprised, but you didn't seem to agonize over it the way I did. For you, it was a joy, pure and simple. Your enthusiasm was infectious, and with every animated conversation that met me at the end of a long day's work, I was able to push the tricky thoughts further and further to the back of my mind.

There were times when I could even have sworn you were more excited than me. I loved coming to bed and seeing you propped up against the pillows, some parenting book folded back in one hand, a Biro poised for underlining in the other. You spent so long researching strollers that I had visions of our son or daughter being at school before you got round to making a decision. It probably would have been the case had it not been for a conveniently timed sale at the baby outlet store.

"Race you for it." You were rocking back

and forth on one foot, both hands on one of our shortlisted prams, doing your best impression of an athlete primed on the starting line. On either side of us expectant parents pushed industrial-size trollies loaded with high chairs and sterilizers and an assortment of other equipment I could barely recognize. The occasional toddler scuttled across the floor. "Loser makes dinner."

I whined something about health and safety. Even as I did, I could see it falling on decidedly deaf ears.

"It's an assault course! To the cots and back," you said, shooting me the sort of wicked grin that reminded me how I'd gotten knocked up in the first place. Some of the braver kids were already gawping at you from behind their parents' sleeves.

"Frank! I am seven months pregnant!"

"Three . . ."

"Frank!" I could feel the smile itching at the corners of my mouth despite myself.

"Two. It's power-walking only. Promise. Nothing too strenuous. One!"

I wasn't going to follow you, I swear. But then you were off on an impressive power-walk, your hips giving that same silly, exaggerated wobble you usually reserved for the dance floor at weddings. It has always been irritatingly infectious.

Customers began to press up against the shelves with surprising good humor. Or perhaps just good sense. You've never exactly been known for your coordination.

"Oh, fuck it." I grabbed the nearest pram. Naturally, it was the most ungainly beast in the shop. It had one of those huge curved awnings over the top, better suited to a café than to a newborn. I refused to let that stop me. "Not so fast!"

On the bus home, we were pressed up against each other, our flat-packed purchase (the winner) squashed against the window. It was cold out, and the windows had steamed up. I wasn't watching what you were doing; you'd exhausted me, and I had my head tipped back on your shoulder, a million miles away, until the driver took a sharp right. Your hand reached out to steady me, and you flung the other over the bump. A total overreaction, but it made my heart soar. I went to kiss your cheek.

That was when I saw it—in big fat capitals, written in the condensation:

MUM + DAD

A photo slips out of the bottom of the planner and onto Frank's palm. He hasn't seen this one in years.

Twenty-five, to be exact. Not since Eleanor was born. The ultrasound image feels a little tacky, the film demonstrating a surprisingly firm grip despite the clamminess of his hands. He angles the bedside lamp so that it shines directly on the image and Eleanor's amoebic form comes into focus, a fuzz of pixels in black and white. He traces the outline of her body, lets his fingers walk along the date stamp, the time too. She is an almost perfect kidney bean. Ironic, really, for a girl who for twenty years of her life would painstakingly pick them out of chili con carne, leaving them on the side of her plate with a look of gross disdain.

Even now, his heart swells looking at a version of Eleanor so unlike how she looked that last time, or any time for that matter. There is something so magical to her body, curved in on itself like a comma, as if to conserve energy for the terribly important business of growth. The scientist in him knows that it is just a collection of cells, reflected as a series of shadows on the film. But the father in him knows it will be so much more. It will be light and it will be laughter and it will be the most marvelous years of his life.

"You are so loved," he says, bringing her bulblike head to his lips.

He goes to tuck the image back inside the book. The

lines at the top of the page leap out at him, underlined with such force that the paper has buckled beneath them: *I was scared, Frank, so scared. We were in this together, but somehow I felt so alone.* When he thinks of Maggie in the GP's office, scared blind and more isolated than ever before, he can't believe she went through it all by herself. He just wishes he could have been there, to squeeze her hand, to fix her a cup of water from the dispenser, to run his hand across her hunched shoulders in the hope of releasing even a few centimeters of her tension.

Frank, of all people, knows how it feels to be isolated by a secret. He can't judge Maggie for that. He knows the fear that it is writ large on your face and the lengths you will go to in order to avoid the subject at all costs. Just the thought of it brings a fresh line of sweat out from under his collar. No, he can't begrudge Maggie the scan he missed. Where would that leave him? He has begrudged her the knowledge of something so much more important.

Four days to go
Then—she was there. Simple as that. Not the labor. You don't forget that, by the way. No, I mean she was at home. Could you believe it? I couldn't. That first week was a pinch-me moment. I'd go to sleep

and wake up wondering if I'd dreamed up this happiness. I never thought it would happen for us.

You know me, not usually at a loss for words. But holding Eleanor was as close as I've ever come. I felt something so fierce for her that it was almost paralyzing. I could have watched her forever, the tiny wrinkle in her nose when she wasn't quite comfortable, the little bubbles of saliva she would blow as she drifted off to sleep. Some nights, I couldn't even bear to put her down, and I'd wander up and down the corridor with her propped against my shoulder, stroking her silky baby hair. Bright red, just like yours.

We got some time as a threesome too, thanks to some accrued annual leave and your very generous boss. We laid her on top of the duvet and watched in awe as she stretched her legs in the air, the flesh bulging in chubby wrinkles at her knees and ankles. I particularly enjoyed your attempts at nursery rhymes. We had incy-wincy spider falling off a wall and into a hundred pieces, and a rendition of "Twinkle, Twinkle, Little Star" that petered out after just a line or two . . . In the end, I managed to drown you out with a blast of ABBA, which got you up and dancing, Eleanor strapped to your front and her feet jiggling with the beat.

Our very own Dancing Queen. The most precious royalty on earth.

It was euphoria. It was the best. It was the highest high I could have imagined. I never can stay there, though, can I? God, I wished I could. More than anything. But then again, it wouldn't be me. I'd never hated myself for it more. I could feel the falling start on the day you went back to work, Frank. You know that sensation, just as you are drifting off to sleep? The one like dropping two floors in the lift with no warning, stomach lurching, legs twitching? That was it, Frank, that day.

I'd had it before—the drop, the fall, whatever you want to call it. That was who I was. I didn't need a name for it, a diagnosis or what have you. I told myself I could manage it. Or so I thought. Now, though, with Eleanor, everything was so much more intense. There was another person involved, one who depended on me entirely. And it had never been that bad before.

Eleanor was what? Three, four weeks old? You came to say goodbye, your cycle helmet already on, and as you kissed the tops of our heads, one by one, Eleanor let out a piercing shriek. I was so close to throwing my arms around your ankles and demanding that you stay. I couldn't do it. Not alone.

I was scared of what I would do. I was scared of myself.

I quickly realized that running through the checklist for why Eleanor was crying was pointless. Clean? As far as I could tell. Warm? Maybe too much so. I checked for fever. Fed? As well as I could. Under my T-shirt, I could feel my nipples cracking, the skin raw. Even the cool air passing over them caused me to wince. I tried everything I could think of—bouncing, singing, stroking, cajoling, begging—and none of it worked. Nothing, Frank. I was trying my best, and still nothing was good enough.

The first days without you passed in a blur. I knew I should be out, in the park, with Edie, at any one of the mother-and-baby groups put on in the local church hall. I couldn't stand the thought of everyone sitting around with their babies calm on their laps, a freshly pressed muslin over one shoulder, while Eleanor screamed blue murder. Maybe they would slip me some tips, some advice on where I was going wrong. Maybe they'd be kind enough to hold those thoughts in and just judge silently. The image alone was enough to make my eyes water. It didn't take much those days. Instead I lay prostrate on the sofa, the curtains closed, Eleanor on my stomach. The two of us stared wide-eyed at each other. I couldn't tell who was more helpless.

Just before you came home, I would muster the energy to open the curtains and fill the kitchen sink for Ellie's bath. Something we could do as a family. The minute you walked in the door, the relief shot straight through me. I've always been able to find pockets of light with you. I'd prop Eleanor up while you splashed water every which way, unleashing a flurry of giggles.

If you had snapped that on a camera, it would have made the perfect tableau. You could have cut it out and used it as a still in a cereal advert or in something about a kitchen renovation that had actually gone to plan. Anyone looking in would have envied us. But you always knew me so much better. You would be drying her off with the hand towel, and I felt like a wanted woman—how long before you guessed?

I didn't say anything. Not to you, not to anyone, certainly not directly. I didn't know how it would come out, and I couldn't stand to lose Eleanor. I loved her, I knew that, somewhere deep within. I just needed to get back to that place, the delight of the first few weeks, and clear the horrible, messy thoughts before someone tried to take her away. It was the sleep deprivation, the hormones, the long hours alone.

Try as I might—they wouldn't budge. Horrible, awful thoughts that would descend on my happy-baby checklist like a swarm of flies, so black they obscured everything else. I imagined her tumbling down the stairs like a rag doll that screamed. I imagined her drowning in the cup of water on the sideboard.

Every thought made me feel sick. But I couldn't shake them; the moment one disappeared, another would appear in its place, somehow worse. There was a whole loop of them—images of Eleanor bruised, bleeding, or in some other form of pain that I had unwittingly caused—and there was no way out. I would squeeze my eyes shut, and still they were there. I checked her tiny body for signs of hurt one hundred times a day. What if I had done something against my will, without knowing? I didn't want this. I would die for her.

Where were they coming from, these clouds, intruding on every aspect of my day? I was going mad, I could feel it, and I couldn't see my way out. When Eleanor was three months old, I nose-dived. I convinced myself there was a virus in our flat and the moment Eleanor drifted off, in my one moment of respite, I set about cleaning the flat from top to bottom. I bleached the bathrooms, twice. I put all our clothes in the washing baskets and threw the rugs outside. I remember exactly where I was when you came home: I was on my knees scrubbing the kitchen floor with my bare hands. Eleanor was screaming, and I couldn't hear her over the sound of dry brushing.

"Maggie. Maggie! Hey, hey, stop a second."

I had scrubbed so hard that my left palm was bleeding.

"Maggie, darling. Up you get."

I couldn't even stop to catch my breath and respond. You had to hoick me up at the waist and physically unfurl my fingers until the brush dropped.

"Maggie—what is it? What's up?"

"I can't do this," I whispered into your chest. "I'm a terrible mother. You'd do better without me. You both would."

Somehow you managed to get me to our bedroom and tucked me into bed. The whole time I could hear Eleanor in distress downstairs. I remember flapping madly in that direction and you just nodding, so serene. Not for the first time, I wished I could be more like you.

I didn't know where I was when I woke up. It was light, and the street outside was quiet, almost empty. I rolled onto my side, facing the cot. She wasn't there. I'll never forget that surge of sheer panic, a jolt of adrenaline so acute that I flew out of bed still naked.

"Frank! Frank! Where are you? She's gone!"

"Here, darling." The kitchen door nudged open. Eleanor gurgled in your arms. "See, she's missed you."

Do you know what I thought in that moment, Frank? You two were better off alone. There was none of the chaos I brought, the panic and the paralysis. I was so scared of doing everything wrong that I could barely do anything at all. Sometimes, when you were holding her and she started crying, you would pass her over to me, almost on a reflex. I took her. But inside? I wanted to run as far away as possible from your outstretched arms and Eleanor in them. I wasn't going to help matters, quite the opposite in fact. I told myself Eleanor could sense my unease, or that she would grow up and realize that was what it was. I couldn't stand that thought of being rejected again, not by her, not by you either.

It got better, eventually. I only noticed we were moving in that direction in earnest once Eleanor was past six, seven months. So, slow progress, but these things don't change overnight, however much we wish they would. You brought in Edie—she came every day until Eleanor was almost one. You came home earlier. But still, even with all your kindness, I could never tell you how dark it had become: just what those thoughts were; how close I had come to giving it all up. What if you left me, the unfit mother? What then?

Now I have broken that. What is running through your mind, Frank? I hope it is not the image of me hurting our precious, precious Eleanor. They were thoughts, Frank, horrible ones, but there wasn't a drop of truth in them. It can't be easy to hear that I held so much of my suffering back from you. You have never been a judgmental man. You have taken me at face value even when that face has been Medusa herself, all chaos and snarling, biting ends. But somehow I thought this was one step too far.

No one wants to hear that the person they have given their life to has the mind of a monster—do they?

Chapter 5

Frank's left foot has gone numb again. He has been meaning to get that looked at, but he has had enough of hospitals for one lifetime, and he has always been at the bottom of his own pecking order. He shakes it out and waits for the inevitable flow of pins and needles to prick their way up to his hip. He ought to take a walk, but it is hardly the time for it—he read somewhere that dawn is when most burglaries and unprovoked murders take place. Not a safe time by any means.

Instead, he shunts his feet into his slippers—horrible, flat, frayed things that Maggie hates—picks up the planner, and heads down to the study. It takes a little while for the computer to wake up. *Like owner, like tool,* Maggie would say, with that mischievous glint in her eye that she has always had. When the screen eventually comes to life, his chess has timed out. A little bubble has popped up in the center of the board: *Game Over!*

Not yet, Frank thinks. Not without a fight.

He exits the window and opens up the photo roll, scanning to the very first image they uploaded. It's a photo of a photo, a reproduction of a disposable-camera shot that is completely unstaged. It is Maggie holding Eleanor, who, according to the date stamp in the bottom right, must have been two months old. Frank zooms in with his mouse.

Not on Eleanor, but on Maggie: Can he see it there? The distress already beginning? He imagines neatly lopping off the top of her skull and peering inside. He would scoop out every last black thought and incinerate them all. They didn't deserve to touch Maggie, and they had no place near Eleanor. *A monster.* Definitely not. We all have darkness in us; he just wishes Maggie could have shared hers.

Frank zooms back out. There was such ease to the way Maggie handled Eleanor, as if she were an extension of her own arm. If she wasn't comfortable as a mother, she certainly put on a good show. Frank cannot work out what it is about him that made it impossible for Maggie to say these things at the time.

His awkwardness? His earnestness? Whatever it was, he knows he has let her down. He loves them both so much—Maggie and Eleanor—and somehow he still disappointed them. We always think love will be enough, but what if, sometimes, it isn't?

The desk chair groans as Frank leans across, tipping as he reaches for the planner. Maggie wanted him to read this, all of this, and he owes her that much. He rubs the grit out of his eyes with his thumb and forefinger; then he sighs, long and hard.

How much more can the heart hold?

Three days to go
I never did feel at home as a parent, Frank. There, I have said it. I could never bring myself to tell you that to your face. Somehow it felt like an admission of failure on my part, even before things started to go wrong. I loved the idea of being a parent so much that it nearly broke us as a couple. And if I had said that when all six pounds, six ounces of that reality hit? It would have sounded capricious at best. Selfish at worst. What sort of mother admits she isn't up to the job? One who didn't deserve her daughter or her husband. I have always felt so unworthy to have you both. I maxed out my quota of happiness, and look what I'm left with.

And why? Why couldn't I feel at home as a parent? I could never quite figure that out, however hard I tried. There was no denying how lucky I was too. I know that. We managed to make it work, me taking time off nursing until Eleanor was old enough for school. Not everyone gets that chance. More than that, I was happy. The happiest I had ever been. Once I was back on an even keel, those days couldn't last long enough. If anything, I felt I had wasted all that time before. Maybe I should have seen someone, gotten it diagnosed, the postnatal depression or whatever they wanted to call it, instead of being so scared and so stubborn.

You told me not to dwell on it. After all, what was the point? There was a lifetime with Eleanor ahead. In the end, I only wished I'd done more to document the sheer joy of those early days. Eleanor padding in to wake me up, Jeffrey tucked under one arm. When the weather was good, we'd have our breakfast sitting on the grass in the garden, Eleanor propped between my legs. When it rained, we'd trace the passage of the drops on the window with her yogurt spoon. We baked cakes, we did crafts, we read books. We went to the meadow and collected daisies and spotted birds and watched the boats. We just were, Frank.

Over the years, I got to see all the milestones, but more than that, I was there for the moments that inched her closer to them too, the seconds when I could chart the contours of her personality coming into focus right in front of me. Eleanor took her first steps just before her first birthday. She would lever herself up, toes splayed, hands pressed down firmly on the floor ahead. For weeks that was as far as she got, an odd, inverted bridge, before she ended up back on her bottom with a thud, a look of mild frustration gliding across her face. You could see it all then, the tenacity, the focus. I could try to distract her all I liked, but it was only a matter of time before she was up and trying again.

Her first words were "mama" and "dada," nothing unusual there. What struck me was the fact that once she found her voice, we never heard the end of it. I'd go to say something and she would be babbling over the top of me. At first, I imagined she was just keen to ensure that her newfound capacities for speech were still working. Then you would get home and the minute I went to ask you about your day, Eleanor would start up again, drowning you out. "Yes, we know you are here," you would say, tickling her sides until the chitter-chatter stopped and her face puckered with the giggles. *As if we could ever forget you.*

I was so captivated by our days together, the two of us, that I wasn't rushing to sign us up for toddler groups. At the back of my mind, I knew I should be. That was motherhood to a T for me— the nagging doubt that there was something I should be doing better. Besides, it wasn't fair for Eleanor to socialize solely with adults. It wasn't her fault we didn't have friends with kids her age. Even if she was so content and cocooned in our love at home, surely branching out was no bad thing? As if in answer to my unspoken neuroses, they opened that big indoor play area ten minutes' drive away just a few weeks before Eleanor's second birthday. Perfect timing for checking it out to see if we could book a party there.

I'd never seen anything quite like it—an aircraft hangar filled with huge plastic slides, numerous ball pits, and nets and flags in the sort of screamingly garish colors that could induce a headache within ten seconds of entry. They had the same three pop songs blaring on a loop. I only realized that after an hour or so, such was the volume of screaming over the top of it. I should have guessed this wasn't Eleanor's scene. One look at the place and she turned her body into me, her nose pressed resolutely against my thigh.

We sat on the edge of a gym mat, rolling a ball between us. I don't know who looked less enthusiastic to be there—me or Eleanor. Still, we were together, and that was good enough for me. A set of twins ran past close enough for us both to flinch. They entered the fray without so much as a backward glance.

"Sorry about them." Their mum appeared behind me and crouched between us. "Can I?" She tilted her head in the direction of the floor between us. There were a few other mums drinking coffee from Styrofoam cups at the back of the room, huddled around what looked like a repurposed picnic table. It didn't look as though there was an open invitation to join.

"Sure." I passed her the ball by way of welcome.

"You don't fancy playing with the other kids?" Eleanor didn't even acknowledge the question that was sent in her direction and shuffled an inch closer to me. Up ahead, the two identical boys I guessed were hers hung upside down from some monkey bars. She turned to me. "Shy, huh? Doesn't seem such a bad thing."

Until then, I had never really thought of Eleanor

as shy. That shook me. It was as if there was a whole other side to Eleanor that didn't exist for us. She was so happy at home, so confident and so loved. It wasn't long before I made our excuses and got out of there. We had the birthday at home. Were we coddling her? I suppose it didn't feel that way at the time. It wasn't as if we were planning on hiding her away forever, homeschooling her and refusing to let her see the real world. Find me a parent who doesn't want to shelter their own child at that age. At any age, for that matter.

Besides, when it was the three of us—in the evenings, at weekends, on the odd week of holiday— that was when Eleanor really shone. I put that photo on the mantlepiece, the one of us all at Iffley Lock, because it showed us that. Surprising, really, that it was such a happy memory, given it was just after my mother had left, that five-day visit that seemed to roll on and on and on. She'd had plenty of opinions on our parenting, none of them favorable. In that visit alone, we were declared *indulgent, fretful.* And the worst? *Overprotective,* as if trying to inoculate your four-year-old against stress was an offense on our part. On the plus side, Eleanor found her amusing—which made one of us—thanks to her bourgeois disdain for bedtimes and bathtimes and dinners with vegetables.

The minute her taxi back to the airport had rounded the corner, I hotfooted us down to the pub. God knows I needed a drink. The sun was shining, and if I shut my eyes now, I can still feel myself drowning in that sky, a perfect cornflower blue. It was so hot, but Eleanor had insisted on wearing her all-in-one polyester dinosaur suit, which we had given her for her fourth birthday just days before, complete with spiky hood and a tail that trailed a good foot behind her. Before we left, she stuck out her gummy little hand and extended you the chimpanzee mask and me the horse. You wore yours very well indeed.

"The three musketeers!" you hollered as I locked up.

My heart swelled walking with you two, and no, not with embarrassment. I was so proud, Frank, of what we had made, of how sensitive and smart and engaging Eleanor was. I watched you, the brilliant father I'd known you would be, and I fell in love with you all over again. I felt giddy, adored. I didn't want the day to ever end.

At the pub, you ordered us chips and cola (mine spiked, thankfully) and while you queued, Eleanor and I lay on the picnic blanket, her head resting on my stomach. I ran my finger down the subtle ski

slope of her nose, lingering on that perfect point
where the cartilage at the end flared up. I fanned
out her hair, with all the knots and the clumps that
formed down the back. I thought she was drifting
off to sleep. Maybe she was. Just before she did, she
rolled to face me.

"I love you, Mummy," she said, with that certainty
children just have. In that moment, my mind was
finally able to stop. I'd spent four years on a carousel,
swung round and round by the constant questioning
of every parenting decision I had ever made—my
own, my mother's, anyone else who felt fit to judge.
Whatever I chose, whatever I did, I always felt I was
falling short of the mark in some way.

But who were those marks really for, Frank?
Surely it was only Eleanor whose opinion mattered.
Being loved by her was the only reward I ever
needed. Her seal of approval was the top prize,
the only thing that could leave me with an
overwhelming feeling of contentment.

I'd give anything for her to come and set my
mind at ease again now.

Frank stands up and makes his way to the living
room, planner open and tucked under his right arm.
It is beginning to get light now, and the woman from

down the road is already up and out with her two elderly Labradors, getting their exercise in before the heat returns in earnest. He bobs his head in recognition as she jogs past. It seems almost unfathomable that life continues around him, when his is in tatters.

It is obvious which photo Maggie was writing about. He suddenly feels very guilty that it is lying facedown. Without it, the whole composition of the room feels off; the photo has occupied center stage ever since they got it printed and framed in one of Eleanor's own creations, a mix of shells and glitter and that strange, fishy-smelling glue that primary schools love. At the time, Frank had felt awkward asking the barmaid to put down her precarious stack of empties and take a snap of the three of them. They swept into formation quickly, keen not to put her out any more than she already was, propping a sleepy Eleanor in front of Maggie in front of him. When they'd gotten the film developed, Frank pointed out that they had formed their very own family of Russian dolls—he couldn't get over how perfectly their life slotted together.

Frank picks up the photo and forces himself to absorb every last detail of it—the trim of Eleanor's T-shirt tangled up in the zip of her costume, a stray strand of hair by Maggie's right ear curling up like a loose spring. For years, it was seeing photos like this that sustained him at the end of a long day at work. It justified the crack-of-dawn alarms and the sleepless nights and the thousands of tiny sacrifices that constituted family life. Until recently, that is. He is ashamed to admit, even to himself, the lengths he has gone to in order to avoid family photographs in the last six months.

There was that incident—the one they would both rather forget. It happened three months ago now, but the shame of it makes it feel as fresh as yesterday. Maggie had caught Frank red-handed. Bin liner in one hand, the photos in another. He couldn't even bring himself to pick them up, instead using the side of his hand like a brush, sweeping away every last hint of his Little Girl Lost. Maggie tried to reason with him. She pleaded. She cried. When she couldn't stop him, there was nothing for it but to leave the room and wait until his uncharacteristic fury had subsided.

By the time Frank got up the next day, every last photo was back in its place. It was as if nothing had happened. The two frames that had been chipped in his frenzy had been mended, the tracks of the super-glue almost imperceptible. Maggie always did do such a good job of holding them together—him, Eleanor. He turns back to that line—*falling short of the mark*. It could not be any further from the Maggie he knew.

There is a crunch. Frank has been holding the frame

so tightly that one of the shells has broken off, leaving a chalky residue in his palm. He puts the frame back before he does any more damage and drops what remains of the shell into his pocket.

"Oh, Maggie," Frank says. "You never had anything to prove."

Three days to go

I often think about what sort of mother *you* thought I was, Frank. I knew all too well how I thought I was: highly strung, cautious, scared out of my mind by the sheer weight of love and responsibility I felt for the part of me that fell outside of my control. I so desperately wanted you to feel that I was doing a good job too, that you could be proud of me.

And I only had the one shot to get motherhood right, didn't I? After Eleanor was born, we didn't mention a sibling. For my part, I worried that if I said it, I might jinx something. We'd had such good luck to have the one child, I didn't want to risk starting a conversation that would make me sound ungrateful or, worse, suggest that Eleanor wasn't enough. If we were trying, it was without ever calling it that. Ultimately, it was nature that ended any potential discussion: a second child wasn't happening for us.

I told myself we had more than enough to focus on with one. If I was disappointed, it was more that my grand plans for a big family were frustrated. Never in you, Frank. Never in Eleanor either. Not back then, at least. At nursing college, I'd envisaged myself with a huge brood, like Edie's, siblings and noise and huge family Christmases with the sort of boundless happiness that I had craved as a child. When that didn't happen, I began to grieve for the life I'd thought I would have. I grieved when we couldn't conceive, and there was a part of me that still grieved after Eleanor was born. There is a special type of grief that comes from packing up your expectations for your own future.

From the off, I worried about Eleanor being an only child. There were the obvious anxieties: loneliness, selfishness, some sociopathic lack of personal skills. Horrible, empty clichés that were easy enough to put to bed the older Eleanor got, simply by looking at how thoughtful and considerate she was. Gradually, when she'd reached five or six, that was replaced by the worry that we had let her down. Doesn't every child want a sibling? A confidant, a playmate, a friend genetically predisposed to make up with you after a fight? I didn't want her to grow up and think we

had denied her that. I couldn't stand the thought
that she might resent us.

I went out of my way to make sure that wasn't
the case. Overcompensating, I'm sure most would
call it, but at the time it couldn't have seemed
further from that. On the weekends, if you had to
work, I'd take Ellie out to the café round the corner
and I'd buy us both buns the size of her face. There
would be sugar all over her, a fine white dust that
settled on the tip of her nose and her cheeks. She
would just talk and talk, mad nonsense mainly,
and I was so swept up in the joy she brought me
that I wouldn't even be dabbing at her with a
tissue or reminding her to chew with her mouth
closed. All the time, there was a smile across her
face, stretching ear to ear. Priceless. It seemed
impossible that she could have been happier, or that
I could have been either.

So, the first time she asked why she didn't have
any siblings with any real seriousness it took me by
surprise, no matter how many possible iterations of
the conversation I had been through in my head.
Eleanor was seven, and I'd just collected her from
Katie's house. It was always so boisterous there, with
four kids under ten and an open-door policy to any
and all of their friends. The noise alone was usually

enough to send the girls up to Katie's room with their hands pressed firmly against their ears.

We were in the car, just out of the traffic at the top of the Woodstock Road and not more than ten minutes from home.

"Why don't I have a brother or sister?"

I was caught entirely off guard. I turned down the volume on the radio and scoured my mind for the most appropriate answer.

"Oh, er, why do you ask?"

"Katie has three."

"Well, not all families are the same. Not everyone wants more than one child."

"Did you?"

I had no idea what to say for best. "It doesn't matter because we are so, *so* happy to have you," I managed, after a pause.

The road ahead was blocked, double-parked on both sides. I let the car ahead try to navigate the chaos and pulled up to the curb. It was dark, and I had to switch on the light above the rearview mirror to see her. Eleanor was staring up at me, visibly puzzled. Her brow furrowed into that wobbly central wrinkle that took me right back to the first time I held her. Every word I'd said was true. It sounds tragic, Frank, but all I wanted then was some affirmation: an "I know that" or "I love you." Even "Thanks, Mum" would have done the trick.

Before I had the chance to dig any deeper, the van ahead flashed its full beams for me to come through. The moment had passed. I was fuming with myself on the drive home, all through supper. I hadn't even had a chance to roll out my ready-prepared spiel: *You are enough. We never needed another child. Our family is perfect as it is.* It was on the tip of my tongue, but somehow I couldn't bring myself to raise the subject again, in case it made it a bigger deal than it needed to be.

Whenever she mentioned being an only child to us in those next few years, it was never as a question, more as a statement of fact. Did you notice that, Frank? That tone when she said, "*I* don't have a brother or sister," emphasis on the "I," as if to suggest this set her apart from her friends, even from us, in some mysterious way. To me, it looked like it had worked out for the best. There was never any doubt back then that Eleanor was secure in her position as captain and mainstay of our hearts. And what greater achievement is there as a parent, really, than to know your child feels utterly assured of your love?

That's not to say we took it for granted. There are a lot of things I can accuse myself of these days, but that is certainly not one of them. Every day we worked to secure that anchor, and each suppertime would be its own Eleanor-focused show-and-tell, you asking the questions in your best impression of a news presenter, Eleanor the interviewee reeling out the details of her day to an enrapt audience of two.

And what of it, for us? Well, we learned a lot, that's for sure. By the time she was eight, we could name and profile every kid in her class; we knew all about the annoying way Josh put his hand up, how Anna could only write with a pencil with a special grip from Japan. By the time she was nine, we'd covered the Tudors, the Egyptians, and the Greeks and could have sailed through Eleanor's pop quizzes on all of them. When she was ten, we heard every point in a yearlong playground argument between Heidi and Jess, two of the most popular girls in her class. We lived and breathed Eleanor and did everything we could to further her sense of stability at home.

More than that, I felt like we learned so much

about Eleanor from her delivery of it all. She was so funny, so entertaining. She definitely got that from you. When she was ten, she had that French art teacher and we had a year of it—Eleanor had her accent down to a T, along with that peculiar way her whole upper body rolled side to side while she talked as if she were stuck on a particularly choppy Channel crossing. Some evenings I wouldn't get halfway through my plate because we would be laughing and laughing and suddenly the food had gone cold. I can still see her now, clinging to my hand the minute I got in the door and dragging me through to the kitchen where she would embark on the latest story. There was nothing like it to make me feel needed, irreplaceable.

I loved that she *wanted* to talk to us. At the time, I never looked further than that. Why would I? Now, though, when I comb through those suppers with as much precision as my mind can manage, it seems so telling that while she was happy discussing her friends, her lessons, the outward trappings of her life, Eleanor never really wanted to talk about herself.

Did you notice that too, Frank? We saw it after Portugal when she refused to admit she was shaken. She was that bit more reserved for a few weeks afterward, on edge, staying close. But things went back to normal and we could have declared it just one bad experience, for Eleanor, for us both.

Only it wasn't the one-off we might have hoped, was it?

They never did go back to Portugal after that holiday when Eleanor was seven. Maggie was very superstitious, and it seemed a small sacrifice not to go back there if it would help put the trauma of the night on the beach behind them all. Or at least as much as possible. Even now, the mere mention of that trip is enough to make Frank shiver, despite the stuffiness of the living room. For so many years that was his worst memory—the empty table and Eleanor gone. The roar of the sea and his own panic screaming in his ears.

These past few months, there is little doubt that Frank has shouldered worse. It has always seemed strange to him how, as a species, humans are so fixated on comparing their misery. The trials and tribulations of now versus then; our suffering versus that of our friends. In the silence, Frank has spent plenty of time mulling which is worse—a seven-year-old Eleanor lost on a foreign shore or the lost girl she became nearly twenty years later. The short, sharp panic of the former or the long, drawn-out decline of the latter? No parent should have to choose.

And in both instances, Maggie is right about Eleanor being so stoic. She never did want to speak about herself. Neither of them could work out why. They provided a happy home, the open environment to talk about whatever was troubling her. It reminded Frank of a phrase his own mother was fond of: *You can bring a horse to water, but you can't make it drink.* He imagines a hidden door inside Eleanor, all her feelings pressed up behind it. They could knock and knock and knock, but only she could let them in.

No—it wasn't a *one-off,* not by any means. Frank can think of a handful of examples where Eleanor deflected the limelight away from her own issues and shone it right back on him and Maggie both.

He smooths down the next page to see which one it will be.

Three days to go
I remember the parents' evening in her last year
at primary school, when we sat, bewildered, as we
were praised for how well Eleanor had handled
one of the boys in her class picking on her after
she collected first prize in a county-wide maths

competition. The next day, when I asked about it, Eleanor insisted it was nothing. Do you know what she said when I asked why she hadn't told us? Can you guess, Frank? Go on, try.

I didn't want you and Dad to worry.

When she moved to secondary school not long after, I was increasingly vigilant for signs that she was holding her problems back from us. That was when a sibling would have been useful. In the absence of one, I found myself craving the same role I imagined one would play in her life. I wanted Eleanor to see me not just as her mother but as a friend. I knew what teenage girls were like, and I couldn't bear the thought of Eleanor trying to navigate the knowing looks and the snide comments without someone to confide in.

I went out of my way to make that happen, organizing trips and activities for the two of us. Always outside the house, in some new environment that I hoped would make her feel mature and give her the nudge she needed to open up and confide in me all at once. And you were so supportive. I never got the sense that you felt left out, but maybe you just appreciated the peace that came with me being out of the house and you being out of earshot.

The Easter after Eleanor's twelfth birthday, we

took a trip up to Edinburgh, just us girls. We walked through the Old Town arm in arm, playing fantasy house-hunting with the big, beautiful Georgian homes. We bought matching tartan scarves and wore them with inordinate pride around the castle. When we sat out the rain in a pub on the corner of the Royal Mile, I let Eleanor try a sip of my whisky, and her response was one of such dramatic disgust— "It's like something *died* in there, Mum"—that I thought we were about to get carted out by the management. On the last day, she managed to get me up Arthur's Seat, huffing and puffing, through the force of her extraordinary good humor alone. When we got to the top, she draped her arm over my shoulders. Not a bead of sweat on her.

"We're on top of the world!" she said, her eyes fixed on the city sprawling below.

"Where you belong." I wrapped my arm around her waist and squeezed her hip. "All I ever want is for you to soar."

It was such a success that we ended up going away annually, the two of us. We did Berlin the next year, Dublin when she was fourteen. I remember getting up the courage to ask her about boys then (better safe than sorry) and was met with such a look of horror that I concluded we were safe on that front. I loved those trips, Frank. I loved how they brought us closer and the way I felt we were forming the sort of mother-daughter relationship I had always wanted with my own mother. I could see us doing this when Eleanor was twenty, thirty, forty. Maybe she would bring her own daughter one day.

We ended up canceling our weekend away the next year, when she was fifteen. She blamed it on exams. I couldn't see how two or three days would hurt, but I wasn't going to push her either. That was the whole joy of those trips—Eleanor wanting to be there. You knew how hurt I was, didn't you? I tried to hide it, to get behind Eleanor's drive for studying at the expense of everything else. She was focused and ambitious—we ought to be proud. That much seemed obvious, and it was, until things started to unravel in earnest.

In reality, it was much harder to get behind Eleanor's drive. We were both on edge, tiptoeing around the house, no radio in the kitchen, no noise whatsoever. I tried to coax her out of her room to give her a break, but all I was met with was her steadfast refusal to so much as glance up from her folders to look me in the eye. When I went to tell her to keep things in perspective, that she would do brilliantly with just a fraction of this work, she would snap. *I didn't understand.*

I flat out denied that at the time. Now, though, when I pick back over those days, hungry for clues to what was to come, I realize she was spot on about that. I didn't understand, Frank, not one bit. How had we managed to raise a child who would crumble under this sort of pressure? Maybe my mother was right when she claimed we were overprotective. We had spent the best part of sixteen years shoring her up, being the scaffolding surrounding the fragile growth of her personality. Wasn't that what it meant, to parent? She was about to turn sixteen, adulthood just around the corner, the passage of life dictating that our metal supports were soon to be whipped away. I hate to say it, Frank, but I didn't trust that she had the resilience not to falter.

We could console ourselves with the fact that the exam ordeal was time-bound. The end was in sight, and with it, we hoped, the old Eleanor, brimming with the lightness and the laughter that had always balanced her out. There wasn't another parent in the world as desperate as me to see their child finally kick back. And when she did? I wasn't naive about her being out, drinking probably. I just wished she could have called or texted, whatever was less mortifying in a public situation where the participants were under eighteen. That way we could have had some rest. I was never able to nod off until I knew she was safely through the door at night. It explains a lot about the frequency with which I have to pick up my prescriptions for sleeping pills nowadays.

That summer of her sixteenth birthday, I think it's fair to say that I was more relaxed than you. Not horizontal. It was far too hot for that, and I've always been a pacer. Just take a look at the carpet under the window. Practically threadbare. No, what I mean is that, at first, I thought it was natural. I saw it as the first step toward getting Eleanor back on track, realigning her energy, her being young and as carefree as she ever could be. I could reconcile myself to the late nights and the half-empty bottles in the alcohol cabinet if it meant she was finding her way back to the girl I knew.

I imagine you are reading this, choking on the depths of my delusion. *Wishful thinking* sounds better, but in light of what came next, it sounds so painfully airy. Everything changed the night of the dinner party. I wonder if you sensed it then, over the wine and the gossip and the piles of dirty plates? While we were playing the consummate charming hosts, something happened that night that robbed us of our little girl forever. It was the moment I began to grieve Eleanor while she was still right before my eyes.

Do you know what happened that night, Frank? Did you ever find out what caused such an almighty change? I did. And it broke me. It broke me that Eleanor asked me not to share it, and it broke me that I kept her trust on that. I never got to test the logic of a problem shared. Even if it hadn't been halved, even if I had borne ninety percent of the load, wouldn't that still have been better?

What, though, Maggie? What? I can see you in my mind's eye, all frustrated, flicking your Biro against your teeth in a bid to get me to spit it out. But now, just before I do, can you take a minute? Please, Frank. For me. Take a minute and just try to hold on to the image of our happy trio for as long as you can. Close your eyes, imagine it.

I don't want what I tell you next to change how you see our Eleanor.

Chapter 6

Frank isn't clicking his Biro, but that was a good guess on Maggie's part. Instead he fiddles with the pages of the planner, concertinaing the edges with his index finger and thumb and then letting the paper spring back against his palm. So, she knew. He is not entirely surprised. There was always that bond between Maggie and Eleanor, that unspoken and unspeakable tie that ran between them and sometimes left him feeling like the piggy in the middle. Had it started in the womb? Or in the early years when it was just the two of them, all day, while he sweated it out on a stuffy minibus somewhere down the M40, en route to yet another conference?

He is restless, desperate to find out what it was

that had drawn Eleanor further away from them and further into herself. It was something she didn't want him to know, clearly. Every time he goes to turn the page, that is what holds him back. In his frustration, he returns to the study. Old habits die hard, and this is his safe kingdom, or rather it was, before the fire alarm and the paramedics and Maggie taken away to the shriek of the sirens.

The computer screen has gone back to sleep, the northern lights swirling in great jade waves across the monitor. Frank jiggles the mouse, and the photos spring back to life. He meant to scroll forward, like Maggie wanted him to, so he could savor their happy trio for a few minutes more: the lazy weekends spent building duvet forts, the camping excursion to Brittany when the tent flooded, the pictures of the three of them in Battleships deadlock. Only with the tiredness, the subtle tremor in his hands that started the moment he found Maggie and will not end until she is back, he has gone the wrong way. The photo reel zooms to the most recent photo.

It was taken by Edie a few Christmases ago, not a comfortable holiday by any standards. It was clear Eleanor didn't want to be there; there was that vacancy in her eyes that showed she was elsewhere, or dreaming of it. At least she had turned up. Frank and Maggie had redoubled their festive cheer in a bid to compensate for her deficit in that department, and both wore gaudy festive jumpers. The lights on Frank's have flashed at just the wrong moment, setting the lighting of the whole shot off, so that their faces are blazingly bright and the backdrop looks like a cellar.

Frank zooms in on Eleanor, scrolling in closer and closer until her face fills the screen and he is looking square at her. *What was it? Why couldn't you tell me too?* He examines the flecks in her irises, the tiny bloodshot veins. Can he find the truth in there? It takes him back to the last time he saw her, and he has to squeeze his eyes shut for just a beat or two to calm the rush in his mind.

Our happy trio. Frank has thought of little else these past six months. He knows that whatever comes next will change his perception of that, Maggie has made that much obvious. It is enough to make him want to throw in the towel, to shove the planner in the bin or on the bonfire. What's to stop him? His own guilty conscience. Perhaps the fact that he has shown enough cowardice already. He said it to Eleanor on their patio nights, and he still stands by it now—it's never too late to change the story.

Frank inhales as deeply as his tight chest allows, and
this time he manages to turn the page.

Two days to go
Did you do it? I hope so. There is so much good
to think about, although, understandably, that is
not what we dwell on. Not now, after everything.
Another mistake, I'd say, but it is not too late to go
some way to correcting it.

So, Eleanor. What happened? We were both so
desperate to know, weren't we? But she wouldn't
open up, no matter how hard we tried in the days
that followed the dinner party. You didn't have any
luck, and mine wasn't much better. She was avoiding
me, Frank, plain and simple. I didn't realize until
then how perfectly possible that was, even under the
same roof. Eye contact cut off, all conversation too;
the very moment I walked into the room she walked
straight out again. She lay in bed and spent whole
days there. A week later, Katie came to the house
to pick her up for something, but Eleanor wouldn't
come to the door and instead insisted I tell Katie that
she wasn't feeling well, that she couldn't go out after
all. I felt awful sending her away.

When Katie had gone, I crept back upstairs. If

she was sick, then the illness was a mystery to me.
The door wasn't quite shut, and there was a gap that
I could see through, a diagonal onto the bed. Eleanor
had pulled the curtains and was just lying there, on
her back, looking up at the ceiling. I was all geared
up to go in, but I got to the threshold of her room
and there was something biting in my chest that
stopped me. Maybe it was the blank stare. I couldn't
stand to have that directed at me. What if I got
turned away as well? I told myself it was fatigue,
burnout, whatever you want to call it. It was best not
to push her any further. I would give her a month to
get back to her old self. I hoped she would speak of
her own accord.

Nothing. Clearly her reticence came from your
side of the gene pool. With a month nearly up,
opportunity presented itself to me. Eleanor's phone
gave up the ghost and she needed it fixed. *Urgently,*
she said, as if the thing breathed for her too. She had
an induction day for sixth form, so it was left to me,
the bill payer, to get it working again. I told her that
I'd use my morning off to sort it and was met with
the warmest look she'd given me in weeks.

The teen behind the counter in the phone shop
took great delight in telling me that it was kaput. I
would need to replace the handset, but they could

transfer the SIM card and any data on it. Numbers, messages, contacts. So long as it was backed up.
It seemed likely enough, and I cashed out for a replacement. He got it all set up for me, finally asking which generic orchid I would like as my background with that slight look of pity that tech assistants seem to reserve for women of a certain age.

"It's for my daughter, actually," I said as he flicked through the options.

"Let's keep the default, then. Everything else is sorted. Tell her she'll need to reset her passcode." He added, "I'll leave it unlocked for now."

I know you won't believe it, Frank, but part of me wasn't going to look. Isn't there a word for that? Evidence procured by such dirty means that even the police reject it? All those years trying to earn my way into Eleanor's trust, and here I was about to break it. I wouldn't have done it had things not been so bad, were we not so desperate to find out what had happened that night to make her retreat right into herself. I got into the car and went into her messages before I had the chance to think better of it.

Most conversations had lapsed a month back.
I suppose it should have made me feel better; we weren't the only ones being locked out. Katie was

320 · ABBIE GREAVES

the most recent text—despite what we'd seen on
the doorstep, she hadn't been entirely pushed away.
She'd been in touch just a day before.

Tried calling but you are still not picking up. If he took
things too far that's serious, you need to speak to
someone. You don't have to tell the police or school
or whatever if you don't want to but tell your mum or
someone. Please Ellie I'm worried about you xxxxxx

Someone might as well have come and slammed
my head into the dashboard. I felt dizzy, hot, and
sick, my ears ringing and the lines of text wobbling
in front of me. I made myself take deep breaths and
scrolled back up through their conversation in case
there was some shred of context I could latch on to
that might lead to an interpretation other than the
one that was screaming out at me. The last few texts
were all from Katie—variations on pick up and r u
OK? Nothing more.

Just then my own phone started going. Sharon
was coming down with something and had to leave.
They hated to ask, on my morning off as well, but
would I mind coming into the surgery a bit earlier?
My noncommittal humming was quickly taken as
a yes. I didn't have the energy to protest. Before I

started the car, I went back to Katie's last message and took a photo of it with my phone.

All afternoon, in between patients, I would flick my phone on and reread the message. On some level, I was hoping that I had imagined it, that it would magically have managed to disappear in the time it took to run a stop-smoking consultation or to change the dressing on an ulcer. I suppose I was also hoping that some answers might miraculously show up, slap-bang between the tightly compacted lines of text. How could I raise this with Eleanor? More importantly, how the hell could I even begin to go about fixing it for her?

I thought about telling you, Frank, of course I did. But somehow that felt like a double violation of Eleanor's privacy. It was bad enough that I had seen, been through her texts—dragging you into it seemed one step too far. And if it was what I thought it was, what then? No sixteen-year-old girl wants her father to be privy to that sort of knowledge. No, I resolved that this was my cross to bear.

A couple of days later, I spent a torturous morning waiting for you to do the food shop. Finally, it was just the two of us in the house. The minute I heard the car pulling out of the drive, I steeled myself against the kitchen counter, ironing in

322 · ABBIE GREAVES

hand, my evidence in my pocket, and took a minute to collect myself. Do you know, Frank, that was the most fearful I have ever been? I was scared of my own daughter. I was scared of what I would learn. I was so scared, Frank, but I had no other choice.

"Can't you knock?" Eleanor dropped her phone to her chest. She had seemed so grateful to have it working again that even if she had been worried about it being temporarily unlocked, she certainly hadn't mentioned it. I suppose she had so much on her plate that the thought of my accessing it had never even crossed her mind.

She watched in silence while I picked my way across her room. I dropped her laundry on the rocking chair in the corner of the room and then sat on the edge of her bed, my hand reaching out to clasp one of her ankles under the duvet.

She flinched.

"What's up, Eleanor?" She had never been odd about touch before. "Is everything OK?"

Eleanor was looking past me, out the window to the playing field beyond. I clung tighter to her calf and felt a shiver run up the back of my own neck as she recoiled again.

"Look, there's no easy way to say this." That got her attention. I lifted my thighs up enough to pull

my phone out of my pocket and flicked through my
album until I found the image. By that stage, it was
in my thumb's muscle memory. I passed it to her and
braced myself for the recriminations.

Nothing.

"They had to unlock your phone at the
shop . . . ," I started, cringing at just how weak the
excuse coming out of my mouth sounded.

I watched as her eyes scanned the text, once,
twice. "I don't know what you want me to say."

"What happened?"

"Just that." She briefly nodded her head at the
message between us, before clicking the button on
the side of my phone so the screen turned black. "A
guy took things too far, at a party. I didn't want to,
but I didn't say no. I should have done. But . . . I
couldn't."

"What?" My voice was barely above a whisper,
all breathy and rasping.

"I don't know what you want me to say, Mum.
I'm sorry. It was my fault. I just want to forget this
ever happened. I want it to go away." Her eyes were
brimming. All I wanted to do was reach out and
wipe the tears away. She got her sleeve there before
me. "Please. Can we stop talking about this now?"

For a minute or so, I watched as she wound a

loose thread on her duvet cover round and round her
index finger. I had never come to terms with how
strange it was to see my own nervous tics played out
in Eleanor. It was the closest I had been to her in
months and in the worst possible circumstances. My
mind was all questions and I didn't know where to
begin or how to phrase them, and suddenly it was all
too much, the itch inside me, the need to know.

"Why?"

"Why what?"

"Why didn't you tell me?"

She shrugged. "I didn't want to let you down."

What was I meant to say to that, Frank? I must
have mumbled all manner of things—that it was
impossible, that we loved her regardless, that all we
ever wanted was to make her happy. None of it went
in. It can't have done, can it? Otherwise how the hell
have we ended up here?

Before I left the room, she made me promise.
Not to tell the school or the police or to tell you or
anyone. Not to try to find out who it was. She was
so adamant about that, gripping my hand, fixing me
with a look that was so hurt and so desperate that
I would defy anyone to have behaved differently.
She told me it was enough that I knew. That we
would get through it OK, together. And do you

know what? I believed her. I'm sorry, Frank, but I promised.

Later, in bed, when I felt my guilt holding you at arm's length, I told myself I was doing the right thing. I couldn't betray her, not when she had confided in me again. That was all I ever wanted. I thought I could solve this myself and bring Eleanor back to us both. I can't believe I was ever that naive.

That night, while you slept, I asked myself if you would have found whoever did that to her and forced him to suffer the way I wanted him to. I have imagined you swinging at him, from behind, and taking a final blow when he was on the floor, man-to-man and face-to-face, every ounce of his flesh screaming for mercy.

In my head, it worked, but in reality? You have never been a violent man, though there is violence in the way that you love us—with an intensity and a ferocity that seem to eat you whole.

Still, I do not think you would wear revenge well. Do you?

Chapter 7

Frank is panting, short, heaving exhalations, each one following so quickly on the last that the stale air is immediately sucked back in, halitosis unnoticed. His pulse is racing like the march of a thousand soldiers, each one on a mission to the brink and beyond.

Oh, Eleanor.

Why couldn't she tell him? He would never have judged her. It just wasn't possible. Not when his love stretched out like the passage of time, not conditional on outside events and impossible to stop. He has spent a lifetime priding himself on being an approachable man, the sort people feel comfortable asking to carry their luggage up the stairs, or to watch their bag while they zip to the loo. Suddenly he feels like the biggest fraud of all.

He'd known there was something wrong. It was apparent that night when she barreled in, so dazed and lost and confused, and it was apparent the next morning too, when she shrank back from every attempt he made to reach out and speak to her. After that, he had been so scared of losing the whisper-fine strands of Eleanor that remained that he had just avoided the subject altogether. There is no denying how badly he has failed her.

Should he have guessed this? A boy. A party. Something that so evidently did not seem to be Eleanor's fault however much she protested to the contrary. Perhaps. You could call it willful ignorance on a father's part or just a blind belief in the goodness of humankind. Either way, he had never come close to this conclusion.

But now he knows, and he can see no way through the barrage of increasingly sickening images—the hands clutching at her, her skirt pulled up. Worst of all, her head turned to the side as if she didn't even want to associate with her own body anymore. He hates it. Hates it. He drags his nails down the page with such force that one catches in the paper and makes a neat vertical tear.

But what Frank hates the most is his failure to protect Eleanor. As a parent you are meant to have a radar for your offspring's troubles. A burbling in your stomach when they are sick, an unshakable headache when they are sad. What's yours is mine and more besides. But that night? While they humored his colleagues and toasted his success over a fleet of inane anecdotes and serving dishes sticky with salad dressing? He'd had no idea. What sort of a parent does that make him?

Frank has been sitting so hunched up that the dull ache in his spine has turned into short, sharp jabs, caused by the compressed discs the physio is forever complaining are a result of his height or the cycling or lifestyle factors that at sixty-seven he has no intention of changing. To shift the pain, he tilts back in the desk chair until he is almost reclining. He shuts his eyes for just a moment's respite from the onslaught of realization and revelation. When he opens them, it is Maggie he sees, chastising him for nodding off again when he said he had things to do. He has never suspected that she knew.

When he asked her—*What happened, Mags? What changed?*—it was always with that rhetorical rush that signals you aren't expecting an answer. He furrows his brow in concentration. He can't remember her opening her mouth to offer up her intel, but he can't remember leaving a gap long enough for her to do so either.

And really, when it comes down to it, why did he feel he needed to know anyway? It is not as if he could have done more than Maggie, who he knows would have tried everything and the kitchen sink, who could not have cared more. No. He wanted to support Maggie. He wanted Eleanor to feel comfortable sharing that secret with him instead of so adamantly denying it to him. Did she think his love was more conditional? If he is honest, really, very honest, there is also a small piece of him that, childishly, feels left out, like the second favorite. That is the issue with the biological necessity for two parents—someone has to come last.

Frank presses his index fingers and thumbs together, the rest of his digits interwoven. When he presses his hands to his forehead, running the fingers up and down his frown lines, he plays with a handgun of his own creation, nestled against his skull. *I do not think you would wear revenge well. Do you?* Maggie always did know him so well. He would have been the worst avenger in the history of the world. He would delay the mission, dither at the point of action, find any excuse to avoid the moment of confrontation. That doesn't mean Frank didn't fight, though, in his own silent, unassuming way.

As he slumps forward, Frank is hit with an earth-shattering tiredness behind his eyes. He felt this fatigue a lot when the fight kicked in with Eleanor, once everything sprinted so far out of hand. In some perverse inversion of expectations, he had slept less the older she got. After that night, he felt his bond with Eleanor disintegrating like a tissue in the rain. He was grasping and grasping after it and still it dissolved into the tiny white fragments too small to collect, let alone keep.

And then, of course, there is the anxiety. Even these past six months, with his own cross to bear, he has worried ceaselessly about her—where she is, who she is with. It never stops, that worry, as a parent, does it?

One day to go
Selfishly, I am glad I am not there to see how you took that, Frank. You have always done such a good job at looking stoical, another thing Eleanor inherited from you, no doubt. But don't forget, I have known you forty years, loved you for all of them: I can read the signs in you better than I can read myself. I know the nervous adjustment of your glasses, your eyes glancing off to the side before drawing back to the problem in hand. That was your default face for Eleanor, when everything started to spiral.

You wear your hurt so very obviously. You have done these past few weeks and months. I know you are suffering. After the initial shock subsided and I realized that you weren't going to speak to me, no matter how hard I tried or cried or begged, I resigned myself to studying you in the moments

when we were together in the house, not separated
by the kitchen or study doors. Over supper, I would
watch as you marshaled the peas onto your fork in
case there was a tremble in your hands that might
give something away, a clue to what, if anything,
might also be awry. When we brushed our teeth in
the bathroom, I would check the tension in your
jaw, on the off chance you might momentarily break
the silence and burble out an apology in among a
mouthful of toothpaste.

I stay awake until you come to bed with that same
hope. Not that I can sleep anyway, not without my
pills. I like it because, when I hear you inevitably
knocking over the washing basket, the buckle
on your trousers making a racket as it hits the
hardwood floor, I know my ears still work. I know
I am not trapped in here, with just my voice for
company. I haven't gone mad. Though there is still
time, I suppose. One day more.

The minute I feel your body melt against mine,
I cry. If not every night, then close enough. I know
you can feel it, because you squeeze me tighter, press
your lips against my neck. Sometimes, at this point,
we have sex. I am never quite sure who initiates
it. Our need is equal. Recently I have wondered
if this has been the only way for us to bridge the

gaping hole between us. For those minutes, those
blissful, peaceful minutes, it is as if none of this
ever happened. We are back before the baby, before
Eleanor, tangled together in the single bed where
we spent our first nights together, with no heed for
Jules's and Edie's sleep patterns.

Just last night, when we lay there, when we were
done, I wondered if it might be the moment when I
would finally hear you again. Six months of dashed
expectations, frustration piled upon frustration to
the point where I could scream just to feel the give
in the air, and still there is a piece of me that thinks
my patience will get through to you eventually.
Why? Why? Why? I don't know why I still get my
hopes up, with so little time left. I convince myself
that I can see your lips about to move, as if an itch
has passed across your face that is just waiting to be
scratched. Then it subsides and there are just those
same blank stares into the darkness that we have
been doing since Eleanor shut off.

That was what it was, wasn't it? Someone had
turned down the dimmer switch on our glowing
orb of a daughter until she was trembling with the
effort of not switching off entirely. After that night,
she began fading into a shadow of her former self, a
hollow cast of the original. It was like living with a

stranger, if it was possible to have birthed and raised an entirely alien object.

We tried to get things back to normal once she started sixth form, in the hope that routine would bring the old Ellie back. We probably needed it as much as she did. At work, I could barely focus on the job in hand. For the first time since Eleanor was born, I had no control over the images that flashed in my mind. I did blood tests and saw Eleanor bleed in the aftermath, over the toilet bowl, scared and confused. Every time I saw a man in his twenties swaggering in, leaning on the reception desk, elbows wide and head cocked at the receptionist, I saw him pulling Ellie away by the hand, her feet hesitating with doubt.

I was trapped, Frank. Who could I tell? Not you, not without the risk of pushing away what was left of Eleanor. Not Edie. Not a colleague. After all, a promise is a promise. Instead, I threw myself into finding her every source of help I could with a compulsion that terrified me in its insistence. I stashed leaflets in her schoolbag only for her to force them into my hand again the minute she was home: *Seriously, Mum. Don't.*

You were out the night I told her. It was about four months after the dinner party, give or take, our desperation by that point well and truly rooted. When I got back from the surgery, I headed upstairs to change but stopped at her bedroom doorway. I took a deep breath, walked in.

"How was your day?" Eleanor was scrolling through her phone and lifted her head just enough to show that she had heard but not enough to convey anything beyond ambivalence.

"I have this for you." I slipped her a piece of paper, hastily crammed into my handbag straight from the printer.

"What is this?" She sat up a bit and smoothed it on her lap.

"Someone to talk to. Privately. Look, I know you didn't like the idea of your dad and me being there too, so I thought . . . maybe this might be better? You can go by yourself; I'll settle up after."

There was nothing and then, miraculously: "Thank you."

I didn't want to push my luck. I turned to leave but just as I did so, she reached out a hand and caught the edge of my jacket.

"Really, Mum. Thank you." She stood up, and we even managed a cuddle, a short one, but for those seconds it calmed the frantic mess of my mind.

Three days later, when the appointment should

just have been wrapping up, Amelia (PsyD) phoned at work. A no-show. I couldn't understand what was going on. I shouldn't have let her go alone, should I, Frank? I didn't want her to feel we had abandoned her, but if I acted on instinct, clung to her like the sole life raft in my ocean of panic, I risked her shrugging me off for good. I never could work out what constituted enough space.

All the time, Eleanor was speeding toward a cliff edge and the brake cable was cut right through. We should have been her brakes, shouldn't we? That is what parents are meant to do. Sometimes you asked me why I didn't come down harder on her when, each evening, she would return to her room the minute we had finished another painful supper, Eleanor answering our questions with little more than the odd monosyllable and pushing her uneaten food around the plate. It wasn't as if you wanted to throw yourself into the ring as the disciplinarian either, but clearly you also needed confirmation that we were doing the right thing by Eleanor.

We started getting letters home from school two terms into that first year of sixth form, alarming calls to my mobile that would flash up mid-consultation and send my stomach crashing to the floor. There was no problem with her work, not by any means, but some teachers had noticed she wasn't participating in class. She seemed tired. The nurse had noticed she was losing weight. I sat through one excruciating weigh-in with Eleanor in the school sick bay—*Now, Eleanor, we all need to eat! I know a lot of young girls aspire to be thin, but that isn't healthy at all*—and hoped she would be condescended back into her previous appetite.

That night, at dinner, she did eat a little more. It was progress, embryonic, but progress nonetheless. I was so desperate not to let that slip that once she was in bed, I got up, went to the bathroom, and then waited outside her door until I could hear her snuffling snores start up. *Our little truffle pig,* you had called her as a toddler. I doubted that would go down very well now. Once I was convinced she was asleep, I edged into Eleanor's room and sat with my back against the crenulations of the radiator until my coccyx felt on fire. I stayed there long after that point too.

"Come back to me," I whispered.

Eleanor didn't wake up. Or if she did, she never told me. Do you know, Frank, what I missed most when she went to university? It was that. The habit I developed, dedicating long nights to a vigil held at the foot of her bed, one hand supporting my own weight, the other reaching out, too scared to touch Eleanor lest she wake up. I never tired of watching her, the subtle inhale and exhale of her breath, the endless thrashing about from one side of the bed to the other.

I thought that maybe, just maybe, if I watched her, at night, nothing else bad could happen. I'm wincing writing that, Frank. Naivety doesn't suit me, as well you know. And I'm not sure that's even what it was. I was paralyzed. I wanted to do it right—being a mother. Now, when I think about it, that is where I know I went wrong—thinking too much, wanting too much—and I hate myself for it.

I will never stop feeling responsible for what happened. Not a day has gone by since she told me when I haven't obsessed over what more I could have done. Frog-marched her to the therapist? Force-fed her three meals a day? Pulled her out of school and sent her somewhere else entirely? I have imagined all these scenarios, but none of them has struck me as the long-lost key to success.

Do you blame yourself for what happened too, Frank?

Through the chink in the study blinds, Frank watches as the neighbor's children traipse to the bus stop. Eight o'clock. The oldest is never unplugged, headphones either in his ears or looped over the top like a bouncer who has yet to grow into his brawn. He has a short-sleeved shirt on, they all do today, and the skin on his biceps is covered in dark pink pimples. He doesn't smile, and he certainly doesn't engage with his siblings. Every time he sees him, Frank feels nervous.

They never did get round to fixing the blinds, so there is no way to shut out the world, now awake and jostling with reminders. Without thinking, he finds himself on the stairs, planner in hand, and pushing open the door to Eleanor's room. He switches on the light. It is exactly the way it was the last time she stayed: sparsely furnished, with very few personal touches anymore.

Frank settles himself, back to the radiator, legs extended straight out ahead of him. He presses his palms into the carpet and feels the soft tufts of pile popping up between his fingers. Maggie did so much—dealing with the therapists, the school, guarding their child when she should have been asleep. She did the lion's share, that was for sure. There was something so very personal about Eleanor's pain. Even whilst it was still an unknown, it sometimes made him feel as if it wasn't his place to be involved. It was that feeling of backing out of a room, hands up in surrender—*Sorry, sorry for asking*—and retreating, redundant, even when he hadn't approached her in the first place. It didn't mean he didn't care, though. Quite the opposite.

And what had he been doing while Maggie sat in this very spot, arms outstretched to their sleeping daughter? The same thing he has been doing for the past six months, albeit to a lesser extent. *Do you blame yourself for what happened too?* That's exactly it. If he had a pen with him now, he'd mark her question with a big fat tick.

"Of course I blame myself, Mags. That's what I was about to say."

One day to go
It's a funny thing—blame. I've had a lot of time to think about it, these last few months. For obvious reasons. For others too. It's there, latent, as you go about your day-to-day. It's in the prickle of guilt that starts the moment the alarm goes off, it's behind every rash or sharp comment that punctuates the working day, it's in the constant treadmill of anxiety that stops me from dropping off at night. And still life has to go on. Eleanor was about to go off to university, whether we could figure out our own chain of responsibility or not.

Parenting would be so much easier if the age-old

adage *out of sight, out of mind* actually applied to
it. If anything, I felt worse when she was away in
Manchester. When she was still at home, I could
comfort myself with the knowledge that, in among
the sweeping differences, there were still so many
little parts of her intact. I could still see the old Ellie
as she cut an apple into four pieces before eating
it. I saw it in the way she licked her bottom lip in
concentration while doing it. That sounds so silly,
written down. Inconsequential. But when those tiny
tics are all you have to hold on to? It's everything,
Frank; you must know that too.

Once Eleanor was at university, those brief
windows into the daughter we knew clouded
right over. She would come home to visit during
those first two years, but the occasions were
so sporadically spaced that the subtle gradients
of change disappeared in favor of fat slaps of
strangeness. She stopped eating with us and
wouldn't come down to watch TV. Even when
she did emerge from her room, she wouldn't
engage with either one of us willingly. There was
withdrawal—we had seen that begin only too
clearly—and then there was this: Eleanor in the
grips of her illness. That was what it was, wasn't it?
It was obvious to us both by then.

In the first term of her third year she came
home not long before she dropped out. We hadn't
seen her since the summer, and even then it was
just for a night. I had envisaged us catching up,
making plans. Instead, she treated the house like a
bed-and-breakfast, if she even managed to rustle
up the latter. A few days in and I was so desperate
to convince myself I hadn't imagined the child I
thought I had that I took the albums out of the
cabinet and pored over the pictures of her when she
was young, before everything went wrong. I looked
for traces of her smile, on a fairground ride or being
swung like a propeller in the park, your hands under
her armpits and her feet spread wide. Where did
she go, Frank? There is no helpline for parents who
cannot recognize their own child anymore.

I ran my hands over every precious, priceless
smile and wished I had cherished them more when
they were there. I missed her laughter and her
curiosity, the way she lit up every room. I missed
the warmth of her trust. I missed her while she slept
just meters above my head.

She caught me there.

"Can I see?"

I was so shocked I could barely speak.

"No worries, then."

"No, no, please." I moved to the corner of the settee to make space.

She turned the pages in silence for a while before she asked me, "What's your favorite?"

"Photo?"

She nodded.

"Hard to say—there are so many." I flicked back through a couple of the pages, the plastic sheets rustling before snapping down flat.

"I like this one," I said, after a while.

It was one of the two of you at the kitchen table. According to my scribbled description beneath: *Eleanor's tenth birthday.* Even without that, you could tell because there was a huge banoffee pie with a candle in it, her favorite, as the centerpiece, or so it should have been. Only something has tickled you both and your heads are bowed, foreheads touching. Neither of you has your eyes open, both laughing so hard that your seams have split, glee pouring out in the breadth of your smiles.

"What about you?" I ventured. "Are there any photos you like?"

There was a second's hesitation before Eleanor reached across to pick up the album. I felt that fragile stirring of hope. So deceptive.

And that was when I saw it—a deep purple puncture in the center of her wrist.

She noticed quickly enough because she dropped her hand, our bonding over, and wrapped the misshapen fabric of her sleeve back around her wrist. She began to stand up, but before she had even managed to get to her feet, I grabbed her. I thought I could feel the mark under the fabric, a drill hole in her skin, but that may just have been my mind playing tricks.

"Eleanor."

"Get off me, Mum."

"No, Eleanor. Not until you explain."

"What is there to explain, Mum?"

"Why?" I whispered.

Was that when I started to cry? Probably. Eleanor inched toward me.

"I never meant to hurt you, Mum. You know that, right?"

I breathed in a lungful of her shampoo, but it only made the crying worse. Apples. Just like you, Frank.

"Don't. Don't do this. Please."

I wasn't making any sense, the words caught up in between sobs. Eleanor leaned closer, kissed me on the forehead. When had she grown taller than me? How had she made me into the child here?

"Let us help," I begged, grabbing fistfuls of her jumper.

That was too much, clearly. She pulled back and went up to her room. She left less than ten minutes later, while I still sat rocking, my head in my hands, on the toilet seat, before I had so much as a chance to say goodbye.

When Eleanor was little, we could fix anything. Cuts and bruises, arguments and disappointments—we could sort them all. Now she was an adult, in body if not in mind, and I couldn't help her. That was what she was saying, wasn't it, when she pulled away? Do you know how that killed me? All I wanted was to make everything all right for her. And I couldn't, Frank. I couldn't.

I failed.

Failed. Frank has thought about that word a lot recently, the long wail of despair stuffed in its middle. No one prepares you to fail as a parent. He wishes he could reach out and touch Maggie again, even if he did have to compete for space with the tubing and the IVs and the rustling of the strange, papery gown. "You didn't fail, Maggie," he would say. "I did."

For a while, Frank thought that he was doing it right. He didn't panic. He didn't push Eleanor away.

Every time he gave in, every time she overstepped the mark and he adjusted his expectations, he told himself he was doing the Right Thing. He thought of their summer on the garden chairs, side by side underneath the stars, and the way Eleanor would talk when she'd wanted to. It had worked once, so surely it would work again. Right?

But Maggie had said it, there in writing—it was an illness. The worst kind. He would have taken anything over this. If it was glandular fever, they could have waited it out. If she'd needed a kidney, she could have had his. Hell, take both. But when it's an addiction, and they don't want help? What then? Well, Frank knows what he did—he fed it because of his failure to know what else to do.

He rereads the last page, Maggie's scribbled transcription of her attempt to get through to Eleanor. He can see her, eyes imploring, a cloud across them that warns of the impending torrent of tears. *Just speak to me. Open up. I'm here for you.* He has heard those phrases all too often since he stopped speaking, especially in the first few weeks, when Maggie swung between burning frustration and a look of disappointment that kneecapped him. It is not just Eleanor he has failed.

As if that wasn't bad enough, there was the whole

sorry debacle at the hospital, his confession on the very tip of his tongue. Then the nail jab and the alarm and the army of consultants. Another string of excuses and another opportunity to let Maggie down. Enough. When Frank is allowed back, he will tell her what he did the minute he is through the door. He will tell her everything, and he will throw himself at her mercy. He will say sorry until he runs out of breath.

He failed to get it out the first time, but he will not fail again.

One day to go

How many times did we see her in the years that followed, Frank? A handful? No more. I have tried counting, but somehow they all blur into one—our desperate attempts to reach out and keep her safe. Our complete inability to do either.

I tried to keep tabs on her, but what little online presence she had went dead. She moved out of the house on Albemarle Street shortly after she dropped out of university. She worked a series of temp contracts and was always on the move. "Couch-surfing," she once called it, which sounds a damn sight safer than it ever seemed to me.

For a while I was determined to report her to the police.

"And tell them what?" you asked, rolling me over
to face you, disrupting our spooning.

"That . . . she's missing."

"No, Mags, she's not. She's just not here. What
could they do, anyway?"

"Find her."

You told me she had to want to be found. You
reminded me that she still texted, infrequently, yes,
but it was hardly the behavior of a missing person.
You told me she needed time.

"How much time, Frank? How much?"

"I don't know."

The bed creaked, equally uncertain.

"I miss her, Frank."

"I know, Maggie. I miss her too."

We would go months without seeing Eleanor,
and the whole time she was away from me, my skin
itched with my need to see her. My eyes watered,
and my whole body ached for her. I barely slept; I
barely ate. She was the only drug I needed. The only
thing I craved. When she was there, I was on my
highest high. And when she was gone? I didn't know
it was possible to feel that low.

So then imagine my guilt, Frank, when I came to
dread her coming home—my Eleanor-shaped hit.
You would make sure to get to the door first—to pave

the way or clean her up. It was one of your greatest kindnesses to me, really it was. I would lock myself away in the bathroom while you carried on with the charade of a welcome and I would run both bath taps at full blast. I would watch the condensation settling on the mirror, the cabinets, the windows. Never once did I get in. What a terrible waste of water.

By the time I came downstairs again, you would have given her cash. You never said as much, but I could tell. Even so, a day or so later, when I popped to the bathroom, I'd come back to find my purse ransacked and the cash gone. I stopped taking out money, and I wanted to tell you to do the same. Only I knew you wouldn't listen, because without it, what would she resort to? I couldn't bear the thought.

I drew the line at bolting her in. You cannot keep your own child a prisoner. We did try an intervention, once. I say "intervention," but that suggests we managed to make her listen when, in practice, quite the opposite was true. It wasn't so much us confronting her as the other way around. And the anger in her then—there's no way you can have forgotten that. Four years after she had left university, and after months of not seeing her, she was basing herself nearby. Temporarily, she said. In reality all it meant was that she was letting herself in and out of the house at all times of the day and night, taking what she needed and then leaving before we could do anything about it.

Do you know, Frank, what I see when I close my eyes? Every night, without fail? It is that evening, the one time you caught her with my handbag. It is Eleanor pushing you by the shoulders, against the wall, to the edge. Your knees buckled against the radiator, braced for a fall.

"Eleanor, please!" I approached her from behind, pulling at her hips, desperate to get her away from you. I had never seen her like this, so physical, so ugly. So far out of control.

"Get off me. Just leave me alone!"

Eleanor had taken her hands off you, but she was still close enough for the spit and the venom of her words to smack you wet in the face.

"Darling, please." I tried to get her to calm down, to take a seat on the stairs, but she wouldn't listen. You were too shell-shocked to say or do anything to help.

She took a step back. "I should go." Her voice cut like a knife across the corridor, slicing through the static. Gone was the fury of minutes before. Eleanor stopped and slumped against the bannister, one elbow jostling with the coats, her head in her hands.

"Really, I should go."

I wasn't about to refute that.

"You don't have to," you said from the corner of the hallway, one hand still steadying you against the wall. Eleanor headed up the stairs.

When she came down a few minutes later, bag in tow, she walked straight past me and toward you. "I'm sorry," she said. She kissed your cheek and then the door swung shut behind her.

We didn't stop her then, did we? Not with proper force, not like a human barricade. No, we could shout and reason and cry and beg, but we could not lock her in. To do that would be to stymie that most beautiful part of Eleanor—her freedom.

But if I had known, known what was about to happen? Well then that would have been different. For six months now I have spent every day considering what more I would have done had I known it would be the last time I would see her. There should be a memo about these things, so you don't mess up your last shot. If I had my time again, Frank, I promise you I would have done it better. I would have kept her for us, even if it killed me.

There's something I want to do, before I tell you what happened, my last confession—the darkest too. Bear with me, Frank, please. Just a few minutes

longer, then I will tell you, I promise. Get a pen and
find a bit of space (there's some in the back here).
I do this every day, Frank, with the hour before
supper. Did you ever notice? I usually find dusk is
best for this, but just do it now, whatever time it is.

When I'm settled, I'll think about Eleanor.
Nothing new there, but in these instances, I
revisit her in the briefest snapshots I can process.
I remember how many moments I told her I loved
her, every time from the moment she was born. I
tally them on paper. Often, I will be so absorbed in
making sure that I have caught every instance that
the bundles of five go right out the window, and
when I open my eyes, I am met by a blur of spindly
marks too tight to count. I am keeping these notes
in the bottom drawer of the dresser in Eleanor's
room. They are still there, if you want to look.
You'll see that some days I do better than others.

I wonder what would happen if I did the same
for you? After forty years together, would there be
more? Then again, we were never very effusive,
not verbally. That was never what love was for us.
We left the giant proclamations to others. What we
have had has been so much quieter, so much softer. I
wouldn't have had it any other way.

Love for a child is different—isn't it? It's a

different love, unquantifiable. It is a taboo to compare the two. Who would you save in a burning building, if you could only take one? The answer's a given, surely, but I would worry about the sort of spouse who would willingly abandon their other half in an inferno. If I imagine you burning, top to toe in flames, I see myself spontaneously combust too.

There are probably only one or two tallies from the last few years that could be attributed to Eleanor. I loved her all the same. I loved her more, if that's possible. More fiercely, more intensely. I told her to her face, knowing she wouldn't say the same back. Because that is what love is, isn't it? Giving without receiving. Of course, there is always the hope of receiving. Tiny, precious, fragile. You can be batted away a thousand times and still it will be there, too small to pick up and dispose of.

I want you to do your tallies now too, Frank, for Eleanor. For me too. I don't want what I did to change your opinion of me, but it will. I know that . . .

In the margins, Frank can see that Maggie has done a few tallies here as well. He was never blind enough to think that the silence was easy on her, but he didn't know it had driven her to distraction either.

He is too on edge to sit there and count. Besides, Maggie said it. It's unquantifiable. He could have told Eleanor and Maggie that he loved them both a million times and still it would have been an insufficient reproduction of how he felt. Instead, he shuffles to Eleanor's dresser. Among the old hairbrushes, an assortment of plastic jewelry, and a stuffed owl that went out of favor, there is a fat stack of curled Post-it notes. A rainbow of her love for Eleanor.

And if Maggie had tried to count for him, how would she have done? Frank can think of maybe one or two times Maggie has told him that she loves him in recent months, always in desperation, as if the appearance of those words in the chokehold of silence would be enough to crack a little air back into the house. Frank could never reciprocate. Not verbally, at least. Instead, Frank tried to *show* Maggie just how much he loved her, whether that meant massaging that same spot under her left shoulder blade that always seized up when she was lying in bed with her back to him, or running his fingers down the inside of her forearm in the way that always soothed her. All that and still he comes back to the same question he always does with Maggie, with Eleanor: Could he have done more?

Frank shuts the drawer and returns to his spot by the radiator. *The darkest too.* Part of him is too scared to read the rest. That would be him all over, spent before the finishing line. His mind flashes back to how he fell, just before the last hurdle, Maggie jabbing his hand and the medical team half hauling him out. *Classic Frank*, as Maggie would say. Only he does not want this to be his defining feature—the falling-short, the just-missing-out, one-second-too-late Frank. No, he does not.

He steels himself and turns the last page.

One day to go
I saw her, Frank.

I had been in the house barely ten minutes when the doorbell went. The boiler was chuntering away with that strange, low moaning—you know the sound, the one that always precedes an expensive call-out. I had rushed off to examine it and hadn't even had a chance to get my coat off. I assumed it was you, that you had left your keys somewhere in the lab again.

"Eleanor! What are you doing here?"

She had her duffel bag slung over one shoulder, weighed down by it so that her upper body slanted like an overburdened coat hanger.

"Yeah . . . er . . . I was in the area. I thought I'd pop by."

She reached up and rubbed her fists into her eye sockets. I could see the imprints of her knuckles on her skin. She looked tired, very tired, but there was some low-level buzz about her; her hands shook; and she didn't seem to want to stay still. I wondered how long she had been waiting for one of us to come home.

"What is it, Eleanor?"

She cast a look over her left shoulder. Then her right. Back again over her left.

"I'm trying to get sorted out." There it was again—the shoulder-checking. What was she looking for? "Look, Mum, it's a long story, but I need a bit of help."

"What sort of help?" I asked, folding my arms. A "power stance" I had read about somewhere. It didn't feel too empowering to me, weak in the face of my only child. All I wanted to do was reach out and pull her into my arms. I shoved my hands in my pockets to suppress the urge.

"It cost to get down here. And there's a few people I need to pay back—Mike, Dan . . ."

She reeled off a list of names I had never heard before. All the time, the twitching, the shoulders. I prayed you would turn up and help me de-escalate the situation. How many bombs could detonate on the doorstep before the whole house collapsed?

"We give you money, Eleanor. Where's that going?"

I thought of the Friday evenings I would spend transferring her £200, £300, whatever I could spare after payday.

"Yeah, it went, OK? I know I need to get sorted. I'll do it, promise. Just, please, Mum, please?"

Eleanor's eyes bore straight into mine. I felt a sharp pain, just below my belly button. The endless pull toward her.

"I can't, Ellie." I could feel myself welling up and willed myself to hold it together. "Your father and I would do anything for you. You know we would do anything for you, right?"

She kicked her trainers against the door frame absentmindedly.

"Darling, please," I whispered. "We can't give you any money. But we can keep you safe."

Her eyes were red, bloodshot, slightly rheumy.

"I've got to go."

"What? You said you were visiting? Wait for your father to get home at least. He'll want to see you!"

She had already turned around, so I couldn't see if she was angry or just jittery, anxious to keep moving.

"Eleanor, wait!" I shouted, raising my voice as

loud as I dared without rousing the neighborhood curtain-twitchers. I put one of your shoes in the door to stop it slamming shut. "I'm sorry. I love you!" I shouted, halfway out into the driveway. "It is only because I love you!"

I ran back to the house and snatched up my keys, kicked the makeshift doorstop away so the door slammed. I was about to go after her, but she was already out of sight. She always was quicker than me. She was gone.

Isn't it strange how your body copes with trauma? In the face of the greatest pain you can imagine, you just keep on, one foot in front of the other. You can be shell-shocked, a husk of your usual self, and still your body keeps marching to its own inner clock. It was just like that then, Frank, although my mind was in pieces. I returned to autopilot the moment I got in. I took off my coat, turned on the oven, and stuck in the first thing I could find. Chicken pie. A nice one too. I went to pour a drink and saw the card for her twenty-fifth birthday tucked between the wine rack and the wall, months overdue. We hadn't the address to send it to.

When I heard the door go, I went to greet you. Just like any other night, I told myself. Just like any other night. All through supper, the confession hovered on my lips. I got halfway through the introduction to my statement ten, twenty times, but just as I came to it—"I saw Eleanor, she was here, I turned her away"—I swallowed the words down again and felt them stinging the back of my throat like a scoop of salt on an open wound. The words have lodged there ever since, Frank.

After we had eaten and you had retreated to the sitting room, I popped three of my sleeping tablets and swallowed them down with a draught of stale water from a cup near the sink. I lay beside you on the sofa, settling my head on your stomach and into oblivion. I was just going under when it struck me that my performance must have passed muster. You hadn't mentioned Eleanor once. I opened my eyes a sliver, the effort nearly too much to bear, just so I could blink you a good night.

Well, Frank, I'm afraid you know the rest. When the police came and asked their questions—*Have you seen her recently? When was the last time?*—I didn't say anything. Not that I could then, not without being carted off under suspicion, unveiled as the most unnatural criminal that I am, the mother who couldn't mother.

But afterward? Even if I didn't offer my confession at the police station, hunched over the reception desk, giving myself up, my words rasping against the bulletproof glass, I could have told you. After all, I had been following through with what we had agreed, in the dark, under the duvet, in the weeks before. We had always been there first to cushion the blow, and nothing had changed. We had to get her to the point where she would start to help herself. We had to let her hit rock bottom.

Do you know what kills me most, Frank? That she must have thought she was alone. That she had no one. And that could not have been further from the truth. Not then, not ever. What if I had said it? *You're not alone.* Better than *I'll fix it.* Better even than *I love you.* Just those three words. Would they have changed anything?

So, there you have it: I saw her, Frank. I was the last person to see Eleanor before it happened.

And worse than that? I turned her away . . .

Chapter 8

I saw her. Frank has read those three little words so many times that he cannot distinguish between them anymore. Somewhere between the looping troughs of the "w" and the tall line of the "h," everything he had thought to be true has fallen apart. There is no axis in his world, no firm ground on which to stand.

Oh God.

He runs over the last interaction, scrawled in handwriting that grows increasingly cramped. He can see it all—Maggie's pleading, Eleanor's restlessness, Maggie hunched over the kitchen table reliving it all in her mind but unable to spit out the words, the gag of a guilty conscience.

Does he blame her? Only as much as he blames himself.

Frank starts the last page all over again, as if by re-reading it he can make up for the fact that he wasn't there. Not when Maggie needed him. Nor when Eleanor did either, for that matter. That was his role in the family—the diffuser, the great diplomat in chief. And where was he that night when they needed him the most? He will never forgive himself.

Somewhere, down below, there is a keening sound. It must have been going on for a few minutes now, high-pitched and relentless. *Maggie,* he thinks, *palms collapsing into her thighs, bent double; Eleanor running off into the distance.* It's his mind, there with her again, hearing things too. Only the noise won't stop, not after another minute, not after another two. There is a second's respite of silence, but it barely lasts a heart-beat before the noise starts up again.

This must be it—madness setting in. Frank has never felt so close to Maggie, or quite so far away. He can swear it is coming from downstairs and wishes it would just stop again, for a second, while he processes and resets and gets back to his rereading.

It takes another five minutes for Frank to be sufficiently irritated into investigation. He has to take the stairs slowly. He hasn't felt steady on his feet for months now, and without Maggie he is rudderless too. Frank reaches the hallway and finds that the noise is louder here and impossible to avoid. He heads toward its source, the kitchen, with a horrible sense of déjà vu.

When he walks in, he sees the light first. *Shit.* His phone. He'd forgotten about it. But clearly Edie hasn't.

Unknown number. Since his first mobile was thrust upon him (by Maggie, obviously), Frank has gone out of his way to avoid calls, even when the caller is most definitely known. That was his awkwardness. But this? He cannot afford to resort to his avoidance tactics again. He picks up.

"Hello?" The voice on the other end is almost shouting over the traffic roaring in the background.

"He-hello?"

"Frank—is that you?"

Ah—he knows that voice.

"Daisy? Yes, it's me."

For a second, Daisy doesn't respond. Frank's stomach plummets. This can't be good news.

"Frank, you need to get down to the hospital now."

"But . . . but they said this afternoon. It's not, what, lunchtime?"

Frank squints out of the window and directly into the sunshine. White spots dance before his eyes, and he has to steady himself against the countertop.

"I know, I know, Frank. And look, I shouldn't be

telling you this, I shouldn't be phoning you, not now I'm off my shift, but something ain't right."

"What do you mean?" Frank leans more heavily into the heel of his palm. He is pressing down so firmly that a hot fizz begins to run up his arm, prickling all the way up to his neck.

"I don't know quite . . . She's not where they want her to be. I left something at work and I had to go in to collect it, so I thought I'd just pop in to see her. I was lucky they let me. Anyway, I told her you've been there. That you hadn't left her side. But there's something not quite right, Frank. It's like she's giving up . . . I don't know how long she—"

The fizz has reached Frank's head. He slumps against the cupboard, and the jammy door by the cereals slams with a bang. She can't be, can she?

"Frank? Frank—are you still there? Look, maybe I shouldn't have called. I just thought you should know—"

"No. No. I need to get to her . . . You were right . . . Daisy?"

"Yes, Frank?"

"Thank you, thank you so much."

Frank hangs up. He needs to see Maggie, and he needs to see her now. Giving up? That's not the Maggie he knows. But after having read every word of that final confession once, twice, to the point that the phrases are imprinted on his mind like the layout of a childhood home, so much of what he had thought to be true about Maggie has been thrown on its head.

There is no more time for this. Frank props himself back up to standing and walks over to the sink. He shoves his head as far under the cold tap as it will go, the water slightly musty from stale days in the tank, and then shakes himself out like a shaggy sheepdog, albeit one with ringing ears and a sharp pain behind the eyes.

Now he feels more like himself. He does that ineffectual patting routine that he always does before he goes out—wallet, house keys. Relieved to find he has both, he stuffs his feet into two shoes by the door and wipes the excess water off his hands and face with the anorak that hangs limply from the bannister. He grabs the car key fob from the hook in the porch and runs out to the driveway, slamming the door behind him.

He twists the key in the ignition. Nothing. He tries again. Nothing. The battery's dead. Frank can't believe it. Sod's law. How long will it take to walk? An hour? More? That is time he doesn't have. Out of the corner of his eye, he sees his bike. Six months it has been rusting outside. No cover, no lock. No wonder no one cared to steal it, with a stone in its back wheel that has left him with a slow puncture.

Needs must. He heads for this next best thing, flinging his right leg over the seat. His torso feels very precarious as it is thrust over the road handlebars, all the more so for having the planner tucked under his right arm. Frank kicks his right foot out a few times on the gravel to get himself started and suddenly wishes he had brought his helmet. As he judders this way and that across the uneven stones, he tries to keep calm and think of Maggie.

At the first traffic lights, he flies straight through a red. Turns out the brake cable needs some work too. The number 4 bus comes to a slamming halt just inches from the back wheel, and Frank is so shaken that he cannot even raise a hand in apology or thanks or a shamefaced mix of the two.

He doesn't remember the lactic acid building up in his thighs so fast. It is far too hot for this, and the exertion is so fierce that his feet seem to have lost all feeling. Every gulp of air he swallows seems woefully insufficient, and his shirt is clinging to his skin with every increasingly sweaty turn of the pedal. "Maggie. Maggie. Maggie," he chants beneath his breath. He will not lose her too.

In a stroke of mad athleticism or sheer desperation (likely both), Frank has managed to make it three-quarters of the way to the hospital. Only there is one hell of a hill standing between him and his goal. To the frustration of the boxy Volvo behind him, he throws himself off his bike and almost into the main flow of traffic.

Frank manages to heave the bike onto the curb and, without so much as a second's thought, drops it into the hedgerow that lines the pavement.

"Hey, mister, that going spare?" a weeny little smidgen of a man pipes up, immediately abandoning his girlfriend's hand in favor of the broken treasure before him.

"All yours!" Frank roars above the traffic.

He takes a look at his footwear and only now notices that he has two different shoes: on his left, his gardening slip-on, on the right, a deck shoe that has never once so much as set foot on a floating vessel. Neither screams running gear. Frank tries to think of the last time he ran properly—school cross-country? He seems to remember going off the route in search of an iced bun instead.

Before he gives it much more thought, he is off. The first few steps feel almost easy. He has a long gait, and he is lean, like a greyhound. Only that is where the similarities stop. After no more than fifty meters, he is spent. He is wheezing like a forty-a-day smoker despite having never so much as taken a puff in his life, square that he is.

The incline is one of those terribly deceptive ones. It doesn't look too bad from the bottom, but get going and it is another story altogether—long and continuous and enough to tax even a serious sprinter. The pavement is unforgiving, and with each step he feels that twinge in his left knee getting sharper and sharper. In life, there are so many things we always think we will get round to fixing—the slow puncture in the back wheel of a bike, the niggling ache, a fractured relationship. If there is one thing the past week has taught Frank, it is that you can never rely on time being on your side.

Frank tries to distract himself from the pain and the sweat coursing down his forehead by running through what he has to say. Maggie emptied herself out to him, all her secrets compressed into rows and rows of lines on a series of wafer-fine pages. All that work to leave him with a clean slate and he couldn't even bring himself to tell Maggie the one thing he had to. If anything will spur him on through the last two hundred yards, it is his own frustration.

He cannot hear anything above the sound of his own panting. It must be loud, because every pedestrian that he passes gives him a wide berth, as if they are worried that he might drop down on any one of them at any second. Frank does not care. He is a man on a mission, and his eyes are trained on the revolving doors of the building at the top of the hill, wavering from side to side like a mirage.

There is a minute, just before he hits the tarmac of the hospital drive, when he thinks he might not make it. He is so light-headed from fatigue, his stomach rattling on the syrupy dregs of just a few fruit chews, that there is just rush. The rush of traffic, the rush of relatives, the rushing rush of a world where he has just one vestige of hope left.

He hits the spinning doors with the full force of his frame. There is a nurse shouting his name as he heads full pelt down the corridor to intensive care, barely managing to weave between the gurneys. At one point his flailing left hand knocks a cup of iced coffee straight out of a woman's hand and down her white shirt. He mumbles something unintelligible about a refund into the air.

Frank manages to weave past a cleaner who has the door to intensive care propped open with a hip. He is so focused on reaching his destination that he does not notice that he has attracted the attention of everyone in reception, their mouths agape. The minute he is within reach of Maggie's door, he grabs for the handle, only his palms are slick with sweat and they slip right off the metal.

Before he can think better of it, he throws his upper body against the door, which shakes on the impact. Or perhaps it is the bones in Frank's shoulder. There is a tremor, and then both give way. Frank lands with his hands over Maggie in a way that could look rather inappropriate to anyone passing by. He spits an unattractive ball of phlegm onto the floor by her bed and slowly eases himself up to standing, trying his best not to lean on Maggie.

"Maggie," he says, the syllables bouncing out between breaths. "I'm back."

Chapter 9

At first, it looks to Frank as if Maggie is sitting up, and he feels a rush of hope. He picks up the planner from where it has fallen at his feet, the page edges discolored with sweat where it has been wedged in his armpit. He tries to dry it off on his shirt, only that is saturated too. He wipes his forehead on his forearm and then, before he forgets, takes the chair from beside the door and scoops the plastic ridge at the top under the handle to buy them a little privacy. To buy himself a little more time too. God knows he needs it.

Frank shuffles round the side of the bed so that he is looking directly at Maggie. After all, what do either of them have to hide?

He notices then that it is all an illusion: four pillows are propped at various angles to keep her up and her eyes are shut. She doesn't seem to have registered his presence at all.

"Maggie? Can you hear me?" Frank reaches out with one hand and slides it under hers. "Squeeze if you can hear me."

Nothing.

"Maggie, please, darling. This is all I'm asking. I know I don't deserve it. I never deserved you, and I certainly don't after everything I put you through. I'm sorry I stopped talking. I'm sorry I had to leave before I got to tell you why I closed off. But if you can do this for me, I promise I won't ask for anything ever again."

Frank's words pour out like a hose on full blast. A long winter when the plastic was frozen solid, and now this—just a few minutes to spill out everything he needs to. No sprinkling of anecdotes, no draining the message.

Frank waits. He has to resort to counting time by the beats of his heart, fat, heavy, painful beats. One, two. Maggie is as still as ever. He will not let this be an excuse again.

"I read this." Frank shakes the planner in Maggie's direction. A few of the photos she enclosed scatter on the sheet; he had not had the time nor the inclination to clip them back in. "I read it all. This, Maggie, this bit about you being the last person to see her. Well, we were in it together. We always were."

Then there it is. A squeeze.

"Maggie? Oh God . . . right . . ."

Slowly, Maggie's eyes flutter. One opens, and then the other. It reminds Frank of the butterflies he and Eleanor watched in the conservatory at the Botanic Gardens, back when she was just nine. The fluttering before the flight.

Before Frank has a chance to check that Maggie is awake, there is a rapping at the door. The handle wavers, but the chair is doing its job. The door won't budge now, not without getting the heavies involved. Through the small glass panel, Frank can pick out the doctor. Dr. Singh is smiling, a little too much, the sort of smile you give to someone unhinged. He wants him to open up.

That makes two of them.

Frank shakes his head and turns back to Maggie, her eyes definitely open now, though glazed. Her gaze has not moved from him. Not to the photos. Not to the planner. Certainly not to the commotion outside her room.

He takes as deep a breath as his screaming lungs allow and looks Maggie square in the face. "You weren't the only one to see her, Mags. That night. I did too."

Maggie pinches his hand. He doesn't have the time to figure out if that is a good sign or not. He has been sitting on this secret for six months now, and it has wrecked him. More than just his voice, it has taken every second of every minute of every day that he has survived, and it has corroded everything.

"I thought I was the last person to see Eleanor. I had no idea it was the last time—how could I? It was definitely her, though—the duffel bag, the messy bun—I'd know her anywhere. I'd just gotten off the bus, it was dark, but I knew it was her. I was standing at the bus stop, and she was at the end of the road, all flustered, you know the way she would be, when she had other stuff on her mind . . .

"She didn't see me. I am almost certain of that. But I ignored her, Mags. I was scared. Scared of her coming home, scared of how it would be. It's not a justification, I know that. But that's why . . . that's why I ignored her. I wasn't there for her when she needed me the most."

There is another rap at the door. Two new gentlemen have arrived, one bearing a walkie-talkie. Security? Let them haul him out; there is no way Frank is leaving voluntarily now.

He crouches down so he is at eye level with Maggie. His hand has not moved from beneath hers.

"There was no way I could tell you, Mags. I didn't want to lose you too. I was so ashamed of myself. That was not the man you married or the father I am . . ."

There are tears coming, sobs that are beginning to break like hiccups in Frank's throat. He swallows them down. Not now, this is not about him. This is his last shot.

"When I went to see her, Maggie, she was in a little side room on her own, and do you know what my first thought was? *God, I hope she won't be lonely.* I was being led down the corridor toward her, blind with terror. We got to the room where she was being held, and the escort stepped aside. He wanted to give me some space, but really I needed him to push me. I don't know how I crossed the threshold, but somehow my feet just kept going.

"I had no idea what to expect. *A body exhumed from the canal.* That was what the police had said, like she was a trainer or a trolley or something. She looked so small on that slab, a doll among the dead. Her eyes were shut, but I made sure to open them, I wanted to see her properly, to make a new last time for us, father and daughter. It took me right back to that first moment when I held her as a baby, when I told myself there and then that I would do everything I could to protect her.

"I stayed and watched her for an hour, maybe more.

I only left when the poor man in the morgue charged with looking after me cleared his throat and said that he had to close up soon.

"You still hadn't moved when I came home that night. And that's when it began, Mags. The silence. I had caused her death, Maggie, ignored her, and I knew that if I told you, however good a person you might be, you wouldn't be able to forgive me. I'm right, aren't I? I couldn't risk that. I couldn't lose you too."

There is no way Frank can hold down the sobs now. They have risen up like dry retches, heaving out of his throat. A tear drops from the end of his nose and lands on Maggie's hand.

"I'm so sorry, Maggie. I am sorry every moment that I am awake. I miss her, and I will never stop missing her—"

There is a crash as a security guard sends the chair slamming across the room. Maggie shudders, as if startled by just the noise. A second later, the door gives way and the doctor enters, flanked by the backup.

All eyes are on Frank. No one moves. No one says a word.

Frank carries on, oblivious.

"I am sorry that I couldn't bring myself to tell you what I did. I'm sorry that you had to suffer in my silence too. I'm sorry for how I let you down. I'm sorry for most things, Maggie, but I have *never* been sorry that I loved you. I never will be either."

At that, Frank's knees give up on the squat and he falls forward, his forehead onto the mattress, his stubble brushing Maggie's thigh through the sheet.

It takes all her strength for Maggie to reach over and place a hand on the top of Frank's back, nestling it between two taut shoulder blades.

"Hush now, Frank," she says.

Epilogue

One year later

From above, Maggie looks like a fifties film starlet, reclining on the bed, a vibrant orange drink to her side. There is jazz on the radio, the melody smooth and full beneath the trumpet's intricate, improvised trails. Maggie's book, *A Rough Guide to the Scottish Highlands & Islands,* is balanced across her thighs and a pen is perched on the cracked spine. In front of her, half-obscured by the ottoman, her not-so-glamorous assistant is rooting around in the wardrobe.

Shuffle in just that little bit more and you'll see the pillow behind Maggie's back isn't quite to her liking. You will notice how she struggles to move herself to a more comfortable position, her biceps tensed but nothing moving quite as it should. Frank looks over from his search every few minutes (less often now than he used to) just to calm his nerves. He does it as subtly as he can manage while he is up to his ankles in discarded bits of clothing; she hates it when he questions her independence.

Those were long, painful days, when Maggie was being roused from the coma, her organs stubbornly refusing to give up the security of standby mode. Then the endless physiotherapy sessions, where a bright young thing lifted her from the wheelchair so that her body was thrust forward over a walker, her feet querying every tiny movement.

It was hard for Frank to watch, but he refused to leave her side, except for when he needed to speak to the consultant. No one had ever seen a man so determined. She would recover, he told him, jabbing his index finger with such force on the desk that the whole thing juddered. People made full recoveries from this sort of thing every day. More than that, Maggie *wanted* to recover.

Frank was right about that. Maggie is nothing if not stubborn, and she was discharged a full week ahead of schedule, albeit with a lot of work still to do. When they got home, the whole place felt brighter. Edie had been round to the house and transformed the living room into a temporary bedroom. There was a new lick of paint and flowers everywhere. Somewhere they could feel proud of when visitors started to arrive.

The nurse, Daisy, was one of the first, a week or so later. She wasn't sent by the hospital; they had someone else for that. It was a courtesy visit then, shall we say, although Frank was struggling so much with the new arrangements that it slipped his mind to offer her a cup of tea or to extend the most basic hospitality. Maggie barked something about the kettle, but it came out wrong, along with a flurry of frustrated tears that broke Frank in two.

Since then, there have been a few wobbles. Christmas was hard, even with Edie and her brood to keep the show on the road. Now it has been and gone (this too shall pass), New Year's too. Everything started to feel more manageable in spring, and now, in high summer, when the days are long and the sun can be out as late as ten o'clock, it feels like a new future is starting to take root.

"Got them!" He holds two straw hats aloft, one with a wide brim and thick green velvet ribbon, the other a trilby, or so it was when they bought it in Spain fifteen years ago, before it was squashed beneath a couple of kilos of cupboard junk.

"Now for a little spray of this!" Frank blitzes Maggie's bare arms with suncream, and she has to bat him away before he can go for her face as well.

"It's nearly teatime!" she protests. "We aren't going to get burned at this hour." Frank runs a hand through his hair. There is still some red in among the gray. "Maybe do yourself. Better safe than sorry," she adds as an afterthought.

Frank draws a line down his nose, two on each cheek. He rubs a little and waits for Maggie's exasperation to kick in. Right on time. She lets out a closed-lip sigh like a lawn mower starting up. Frank crouches down and lets her finish the job. He could have done it himself, but there is nothing quite like the tenderness that she has always applied to him, even to his factor fifty. When she is done, he sneaks a kiss and stands up to collect the bag he has prepared.

"We're going to be out for a little while tonight. I think we should take the chair. I can put the stuff on your lap."

Maggie isn't as reluctant about that as she used to be. She nods and points at her sandals in the corner of the room. It is a beautiful August evening, perfect for an excursion. She is eager to get out—of the house and her head—and she is down the stairs, shawl on and at the front door, before Frank has had so much as a chance to offer any assistance. If Frank has seemed distracted today, Maggie hasn't picked up on it. She has always had a lot on her mind, and today was never going to be easy on either of them.

It is six o'clock by the time they reach the kissing gate at the entrance to the meadow. Frank can hear the peals from St. Giles's starting up, the sound muffled by the distance between where he is standing and the church on the far side of the fields. Maggie does not appear to have noticed. She is focused on standing up and making her own way through the narrow gap. It isn't the swiftest process, but even so, there is no way Frank is missing his opportunity to pucker up.

"Incorrigible," Maggie tuts, once she is on the other side. I can see her smile radiating, even from here.

She has decided she doesn't need the chair for this stretch, and once he has lifted it up and over the cast-iron railings, Maggie lets Frank steer it down the gravelly path with his left hand, his right held in hers. She isn't as fast on her feet as she used to be, but there is no doubt that she will get there. A few months ago, the thought of Maggie walking was unfathomable. The doctors had all manner of charts to map progress and to temper expectations. Maggie has reveled in confounding them both. It is easier when you have a focal point that calls to you. Frank has done everything he can to show that Maggie has much to look forward to. That they both do, together.

They stop at the bench by the side of the Thames. To the untrained eye, it is just another stretch of grass in a sun-parched field. For us, it is a first walk, a space to learn to ride a bike, the venue for a hundred family picnics. A canoeist glides between the sailboats on either side of the bank, one hand raised in greeting. Frank responds with a nod, but Maggie is too absorbed in memories to notice.

He is cautious of rushing Maggie's reflection. He knows all too well the pull that the past will always exert, the way it frames their present. But that is just what it is, a frame, the surround for the new day they meet every morning, one foot in front of the other, hand in hand. They have suffered beyond comprehension. They can never forget. But there is still so much more beyond that. And what will it be like? No one can say for sure, although one thing remains certain—it is never too late to change the story.

"Here, Mags. Try some of this." Frank extends Maggie a tinfoil parcel with a molded plastic handle sticking out of it. The bowl of the spoon has already sunk into its contents—a banoffee pie.

"I didn't know we would be celebrating."

It was Maggie who used to make one every year for

Eleanor's birthday. But today? The second birthday since they lost Eleanor? The first they have endured since Maggie left hospital? Frank felt it was time for him to step up to the plate. While Maggie took a bath that morning, he swept into action. It took the best part of half an hour to whip the cream, and most of it ended up outside the bowl. It's a good thing Maggie hasn't been into the kitchen since.

"Commemorating and celebrating," Frank says. He can see her mouth trembling and reaches out to cup her chin. "We owe it to Eleanor. We owe it to ourselves."

Maggie turns, gently, and stares into the river. She spoons some of the biscuit base into her mouth. Half the crumbs settle in the corners of her mouth.

"Do you remember that bike ride we took where she nearly fell in here?" Maggie says, brushing away a few crumbs with the edge of her shawl.

"Like yesterday." Frank lets out a small snort of laughter. "Trying to do an impression of—who was it? Katie's mum?"

Maggie nods. She can see Eleanor like a mirage in front of her, both hands off the handlebars, zigzagging at an alarming speed. Eleanor was oblivious to Maggie's protestations from twenty feet behind. When Eleanor hit a pothole, both she and Frank were braced for her to be thrown sideways into the river.

"She salvaged it right at the last minute!"

There is a pause when they know they are thinking the same thing, about the same secret they held, separately: that they both saw Eleanor in her own last minutes; that neither could save her.

Maggie looks up at Frank. "Do you . . . do you think she knew?"

"What, darling?"

"That we loved her." Her voice is quiet, the words melting into the breeze.

"Of course, Mags. She always knew that."

Frank bends his head to kiss Maggie. I can see Maggie lingering; she doesn't want that contact to end. There has always been such hope in Frank's touch, the sort that is every bit as fresh as when she first felt it forty years ago.

"She would want us to be OK, you know that, don't you?" Frank says as he pulls away. He keeps his forehead pressed against Maggie's and imagines he is pressing that belief right through the lines in her skin and into her skull.

Maggie blinks her eyes open and locks them on Frank. He is close enough to see the exact point at which the lashes cross, the folds at the hoods of the lids. And when he looks deep into her pupils—what there? Four decades of soaring highs and devastating lows, the fights and the routine and the joy and the light on which they have built a life. He sees everything they have been. He sees everything they are. He can see everything they can still become.

There is a scattering of pebbles around their ankles, followed by a cloud of dust, enough to cause them to pull apart and for Maggie to cough. A little girl, no more than three, rushes past on a bike. Only one wheel of the stabilizers is making contact with the ground. Her thighs are pumping and pumping, the glitter on the orange plastic frame reflecting the sunlight so that she is bathed in an amber halo.

"Tessa! Watch out for the nice people on the bench!" Her parents are jogging in her wake. Tessa's mum has her arms spread wide at her waist, palms up, the gesture that says she will try to catch her daughter wherever she falls, if only she can. "Sorry!" she says as she trots past. "I can't keep up with her!"

Frank and Maggie both smile. It is a knowing curl at the corners of their lips that takes them back twenty-odd years and makes them savor every second of them.

"She would, wouldn't she," Maggie says, when Tessa and her harried parents are out of sight. Then firmer, louder: "She would want us to be OK."

Frank covers Maggie's hand with his own. She can feel the wood on the slats of the bench, rough and splintered, pressing into her palms as she gathers the strength to continue. "I miss her, and I will never stop missing her, but we have to carry on, for her sake. I just wish she was still here."

"Me too. But she is, somewhere."

Frank gives Maggie's hand a light squeeze and, with the other, wriggles a photo out of the pocket of his chinos. He unfolds it down the center crease, revealing a shot of the three of us. It was taken before everything unraveled. Before the darkness that settled and the years when they tried desperately to lift it and when whatever they did, however hard they tried, it was never quite enough. It is human nature to want something, someone, to blame. Sometimes that simply isn't possible.

I am thirteen, not quite adult-size yet, and am squeezed between the two of them on the rickety bench of a fishing boat off the Cornish coast. Both of them have their arms wrapped tight around me, as our scarves all half trail into the sea. They cannot let go. They did all they could to hold on to me. Now it is up to them to do that for each other.

In turn, the two of them will kiss my face. Frank lets his forehead collapse against Maggie's.

Neither of them says a word.

Acknowledgments

Thank you to my agent, Madeleine Milburn, for your unwavering support for my writing, your ambition for it, and for all your tireless work on my behalf. Thanks to Giles Milburn, Hayley Steed, Alice Sutherland-Hawes, Anna Hogarty, Liane-Louise Smith, and Georgia McVeigh for making me feel so welcome and for being the very best champions.

I feel incredibly lucky to have not one but two extraordinary Emilys in my life—Emily Griffin at Cornerstone in the UK and Emily Krump at William Morrow in the US. Your editorial input has been invaluable and there have been times when I have felt you understood what I was trying to say better than I did myself! This book is immeasurably better for your insights and I am so grateful for your vision and determination to make this a success. At William Morrow, thank you to Julia Elliott, Liate Stehlik, Jennifer Hart, Molly Waxman, Brittani Hilles, Stephanie Vallejo, and Ploy Siripant. It is a pleasure and a privilege to work with such talented people.

Closer to home, many thanks to the friends and extended family who have endured my tall tales for long enough and who weren't altogether too surprised when I announced, out of the blue, that I had written a novel. Not least to Sheila Crowley for her boundless faith that she would be seeing my name on the shelves before too long.

Special thanks to my mum and dad, Stephanie and David Greaves, for your generosity and good humor. I could not have wished for more supportive parents and I think I speak for both myself and my brother, Nathan, when I say we wouldn't be where we are now without everything you have done for us both. Thank you for knowing it was only ever a case of when, not if, you would be reading my debut novel. Your faith in my capabilities means more than I can say.

And finally, my thanks to John Russell for not complaining too much about the crack-of-dawn writing starts and for delivering the porridge to sustain them.

Thank you for your confidence that the future looks bright and for reminding me to leave the computer and get some fresh air every now and again. Above all, thank you for showing me a love that speaks louder than words.

About the Author

ABBIE GREAVES studied English literature at the University of Cambridge. She worked in publishing for three years before leaving to focus on her writing. She now lives in the U.K. *The Silent Treatment* is her first novel.

HARPER LARGE PRINT

We hope you enjoyed reading
our new, comfortable print size and found it
an experience you would like to repeat.

Well – you're in luck!

Harper Large Print offers the finest in
fiction and nonfiction books in this same larger
print size and paperback format. Light and easy to read,
Harper Large Print paperbacks are for the book lovers
who want to see what they are reading without strain.

For a full listing of titles and
new releases to come, please visit our website:
www.hc.com

HARPER LARGE PRINT

SEEING IS BELIEVING